NOBODY'S PRIZE

"Helen is the original 'girl power' heroine! She hungers for adventure like some people hunger for a new pair of cute shoes. . . . If you are a fan of the romance, adventure, and intrigue in mythology, but would like to look a little deeper to humanize the characters from your favorite stories, this is the book for you!"
—Justine *Magazine*

"Friesner is an accomplished writer who is able to interweave a contemporary feel for these ancient characters with pieces of history and mythology. She can also be funny, as readers can virtually feel Helen rolling her eyes during the course of her narration."
—Voice of Youth Advocates

"This fresh take on a familiar woman . . . will intrigue both mythology fans and those readers who can't get enough of tough girl heroines, regardless of setting or genre."
—The Bulletin of the Center for Children's Books

"Readers may be familiar with the legends and myths of Jason and the Golden Fleece, Medea, Hercules, and Helen of Troy, but Esther Friesner weaves these characters together in a teen novel that lifts them off those dusty pages and into a re-imagined tale of adventure and intrigue. . . . It is a thrilling coming-of-age story that will undoubtedly please fans of Nobody's Princess and garner new fans."
—Historical Novels Review

Nobody's Prize

Prize

∙◦► ◦◙ ◙◦ ►◦∙

Esther Friesner

Random House ⌂ New York

Text copyright © 2008 by Esther Friesner
Cover art copyright © 2008 by Larry Rostant

All rights reserved. Published in the United States by Random House Children's Books, a division of Random House, Inc., New York. Originally published in hardcover by Random House Children's Books in 2008.

Random House and colophon are registered trademarks of Random House, Inc.

Visit us on the Web! www.randomhouse.com/teens

Educators and librarians, for a variety of teaching tools, visit us at www.randomhouse.com/teachers

The Library of Congress has cataloged the hardcover edition of this work as follows:
Friesner, Esther M.
Nobody's prize / Esther Friesner.
p. cm.
Sequel to: Nobody's princess.
Summary: Still longing for adventure, Princess Helen of Sparta maintains her disguise as a boy to join her unsuspecting brothers as part of the crew of the *Argo*, the ship commanded by Prince Jason in his quest for the Golden Fleece.
ISBN 978-0-375-87531-1 (trade) — ISBN 978-0-375-97531-8 (lib. bdg.)
1. Helen of Troy (Greek mythology)—Juvenile fiction. [1. Helen of Troy (Greek mythology)—Fiction. 2. Jason (Greek mythology)—Fiction. 3. Argonauts (Greek mythology)—Fiction. 4. Sex role—Fiction. 5. Adventure and adventurers—Fiction. 6. Mythology, Greek—Fiction. 7. Mediterranean Region—History—To 476— Fiction.] I. Title.
PZ7.F91662Nod 2008
[Fic]—dc22
2007008395

ISBN 978-0-375-87532-8 (tr. pbk.)

Printed in the United States of America
10 9 8 7 6

First Trade Paperback Edition

This book is dedicated to
Erica Christine Sullivan

Strength, style, and true beauty

CONTENTS

PART 1
IOLKOS

1

COMING TO IOLKOS

I stood in the bow of the little fishing boat and gazed at the glittering city high on the bluff ahead. Even so late in the day, with the sun setting and the early summer light fading from the sky, I could see how tall the palace walls stood. I marveled at how many buildings clustered at their feet. Only the richest cities were so crowded with houses and shops and temples.

Iolkos! I thought happily. *It must be Iolkos. After so many days' sail from Delphi, the gods grant it's no place else.* My heart beat faster as I scanned the harbor that lay in the shadow of the citadel, seeking one special ship among all the rest. Where was it? Where was the vessel that would carry me off to adventure? Was it that one, with the almond-shaped eye painted in red just above the prow? Or that one, with a swarm of men busily at work, taking down its blue-bordered sail? Where was *my* ship, the ship Prince Jason was going to sail to the farthest shores of the Unfriendly Sea, the ship of heroes who would dare anything to fulfill the quest for the Golden Fleece? Where was the *Argo*?

"There she stands, lads, Iolkos!" the fisherman called out to Milo and me from his place at the steering oar, confirming my hopes. "And less than a day's sail away." He winked at me when he said "lads," and I grinned back. Though I wore a boy's tunic and my skin was deeply tanned from our voyage, I was no more a lad than that man's daughter.

The fisherman knew my true name and rank—Helen, princess of Sparta, Lord Tyndareus's heir, Queen Leda's daughter—but I'd spent so much of our voyage from Delphi teaching him to call me "Glaucus," the boy's name I'd chosen for myself, that it came to his tongue naturally. He'd keep my secret. The real question was whether I could do the same. My brothers, Castor and Polydeuces, waited behind the walls of Iolkos, waited to sail with Prince Jason on his quest for the Golden Fleece. I intended to join them on that quest, but for that to happen they must not recognize me as their sister or my adventure would be over before it began.

I leaned as far forward from the prow as I could without toppling out into the waves. Sea spray was cool and salty on my lips. There was a fine breeze filling our sail, and the sky swirled with squawking gulls. Soon we'd land, and I'd put the next step of my plan into action.

I wasn't the only one in a hurry. "Is it true?" Milo exclaimed eagerly, scrambling to stand beside me. "Are we there at last?" My friend was *not* the world's happiest sailor.

"Soon enough," the fisherman said. "Tomorrow morning." He leaned against the steering oar and turned our boat's nose toward the shore.

"'Tomorrow'?" I echoed. "Why not today?"

The fisherman chuckled. "You know the answer to that."

So I did. "Always keep the shore in sight," I recited dutifully. While I'd spent our voyage from Delphi teaching the fisherman to call me by a boy's name, he'd spent it teaching me the basics of sailing. "A strayed boat's a doomed boat."

"And——?" he prompted.

"And only owls and foxes can see in the dark," I went on. "The wise sailor beaches his boat by dusk."

"Good. Now come here and show me what else you've learned." He stood to one side and patted the steering oar that guided our little vessel.

"You want *me* to beach us?" I could hardly believe it. I'd never expected such a privilege. My father could buy a dozen great ships with the oil from just one season's olive harvest, but for the fisherman this lone little boat was his entire existence, his livelihood, his only way back home.

"Are you *sure?*" I asked.

"I know this shore. It's friendly enough. Go on, steer us. I'll mind the sail, but I'll step in if I see you doing something wrong."

I said a prayer to Poseidon as I took the steering oar with both hands and braced my bare feet against the boat's sun-warmed hull. I leaned against the long wooden oar and felt the power of the waves pushing back against me. There wasn't much resistance, just enough for me to feel the message of the sea: *I am immortal, endless, stronger and wilder than a thousand bulls. If you think that you've tamed me because you've made me carry you where you want to go, you're a fool. Respect me, or pay for your pride.*

Yes, Lord Poseidon, I thought as I turned the boat toward shore. *I hear. I know. I ask your blessing.*

The god answered in his own way, by letting me beach the boat without much trouble. When I felt the bottom grate along the sand and pebbles, I took a deep breath of relief.

Milo was the first to leap from the boat. "I'll make the fire!" he called out, racing away to gather bits of wood.

"Helpful, isn't he?" the fisherman remarked as we dragged the boat a safe distance onto the beach.

"He'd volunteer to kill a dragon if it meant he'd have solid ground under his feet," I replied.

After Milo got the fire started, we cooked some red mullet we'd caught and ate them along with the last of the bread and cheese we'd bartered for at a small village two days' voyage south. I was convinced that I'd be too excited to eat or sleep that night. My mind rang with *Iolkos! Iolkos! Iolkos!* My body had other ideas. I gobbled up every bit of food in front of me and my eyes closed as soon as my head touched the ground.

That night, my dreams were strange and terrifying. I was back in the forests of Calydon, once more running with the hunt for the monstrous boar that was ravaging the land. The beast rushed out of the darkness the same way that he'd come when I'd helped the great huntress Atalanta meet his attack.

In my dream I stood alone.

Stop! I shouted at the charging beast, holding the great boar spear steady. *Stop! I order you, as Sparta's future queen!*

The boar kept coming. I jammed the spear's butt against the earth and dug in my feet to meet his attack, but when I glanced down, I saw a blood-chilling change. Instead of wearing a boy's tunic, I was weighed down by a heavily flounced dress. Instead of a spear, I held a spindle tangled with gleaming gold thread.

A strand leaped out and lashed itself around my wrists.

Then the boar struck. One moment I was standing, the next I sprawled across the beast's back. The boar tore on down the mountain, through the trees. My thoughts were thunder. With one win-all/lose-all motion I jerked my bound hands down and slashed the thread apart on the boar's own tusk. I gave a shout of triumph as I grabbed the creature's shaggy pelt and threw one leg over his spine, ready to ride him to the edge of the world.

"Wake up! Lady Helen, wake up! You're having a bad dream." A strong hand on my shoulder shook me. I bolted upright. The sky was just beginning to turn light, the horizon shimmering with a pearly glow soft and rosy as the smile of Aphrodite. As I rubbed grit from my eyes, I felt my hair stir in the dawn breeze. My nostrils filled with the clean, briny smell of the sea, my ears with the cries of gulls and other seabirds.

"You've *got* to stop calling me 'Lady Helen,' " I said drowsily.

"I'm sorry, Lady Hel—" Milo squatted beside me on the beach, biting his lower lip.

"Never mind, it's all right." I wanted to take that look off his face. Milo was my friend, but he always took anything I said to him much too seriously. It was as if I were already queen of Sparta instead of just fourteen, probably not much older than he was himself. Of course, it was impossible to say exactly how old he was: No one kept track of a slave boy's age.

Milo was no slave now. I had bought his freedom from my uncle, the king of Calydon. I had bought my own freedom as well, freedom from skirts and spindles and the life everyone said a royal daughter *must* lead, but I hadn't made that bargain using gold. I'd bought my liberty with a decision, choosing to turn away from the safe road home to Sparta to go on the quest for the Golden Fleece.

I got up and stretched, then patted Milo's shoulder. "There's no harm in you calling me by my real name when there's only the two of us. I'm just worried about what could happen if you slipped up in front of other people."

"You can trust me," Milo replied. "I'd die to protect your secret."

"You won't have to." I spoke quickly. "Just watch how you speak to me. The moment we set foot in Iolkos, there is no Lady Helen of Sparta, understood?"

He ventured a small smile. "I'll guard my tongue, but who's going to guard yours?"

"What do you mean?"

"When you were asleep, you kept yelling about who you are, how you're Sparta's next queen——" He spread his hands, letting go of any blame. "It woke me up."

It was my turn to feel embarrassed.

"People say all sorts of things in their dreams," he reassured me. "Once we're aboard the *Argo*, I'll look out for you, awake or asleep."

"And what happens when you topple overboard and drown because you've spent your nights standing guard over my dreams?" I teased.

"If it was for your sake, I'd be glad to——"

"What are you two jabbering about?" The fisherman appeared from behind the far side of his beached boat, a wooden spear in one hand, a string of fat fish in the other. "Not bad for a little wading in the shallows, eh?" He held up his catch proudly. "Now build up the fire or we'll have to eat these beauties raw."

Later, as we picked the last of the fishes' meat from their bones, our host looked at me and said, "Today we part ways. You've brought me good fortune and safe seas on this journey . . . Glaucus. Is there any favor I can do for you when I return to Delphi?"

I didn't have to think twice to answer that. "Tell Eunike I send her my love and thanks for everything she's done for me," I replied. "Tell her that you left Milo and me well, safe, and happy at Iolkos."

The fisherman made a face. "As if it's that simple for a man like me to get an audience with the holy Pythia."

I gave him a knowing smile. "You'll be able to do it easily enough if Lady Helen of Sparta puts in a good word for you."

Then we both laughed, for we shared a secret: The only reason I'd been able to steal away to Iolkos was because people have eyes and ears, yet most don't use them. My friend Eunike was the Pythia, priestess and prophet of Apollo's shrine at Delphi. When she spoke, people heard the all-seeing sun god's own words, predicting the future. When she declared that Lady Helen would not leave Delphi when her guardsmen headed home, everyone assumed it was Apollo's will. (She didn't lie: My guards marched off to Sparta one day before Milo and I sailed for Iolkos.) After that, whenever any of the priests who kept Apollo's shrine saw a royally dressed girl walking through the temple grounds, who else could she be but Lady Helen? In reality she was the daughter of the same fisherman who'd brought me this far in my journey.

I hoped that the same trick that let a fisherman's daughter pass for a Spartan princess would also fool my brothers on the *Argo*. Even the largest ship is a small, enclosed world. We *would* run into one another, unless I spent the whole voyage hiding in a chest, and what would be the point of that? When my brothers saw me, I wanted them to look right at me and say to each other:

Is that our sister?

What, here? Did you get too much sun? That's just one of the other men's weapons bearers.

I was very confident that was exactly how things would work out. I was so eager to see it all unscroll smoothly that after breakfast I danced around our smothered fire, urging the fisherman to launch his boat. I wanted to be in Iolkos *now*.

The winds were with us. The sun wasn't even a hand-span above the horizon by the time we beached on the strand at the foot of the great city on the Wavy Sea. I reached into the leather belt-pouch I carried and pulled out a little golden disk as big as my thumbnail. My best skirts from home were trimmed with a fortune in such charms, dresses fit for a princess. Before we left Delphi, I'd harvested the gold, silver, and gemmed ornaments to trade for necessities. I tried to give this one to the fisherman, but he refused it.

"Pay me back by coming back," he said. "My daughter's life is in your hands. That's worth more to me than a fistful of gold." He threw his wiry arms around Milo and me in a quick hug, and walked away.

Milo turned to me with a *Now what?* look in his eyes.

"Now we go up there," I said, pointing to where the citadel walls of Iolkos shone in the early morning sunshine. "We'll find a pair of warriors who've come to Iolkos to sail with Prince Jason but who haven't got weapons bearers to serve them. This quest may fetch more men than the Calydonian hunt. We'll get to pick and choose from a whole mob of masters."

Milo and I had to hike a fair distance along the shore before we reached that part of the waterfront where the great ships and their crews waited. Once again I felt my heart beat faster as I looked from one grand vessel to the next.

"Glaucus, put on your shoes," Milo said. I ignored him. Men scurried here and there on a hundred unknown errands, or grunted under the burden of massive clay amphorae and wooden chests. Some sat mending nets, others untangling lengths of rope. The reeks of fresh pine pitch, salt, and sweat fought each other, no one winning.

"*Glaucus . . .*" Milo's hand fell on my shoulder and gave me a little shake.

"Oh! Sorry. Were you talking to me?"

"Were you listening?" he countered. "If you won't answer to 'Glaucus,' why insist I call you by that name? I said, put on your shoes." He gestured at the pair of sandals I was carrying slung around my neck. On the fisherman's boat, I'd gone shoeless for better footing.

Now I was ashore, and it was pure luck that I hadn't stepped in something disgusting or rammed a chunk of broken wood or baked clay into my foot. I knew from painful past experience how long such wounds took to heal. What warrior would hire a lame weapons bearer? I leaned against a building and put on my sandals, then announced, "Let's get started. If the gods are with us, we'll be serving good masters before the sun's overhead."

"The gods grant it," Milo said. "How do we find *good* masters?"

"First, by finding the *Argo*," I replied.

"And how are we going to do that?"

I waved away his question. "Easily." I set off with a light step, arms swinging, heart full of confidence.

It didn't last. I can't tell you how many ships, great and small, we passed. The longer we walked along the water, the less certain I felt. I began to stare at every vessel, struggling to find a clue that would tell me beyond any doubt that it was the one we sought. All I knew was that the *Argo* would have to be *big*. Before my brothers went off with Prince Jason, all they'd talked about was how their ship would sail crewed by *fifty* heroes. I thought it would be easy to find a single vessel large enough to carry so many.

There were many big ships at Iolkos, all pulled up onto the shore to keep them safe. Their sails and masts were down to keep any sudden strong winds from carrying them away.

Then Milo said the unthinkable: "What if the *Argo*'s already sailed?"

My heart went cold. Could he be right? It was

possible. It could've happened the day before we arrived, for all I knew.

Lord Poseidon, help me, I prayed, fighting back the ghost of bitter disappointment. *Grant that the* Argo *hasn't sailed without us. Master of the seas, send me a sign and I'll make a rich thanksgiving sacrifice to you as soon as I have something worthy to offer.*

Suddenly Milo tapped my arm and pointed farther down the strand. "Look there, Glaucus," he said. My false name no longer sounded forced on his lips. I shaded my eyes and let out a yelp of joy when I spotted what he'd already seen: the ram.

It was painted in mid-leap on a green sail edged with blue. Its fleece wasn't golden, but the next best thing, a crocus yellow brilliant enough to dazzle the eyes. You could tell that sail was still waiting to see its first voyage. When the wind blew toward me, I swear that I could smell the newness of the cloth, the tang of the dyes.

The ship itself was the largest craft in the harbor. The only reason I'd missed seeing it before was that it lay beached between other vessels, around a curve in the shoreline that disguised its length. The shallow black hull was as newly made as the sail unfurled from the single mast, the gleaming prow freshly painted with a long blue-and-red-rimmed eye for luck, to watch over the waves ahead. The prow itself curved up like a beckoning arm, and was decorated with carvings from base to tip. I was standing too far away to see whether they meant anything or were just for decoration, but I was positive that I'd get a close enough look at them soon.

"That's it, Milo," I said as we walked a little closer. "That's got to be the *Argo*. I thought those other ships harbored here were big, but this . . ." I couldn't help counting the short wooden poles sticking up in pairs along the side rails. I'd overheard enough sailors' talk on the few voyages I'd made to learn those were called thole pins, and that they were used to hold the oars steady when the crew rowed. "Enough of them on this side to hold twenty-five oars steady, so there must be the same on the other. Fifty oars, fifty men, just as my brothers said. And the picture on the sail—"

"Why have they got it unfurled?" Milo asked. "The ship's not going anywhere."

"It must be Poseidon's doing, a sign that he *wanted* us to find this ship," I said. "We couldn't ask for a better omen! Now let's see whether the god will also help us find our new masters." I started toward the ship, only to have Milo's hand close on my shoulder yet again and hold me back. "What's wrong?" I asked.

"Let me go first."

"Why should I—?"

"In case your brothers are there."

I could see he was right. The ship wasn't deserted.

My brothers very well might be there among the men who were swarming everywhere, bringing aboard and stowing supplies. I grabbed the side of another beached ship and pulled myself up to get a better view of what was happening aboard the *Argo*. Craning my neck, I caught sight of wooden storage chests being set down alongside the oars so the crew would have places to sit while they rowed. One man was examining the ropes that controlled the single sail. Another was stowing clay amphorae under the small wooden shelves at either end of the ship, as well as in the bottom of the shallow hull, taking care to distribute the weight evenly.

I let go of the other ship's side and dropped back to the beach. "All right," I told Milo. "You go ahead. I'll be waiting for you over there." I nodded toward the row of buildings along the seaside. "Bring me good news."

It was a hard thing to have to let Milo approach the great ship without me. I loitered well out of sight, between a stone building and a shed that smelled of fish and sour wine. I didn't like being left behind, waiting. I wanted to meet my fate head-on. I also wanted to examine every hand-span of the ship's body to see where I'd best be able to lie low once we set sail and my brothers were on board. A smart rabbit doesn't wait until the hounds are on her trail before she digs her burrow.

Milo came back quickly enough. He wasn't smiling. For a moment I was terrified, imagining that the big ship with the yellow ram painted on its sail wasn't the *Argo* after all.

"What did you find out?" I asked.

"That's Prince Jason's ship, all right," he replied. "I talked to one of the crewmen overseeing the work. That is, *he* talked to *me*. Yelled at me, I mean. Told me to get out of the way so Lord Pelias's slaves could do their work."

"Is that why you're wearing such a long face?" I asked. "I'll teach him better manners."

Milo shook his head. "Forget him. He's nothing. The man with him, the one who called him 'brother,' *he's* why I'm worried. He said, 'Let the boy be. Can't you see he's only hoping for a handout?' And when I told him I wanted to earn my keep as his weapons bearer, he answered, 'Better look elsewhere. This ship's fully manned. We're not looking for any extra hands.'"

"Maybe he only said that to get rid of you," I suggested hopefully.

Milo shrugged again. "They're still there, by the ship, and plenty of others who don't look like slaves. Talk to them yourself. Maybe they just didn't like my looks."

"Then they're fools and I wouldn't waste my breath on them," I said.

"You're always too kind to me, La—Glaucus. But

you mustn't worry. Someone's got to be ugly in this world." He grinned.

"You're *not* ugly," I said hotly. And that was true. The same harsh slave's life that had left Milo so skinny had also given him wiry muscles under sun-browned skin. He reminded me of images I'd seen of the young Hermes, thin but fit and graceful. His dark hair was growing longer, like a noble's, and his brown eyes shone when he smiled.

"Have it your way," he said good-naturedly. "But in case they do prefer your looks, see if you can persuade them to hire me, too. It's safe, your brothers are nowhere in sight. I'll wait here."

I raced off to the *Argo*. There must've been at least a dozen men working on board, continuing to secure the supplies. They were all strong and carried themselves with pride, even while they labored. They didn't have the hungry, harried look of slaves. Eight more stood aside in scattered pairs on the shore, talking earnestly. They could hardly take their eyes off the ship. Most of them smiled when they looked at her, but I noticed one or two whose expressions said, *What have I gotten myself into?*

I approached one of those men first. "The gods give you a good day, sir," I said cheerfully. "Has Prince Jason come down to the ship yet this morning?"

"How's that any of your business, puppy?" he replied sourly. He had short hair, unlike most of the other warriors and nobles I'd met. It was silver-tipped and so bristly that he reminded me of a hedgehog.

I kept smiling. "I heard that he's manned his voyage with plenty of heroes like yourself, but that the call came so quickly that you could do with a willing lad or two for the drudge work. Any Mykenaeans here?"

Hedgehog-hair scratched his head. "Those braggarts? I don't think so, or we'd've heard their crowing by now."

"Ah, too bad." I pretended to be downcast. "They might've vouched for us."

"'Us'?" the man echoed. A trio of his friends were also beginning to pay close attention to what I had to say.

I jerked my thumb back over one shoulder. "My friend Milo. He's down that way, out of sight, watering the wall to make it grow. The wall, I mean. Not much hope for the other." I made an unmistakable gesture at the hem of my tunic. I'd seen and heard more than my share of such crude jokes passed among the Spartan soldiers. The men roared with laughter. "We were serving a pair of young warriors, Tantalus and Pelops, distant relatives of the Mykenaean royal house. They heard about Prince Jason's quest. They were so eager to set out that they didn't make a fitting sacrifice to Apollo before we left."

"What's Apollo got to do with journeys?"

Hedgehog-hair demanded. "A prayer to Hermes, that's what you need if you're going on foot, or Poseidon, if you're traveling by sea."

I shook my head. "That's what they said, even when I told them that the sun god watches over *all* travelers."

"So, now you're a priest, too?" This time the men's laughter was at my expense.

I let them have their fun, then softly said, "It doesn't take a priest to know which god's been offended when men die sunstruck."

My words sank into their minds, dragging down the corners of their mouths. One of them clutched an amulet he wore around his neck. Another muttered a few words under his breath. I worked hard to keep my face solemn. If I could spin thread as skillfully as I spun words, my sister, Clytemnestra, would die envying me.

"That's harsh, lad," one of the men said, patting me on the shoulder. "Where did it happen?"

"About five days' march south, in wild country." I took care to have our masters die too far away for anyone to bother confirming my story, just as I'd first made sure there were no other Mykenaeans around to call me out for lying. "We covered them with stones and made the proper sacrifices, then decided to honor our masters' spirits by finishing their journey for them."

Hedgehog-hair rubbed his chin, where a small black beard straggled around his jawline. "That's noble of you, boy. Pious and practical at the same time. I wish you luck." With that, he and the other three turned their backs on me and walked away.

I scampered after them. "Wait! Can't any of you use a pair of able-bodied weapons bearers? The gods will reward you, for our masters' sakes."

The men stopped and gave me pitying looks. The shortest of the four spoke: "Lad, how do you know *what* the gods will do?" He managed a wobbly smile. "Apollo himself might still be angry. Your masters are beyond his reach, but what's to stop him from taking it out on you?" He shook his head. "This voyage we're about to take is off over unknown waters, to lands full of fierce barbarians, monsters, dangers so great that the praise-singers will go crazy trying to find the right words to describe our glorious deeds. We can't afford to bring along two boys who might be carrying a god's displeasure. Sorry, but we can't risk it."

The four walked on. I stayed behind, seething. "Pork-brains," I snarled under my breath. "*Unknown* waters, yet you know there are monsters and barbarians on the other side?" I went to report my failure to Milo.

"At least you came up with a good explanation for who we're supposed to be and why we've come here alone," he said when I finished. "Which one was my master, Pelops or Tantalus?"

"Pick one and give me the leftover," I grumped.

"Pelops, then; easier to remember. Look, it's a big ship with a big crew. You only spoke to, what, three of the men?"

"Four." I thought about this, then said, "You're saying that one bad olive doesn't mean the whole crop's rotten, right?"

"One or even four, yes." One corner of his mouth curved up. "Unless you're used to getting your own way easily."

"I am not!" I took his light teasing to heart. "The things I've wanted *didn't* all come easily. I had to fight to learn how to use a warrior's weapons. I had to work to convince Atalanta to teach me how to ride a horse."

"Then fight for this, too," Milo said. "I'll help, if you'll let me. Tell me again about our dead masters."

We went over our story several times before we split up to seek other crewmen from the *Argo*. We agreed to meet in the alley when the sun was directly overhead. "Talk to the men still down by the ship," I told Milo. "I'll try my luck closer to the palace."

"Do you think that's a good idea?" Milo looked doubtful. "Your brothers might be up there, if they aren't here by the water."

"It's time I started to practice dodging them. If I can't do that now, what hope do I have of doing it once we've sailed? And don't forget, they know your face just as well as mine. What *are* you going to say if you meet them?"

Milo nibbled the corner of his lip in thought, then brightened and declared, "I decided that it was no use having my freedom if I didn't use it, so I left you in Delphi and struck out on my own. And don't worry, I know the rest." We parted, he for the waterside, I for the palace within the citadel atop the heights of Iolkos.

The sun was beating straight down on the dirt streets when we met back in that alleyway, tired and hungry. Even the rats had taken shelter from Apollo's burning arrows. Our faces told the whole story before either of us could speak: No one wanted to hire a weapons bearer for the *Argo*'s voyage.

"That was a waste of sandal leather," I said, wiping sweat from my brow as I leaned against the barely shaded side of the alley. "I lost count of how many men I spoke to. Every one of them turned me down. The *Argo*'s crammed with heroes, but they're all determined to look after themselves."

"Same here." Milo tilted his head back and took a long drink from the water-skin slung over his shoulder. I had one as well, but it had been empty since the morning. I'd been so impatient to find us a place on the *Argo* that I'd neglected to fill it. "It's funny," Milo went on. "The more men I questioned, the more their reasons for not hiring us sounded . . . false. False and forced, as if they were repeating words they didn't want to say."

My brows drew together. Milo's words made sense, but they buzzed strangely in my ears. His face looked odd as well, dark as a dried fig, his eyes two smears of wet clay that began to trickle down his cheeks as I watched. What was wrong? I closed my eyes and shook my head vigorously, fighting to banish the illusion.

"I agree." I spoke loudly, as if noise would scare off the weird vision. "There's a secret at work among the *Argo*'s crew, but finding it out can wait until we've had some food and drink. I'm so famished my head's spinning." I pulled a fistful of ornaments from the pouch at my belt. "It shouldn't be too hard to find a tavern in a city like this." I started back toward the water, jingling my riches boldly in my hand.

Milo grabbed me and hauled me back so fast I almost scattered the gold bits like grains of barley. "Are you crazy?" he demanded. "What do you think you're doing, showing off that kind of wealth?"

"I *think* I'm about to get us a decent meal," I snapped. I wanted him to be quiet. His voice had taken on a thunderous echo that made my head throb. I was sure he was doing it on purpose, to annoy me. I squirmed out of his arms and chinked my gold under his nose. "Am I the only one who's hungry and thirsty?"

His hand closed over mine, muffling the high, sweet ringing sound. "If you go into any wineshop and put even one of these on the table, it'll be the same as slitting our throats," Milo hissed. "We're supposed to be servants. Servants don't have gold, especially not a pair of boys."

"You worry too much," I told him, tossing my head. "Any tavern keeper will be happy to take this as payment, no questions asked. Let me *go*."

I jerked my hand away so hard that I lost my grip. The ornaments made a golden rainbow that arced out of the alley and across the path of a pair of thickset men. The smaller of the pair dropped to his knees and began scooping up handfuls of dust and dirt, rubbing them through his fingers to sieve out the gold. His companion turned his attention to Milo and me.

"This yours, lads?" he drawled, gesturing at my fallen fortune.

Milo said "No" and I said "Yes" loudly, quickly, and at exactly the same instant. That made him laugh.

"Well, one of you's lying. You, boy." He nodded at me. "How'd a little donkey-turd like you get your hands on such riches?"

"The same way I got my hands on this," I replied,

drawing my sword. My words came out slurred. The buzzing in my head was growing louder, and my sight painted four ugly men where there were only two.

Our confrontation began to draw attention along the busy waterfront. Faces and bodies blurred into a murmuring cloud of people just outside the mouth of the alley. The stench of sweat and rotten fish stabbed up my nose so painfully that I had to grit my teeth or scream. My ankles wobbled, but I forced myself to stand fast.

"You!" I jabbed my sword in the direction of the man who was still harvesting the fallen gold bits. "Give back what's mine and I'll let you keep a couple of pieces for your trouble."

The two men exchanged looks of disbelief. The one still standing laughed, though it sounded more like a bull's bellow. "You hear that? The prince has spoken! Obey him and he'll let you keep your own gold. Sounds like that outlander Jason's not the only one to come swaggering into Iolkos, laying claim to honest men's property!" He glanced down at my feet and sneered. "Hunh. Two sandals. I was expecting only one. Seems like that's the fashion for all great liars, these days."

The crowd laughed at that. Why? It sounded like nonsense to me, but it won them over. Some of them shouted insults at me, calling me thief, liar, fraud. Only one voice was raised in my defense.

"Who do you think you are, calling my friend a liar?" Milo yelled. "And Prince Jason, too? Say that to *his* face, you coward!"

The man ground his teeth together. "Think I wouldn't? It's only because Lord Pelias is such a pious man that he didn't have that so-called *Prince* Jason put to death as soon as he claimed to be our king's nephew. Everyone knows the *real* Jason's dead. The boy's own mother said so!"

A shrill, cracked voice rose from the back of the crowd. "The boy's own mother lied to save her child, and you know it!" The people stood aside to let a gray-haired old woman come forward, bent double by the weight of a basket on her shoulder. "And *I* know *you*, you good-for-nothing ruffian! Take your worthless crony and leave the boy alone." She glowered.

For an answer, the bully knocked the old woman's basket away with one blow of his fist. Fish scattered in the dirt. "Mind your own business, hag," he snarled. "Next time I won't hit the basket."

"Next time you'll hit *nothing*." I darted forward and brought the flat of my blade down on the man's forearm, making him yelp. "Pick up what you spilled."

"Or what? You'll cut my throat in front of all these people?" His mouth stretched out in a rotten-toothed leer. He rubbed the arm I'd smacked and added: "Curse it, that hurts. Where'd you steal that sword, you lousy little—? Ow!" A rock flew through the air and bounced off the side of the man's skull. It was too small to do damage, but it got his attention. He whirled around, cursing, just as a second rock whizzed past his ear.

"Pick up my fish, you ox!" the old woman yelled, shaking her fist. It already held a third rock, ready to fly. "Pick them up or I'll lay you out on top of them; see if I won't!"

He growled and charged. The old woman stood her ground, but her courage wasn't going to shield her skinny limbs from a bad bruising, or worse. I couldn't let that happen. I leaped onto his back, grabbed his filthy hair in my free hand, and yanked it hard. Furious, he reached back, seizing my shoulders and flinging me forward, over his head. It happened so fast that I couldn't even think about using my sword. I went sailing straight for the thickest part of the crowd. Men and women scattered left and right, but I bowled into one slow-footed fellow. The pair of us tumbled heels over head, churning up a small dust cloud, until we stopped halfway to the water.

"Get off me!" The man shoved me away and clambered to his feet, grumbling. "A fine thing, when every tadpole fresh from the egg's got a sword."

"A bad thing," my opponent said, suddenly behind me. "Give it here, boy, before you hurt yourself." He bent over and tried to take my blade.

That was a mistake. I got my feet under me in a

crouch and deliberately stood up fast, shooting the top of my head against the bottom of his jaw. The impact was jarring. His teeth slammed together and I ran a few steps clear of him. I whirled around just in time to see him stagger backward and collapse right on top of his companion, still grubbing in the dust.

"You should've picked up those fish," I cried gleefully. I pointed my blade at the pair of would-be bullies and added, "Now empty your hands and get out of my sight!"

The crouching man stood, letting the gold drop back into the dirt, then slung his partner's arm over one shoulder and helped him away. The crowd cheered and clapped their hands. Now that I'd given them a good show, they were all on my side.

I turned to the one person among them who'd first stood up for me. "I'll get your fish for you," I told her, going after the basket.

"Poseidon grant they're still worth trading," she said, folding her arms over her bony chest.

"You won't know until you—" I began. Suddenly I froze. The fallen basket lay a hand-span from my reaching fingertips, but as I looked at it, it began to swell like a water bubble, a weird red light crackling around its wavering edges. I only had a moment to think, *Gods help me, what's this?* before the bubble burst and flooded my head with darkness.

2

MASTERS, SERVANTS, AND SLAVES

I opened my eyes to see a man's tanned face backed by a soot-stained wall. I knew those eyes, but my head was still twirling, and when I attempted to remember where I'd seen this person before, my thoughts danced away, windblown wisps of smoke.

"Who—who are you?" I asked. "Where are we? Where's Milo? Where's the ship?" My voice came out raw and sandy. Wherever I was, it was dark and smelled like fish seasoned with a little sour wine and rancid oil. When I tried to sit up, the world tilted sharply and I fell backward.

"Ah, careful there!" The man thrust his arm behind my back and braced me. "If you fall over, you might hit your head. Then what will I tell your brothers?"

"My . . . brothers? How—" I took my first real look at him. My spine stiffened, moving me away from his steadying arm. When I spoke his name, it was a gasp: "Iolaus."

"That's me." He smiled and ran his fingers through his hair. We were both on the floor, he on the bare, beaten earth, I on a woolen cloak thrown over a thin pile of barley straw. "I was worried that you'd forgotten me. Memory loss is a bad sign when you've been sunstruck. I don't flatter myself to think I'm worthy of your royal notice, Lady Hel—"

I lurched forward without thinking and clapped my fingertips to his lips. "I'm *Glaucus*," I whispered fiercely as the room spun. "Please."

He was very gentle as he clasped my wrist, lowering my hand. "My mistake," he murmured. "Your slave told me that, but it slipped my mind."

"Milo's not my slave," I said sharply. I looked around the room, which had steadied. It was bare except for some baskets, a few clay pots, one plain wooden storage box, and a tiny hearth well away from the straw where I lay. Light and air came in through the smoke-hole in the roof. The reek of fish and the sea clung to everything. "Where is he? Is he all right?"

"He's fine. You're both safe and there's no one near to overhear me call you by your true name. The old woman went off on her own business after insisting I bring you here. This is her home."

"The fishwife?" I asked.

"She told me her name's Melitta." He took a damp scrap of cloth from a shallow bowl on the floor and dabbed it softly across my brow. It felt good. Iolaus was a warrior, the nephew of the great hero Herakles himself, yet he had a light touch and a kind heart.

"How did you find me?" I asked him.

"I was coming down from the palace to have another look at the *Argo* when I saw the crowd you'd attracted. There were too many people to see what was going on, but I had a fine view of things when you collapsed. I thank almighty Zeus that I recognized you, because you were the last person I'd expect to find in Iolkos, in the middle of a brawl. I almost had to get into one myself with that slave of yours. He was ready to fight me to the death when I tried to pick you up and get you out of the sun."

"*Stop* calling Milo my 'slave.' He's my friend, and he's as free as you are!" I spat out the words with so much force that Iolaus raised his hands to ward off my anger.

"Lady—Glaucus—what can I say? I only remember him from King Oeneus's palace in Calydon, where there's no denying he *was* a slave. And he certainly is your friend. He let me carry you away only after I whispered your true name."

"Where is he now?" I asked, placated by Iolaus's explanation. "You never told me."

"I sent him for more water."

"Oh." A fresh thought came to my mind. "Iolaus, you spoke of my brothers. You can't tell them I'm here. Please."

He looked puzzled. "I thought you came to Iolkos to find them. I'll tell you the truth, I've been sitting here wondering what could've happened to make a girl like you risk the journey here. When your brothers showed up in Prince Jason's company, they told me how you'd all traveled together as far as Delphi, where they'd left you safe, yet now . . . here you are."

I told Iolaus the whole story behind my decision to come to Iolkos and how I'd accomplished it. While I was talking, Milo returned. He was carrying a deep bowl filled with water. I took it from his hands with thanks and drank greedily. I'd never tasted anything so delicious!

"Slowly," Iolaus cautioned me. "Gulping cold water can tie your guts in a knot."

I set the bowl aside reluctantly. "I guess sometimes I need to be protected from myself." I looked at him steadily. "But who's going to protect me from you?"

He reacted as if I'd slapped him. "Why would you say such a thing?"

"Forgive me, that came out badly. You helped me today, and you were a good friend to my brothers and me when the boar hunt ended in disaster."

"All I did was bring you terrible news," he said. "Your cousin's death, and then how his mother died by . . ." He sighed deeply, turning away from the memory of my aunt's suicide.

I shook my head so that my sunstruck vision reeled. I'd have toppled sideways if both Milo and Iolaus hadn't grabbed me at the same time. My friend shot a poisonous look at Iolaus, who let go of me and edged away from us, even though he could have shattered Milo's wrist with one hand.

"Milo, *no*," I said, shaking my head more cautiously this time. "I don't need anyone to protect me *from* Iolaus. Since he's recognized me, I need *him* to protect my secret."

"What are you talking about?" A deep crease showed between Iolaus's brows.

"When we sail on the *Argo*—" I began.

" 'We'?" He cut me off at once. "No. Out of the question. It's too dangerous."

"Why?" I asked. I spoke softly, but my pulse was racing. "This will let me join Prince Jason's quest safely." I gestured at my boy's clothing. "The only reason you discovered me was because you know me and got a close look. Trust me, I won't give Castor and Polydeuces that chance."

"That's not the danger I mean," he said. "If I don't stop you now and some dreadful fate befalls you on this voyage—the gods forbid it!—I couldn't bear the guilt."

I took a deep breath and tried a different tactic. "Iolaus, do you hate my brothers?"

" 'Hate' them?" he echoed, puzzled.

"If you tell them I'm here, they'll want to get me home. Whether they hire armed men to escort me to Sparta or take me back themselves and abandon the quest for the Fleece, it will draw attention. I'm not ashamed if people gossip about what I've done, but *they* will be."

"I doubt you cared this much about their feelings when you chose this path," Iolaus said. He didn't raise his voice. The truth doesn't need to be shouted.

"Maybe not," I answered, looking him in the eyes. "But I had to choose it."

"That's ridiculous."

"No more ridiculous than why *you're* ready to sail into the unknown. The only person who *needs* to chase after the Golden Fleece is Prince Jason, yet you and all the others are joining him for the sake of pure adventure. You hunger for it! Why can't I?"

"Enough." Iolaus raised his hand. "You win, for your brothers' sake and because I've got the feeling you'd find a way to sneak aboard no matter how much they or I try to stop you. I wish some of the men I know had half your boldness. It's strange to see it in a girl. Perhaps you're really Atalanta's daughter."

My smile answered his. "My nurse, Ione, said I was Zeus's child."

"My uncle Herakles is supposed to be Zeus's son. You two must be related. He's a great one for following his heart first and thinking about the consequences afterward. Or never." His teeth flashed in the shadows of the old fishwife's home. "I'll keep your secret."

"Thank you. You won't have to do it for very long. You said I didn't care about my brothers' feelings when I decided to join this quest. You were right. I've only been thinking about what *I* want." I took a deep breath. What I was about to say tore at my heart, but I couldn't escape it. "I'll go back to Delphi. It's one thing to take a chance with my own life, but not with so many others'."

"Oh, I agree," Iolaus said. "Which is why I intend to take very good care of my new weapons bearers."

It was sunset when Iolaus left us. He waited until Melitta returned to ask if we could stay with her for one more night. "These boys work for me," he told her. "We were separated on the road. I'd bring them up to the palace, but I get the feeling that Lord Pelias wouldn't welcome the surprise of two more mouths to feed."

The old woman snorted. "You don't have to tell me about Lord Pelias. His fingers clench around every crumb. They won't uncurl until he dies."

"The lads won't be a burden to you, Mother. I'll bring you plenty of extra food and wine for them."

"Keep it." She nodded at me. "They're welcome under my roof."

"Spoken like someone who's never seen them eat." Iolaus chuckled. Then his voice turned serious. "Can I trust you to keep their presence here a secret?"

Melitta's eyes narrowed. "Why?"

"Unless Iolkos is the only city where no one gossips, word could reach those men, the ones who scuffled with Glaucus. They might decide to stir up trouble."

"Hunh! Not likely, the cowards," she said.

"Cowards don't pick fair fights," I pointed out. "They might do something nasty and sly if they find out we're here, something like . . . like—"

"Like starting a fire," Milo piped up.

"That sounds like just what they *would* do," the fishwife agreed, and promised to let no one know we were her guests.

That night she fed us flatbread and fat anchovies she'd broiled on a rock in the house's fire pit. "Here, boys," she said, holding out portions to Milo and me. "I'll cook more soon enough. There's plenty, thanks to that good master of yours. He's no Lord Pelias, that's for sure. Our false king wouldn't give a bone to a starving dog unless he was planning to take its pelt to market and boil its bones for soup. Eat, eat!"

"Why do you call him 'false'?" I asked, taking a bite of my bread.

"Because he's got no more right to rule this land than I do, since Prince Jason returned. Child, surely you know the whole story behind that great ship, the one that waits for you and your master?"

"I know that Prince Jason ordered it built and manned it with heroes to bring the Golden Fleece back to Iolkos," I replied.

"Zeus bless you, is that what you believe?" Melitta clucked her tongue as she arranged a fresh row of silvery fishes on the hot, flat stone. "Prince Jason's father was our king. They say the shock of Lord Pelias's treachery killed him. His widow claimed that the infant prince had died as well. Truth was, she sent him to safety far from here."

"Why didn't she go with him?" I asked. "How could she stand to lose her husband and her child, too?"

"She stayed in Iolkos so Lord Pelias would believe the lie that saved her baby's life." The old woman looked grim. "I wish the gods had let that brave woman live to see her son return. And what a return, on the heels of the Pythia's prophecy!"

My ears perked up when she mentioned my friend Eunike. "What prophecy?"

"Last year Lord Pelias sent a rich gift to Delphi and asked about the future of his reign. The god replied that Lord Pelias should fear nothing but this: a man who'd come to Iolkos wearing only one sandal, but who'd have the protection of Hera." Melitta turned the fish with a charred wooden spoon. "Exactly how Prince Jason arrived, half shod, but bold as if the queen of the gods held him in the palm of her hand."

Now the bully's comment about liars wearing only one sandal made sense. "If the Pythia's prophecy told Lord Pelias to fear a man wearing one sandal, I'm surprised he didn't have Prince Jason killed."

"Oh, he would have, if he'd dared. But Prince Jason first made sure that plenty of powerful folk knew who he was. Many of our nobles don't care for Lord Pelias and stand ready to welcome *any* change. Prince Jason's got their protection against *direct* attacks." She gave the anchovies one more turn with the spoon and slid them onto her own piece of flatbread.

Milo was bewildered. "If Prince Jason came to claim his throne, why is he sailing off to Colchis?"

The fishwife took a bite of her dinner. "Our prince is smart, but our king is crafty," she said with her mouth full. She swallowed, then added, "He pretended to welcome his nephew home and pledged to make him heir, even before his own son. But I hear that at the banquet that night, he kept Jason's wine cup full and turned the talk to heroes. He twisted things until our prince found himself trapped by his own inescapable oath to fetch the Golden Fleece."

"Why would he vow to do something that risky, just when he'd gotten everything he wanted?" Milo asked.

"Here's a lesson for you, lad." Melitta leaned forward and poked him sharply in the ribs with one gnarled finger. "Don't drink heavily at your enemy's table, especially when your enemy claims to be your friend. The instant that Prince Jason swore he'd bring back the Fleece, the king quickly promised his nephew a fine new ship and supplies." She took another bite of fish and bread before concluding, "If I had a sheep for every man who made his own trouble by swearing a stupid oath while drunk, I'd be a rich woman."

PART II
ABOARD THE ARGO

3

SHIPMATES

Iolaus came for us the next night. The *Argo* was to sail at dawn. He brought Melitta a jar of the finest barley and another one filled with olive oil. She tried to refuse the gifts, but Iolaus could be very persuasive and charming. I liked him more and more for the kind and honorable way he treated someone who clearly had no power over him, for good or ill.

I dug into my belt-pouch and gave her one of my silver charms. She wanted to refuse that too, on the grounds that she wasn't a beggar or a weakling and could still support herself with no one's charity. I told her it wasn't payment, but a keepsake, and asked her to remember us in her prayers to Poseidon.

There was more than moonlight brightening the harbor that night. The *Argo* was no longer beached beside the other ships but rocked at anchor some distance from shore.

"The king's orders," Iolaus whispered. "He thinks that once the ship's got all her supplies aboard, she'd be too heavy for us to launch. That shows how little he knows of ships, or how little he thinks of us!"

"Or how eager he is to be sure nothing keeps Prince Jason here," I murmured.

Torches lit the shore near the *Argo*, with a strand of flames trailing down the path from the citadel. Sentries stood watch while slaves laden with the last provisions waded out to the ship. At Iolaus's direction, Milo and I waited in the shadows until he came back for us with two of the slaves. "Climb on their shoulders and they'll get you on board."

"I can get there myself," Milo said. He sounded determined, but I pointed out that the water was over his head. If he began to flounder, he'd draw unwanted attention to us both. He saw the sense in that, and soon we found ourselves carried safely through the water and deposited over the side of the *Argo*.

I started exploring the ship the moment my feet touched the planks. The scent of pine pitch filled my nostrils immediately, though I soon saw that the timbers had been so cunningly fitted together that the ship might have stayed watertight even without that gummy stuff to seal her cracks. I made my way to where the mast towered above the framework that let the crew brace it in place when needed or take it down when it was time to beach the ship for the night. Tilting my head back, I gazed up to where the great sail was bundled to the crossbeam. I glimpsed the long, leaf-bladed oars, piled against the *Argo's* low sides, and noticed that the wooden chests where the rowers would sit had all been covered with thin cushions. My inspection was cut short when I caught sight of my brothers. Luckily for me, they were busy inspecting the leather straps that would help secure the oars between the thole pins. I retreated to the rear of the ship, where the big steering oar rested. There was still no call for the helmsman to begin his duties, so I was free to investigate the space beneath his post. A wooden platform covered a small part of the ship's stern, making a covered storage space for gear. Someone had curtained it off with ox hides. It was too dark for me to tell what was being stored there, but it was a sheltered space where we could stay completely out of my brothers' sight. I nearly danced for joy.

Even though I'd found a secure place for Milo and me to lie low, I continued to explore, making the *Argo* mine. There were plenty of people on board besides my brothers, but they also all had their own work to do and had no time to notice me. I was able to sneak from the stern to the prow and back again at least twice before I realized that Milo hadn't moved.

He stood where the slave had left him and stared at the lights onshore.

"Milo, good news," I said softly in his ear, and proceeded to tell him about the haven I'd found for us. "We'll be under the helmsman's nose, but he'll be too caught up managing the steering oar to be a threat. If we keep quiet, he'll never suspect we're there. Now come help me find some provisions. I should get an empty pot as well, for night-soil. I may be dressed like a boy, but I won't be able just to lean over the rail and—"

"Well, hello!" A new voice sounded behind us, young and friendly. "What are you two staring at?" I turned around to see a boy so handsome I forgot to breathe. His thickly curled black hair had a blue sheen in the moonlight, and his eyes held flecks of silver. He wore nothing but a short sea-green kilt in the Mykenaean fashion, and though he was years away from having a grown man's muscles, his body looked strong and striking as a young lion's.

"Just wondering where to—what to do next, now that we're on board this—the *Argo*," I replied. I stumbled over my own words just a bit and felt my cheeks go hot and red with embarrassment. *Aphrodite, Artemis, please grant he didn't see that!* Suddenly I wanted to know this boy's name as desperately as I'd ever wanted to join the quest for the Golden Fleece. I hoped fiercely that he was going to sail with us. If he turned out to be an Iolkan slave, bound to stay behind, I'd die.

Idiot! I berated myself. *Since when does a slave have the time or freedom to strike up conversations with strangers? Just look at him! He can't be more than a couple of years older than you, so if he's part of this voyage, there's only one reason.* Aloud I said, "My name is Glaucus and this is Milo. We're weapons bearers, like you."

It was a good guess. "Thank all the gods, I thought I was the only one!" he exclaimed. "Lord Pelias didn't want any of us aboard."

So that's *the secret,* I thought, remembering how Milo and I had been rebuffed when we'd approached those other crewmen. "Why's that?" I asked.

"I heard it's because he meant to make the voyage as rough as possible for Prince Jason and his men, but some of the other crewmen say it's because he didn't want to provide supplies for more mouths than necessary. You can imagine how well my master took *that* news." Even his laughter was beautiful. I hoped he wasn't going to turn out to be like Theseus. I'd thought the king of Athens was handsome too, until he showed his ugly personality. "*You* tell Herakles he can't bring me along!"

"You're *Herakles'* weapons bearer?" I must have goggled like a strangling fish.

"You sound surprised. I'm Hylas of Trachis. Where are you two from? Who d'you serve?"

It was my turn to chuckle. "Iolaus of Thebes, your master's nephew. We're from Calydon. He took us when he came there to hunt the boar."

"Ah! A fine adventure." Hylas nodded knowingly. "Herakles and I heard more than one bard sing about that heroic hunt. I wish we could have been there. Is it true what they say about Atalanta?"

"If they say that she was brave and beautiful, yes," I replied.

Hylas sighed. "She must have been wonderful. I wish she were sailing with us tomorrow. Did you know her well?" He addressed the question to Milo, trying to draw him into our talk. It seemed that Hylas was as good-natured as Theseus had been overbearing. I was pleased, but Milo only pressed his lips together. Hylas raised one eyebrow at this chilly response. "What about you, then?" he asked me.

It was so good to be able to talk about Atalanta! Hylas listened attentively while I told him as much about my huntress friend as I could without betraying my own secret. I don't know how long I would have stood there, jabbering away, if Milo hadn't spoken up.

"It's late, Glaucus. If you don't show me that place you found for us, we won't have time to get food and settle in." His eyes were flinty when he regarded Hylas. "Our master told us to keep out of the way when the ship sails and not to show ourselves for two or three days, not even when the ship's beached for the night."

"That's strange," Hylas said. "Why?"

"I don't question my master," Milo replied crisply. "We have to go. Come on, Glaucus." He started for the stern.

"Wait a moment." If Hylas noticed how rude Milo was being, he seemed willing to overlook it. "Iolaus probably doesn't want the other men to know he's got two weapons bearers when they can't have even one. Let me help you."

"We don't need any help." Milo crossed his arms. "We have a place at the stern. Glaucus said——"

"I *say* we listen, at least," I cut in. "What can you do for us, Hylas?"

The beautiful boy smiled, dazzling me. "Show me this hiding place of yours first, then I'll do as much for you as I can. We're all brothers on this voyage."

Just what I needed: another brother.

We all headed back toward the helm of the *Argo*. We passed the rowing benches and I spared a moment to pray, *Lord Poseidon, grant that Castor and Polydeuces have become good oarsmen.* I didn't want my brothers to be humiliated among their new comrades.

"Ah, you do have a good refuge," Hylas said, lifting one of the ox hides and peering into the darkness. "This is where I stored Herakles' things, safe from sun and sea."

"Only *his* things?" I asked. "No one else's?"

"The other men store their belongings in the chests they sit on to row. Herakles demanded more, and he got it." Hylas's amused expression added, *Could you ever doubt that?* "He and I are the only ones who'd have reason to go under there, and he won't unless there's a call to arms. If you only need to keep out of sight for a few days, this is the best place for you. You'll be comfortable as kings. I'll bring you food and drink. No one will suspect anything. They'll think I'm carrying it for myself, to eat while I'm looking after Herakles' weapons."

"Will we have to sleep on spear shafts?" I asked, joking.

Hylas laughed again. "Feel free to make a bed out of any spare clothing you find. What do you say?"

"That the gods are being very kind to us. So are you, and we thank you." I cocked my head at Milo. "Shall we?" He shrugged, then stooped to shoulder past me, between the hanging hides.

"Talkative, isn't he?" Hylas remarked.

I didn't know what to say. What was the matter with Milo? He was in a foul mood. "He gets seasick," I said at last. "He's afraid it'll keep him from doing his best for our master on this voyage." It was a weak excuse, but Hylas just nodded.

I ducked into the little space under the helmsman's post. It was dark as Hades' kingdom. I felt a pair of sheathed swords, some spears, and a couple of leather bags before I found Milo. He pulled away from me as soon as my fingers brushed his skin.

"What *is* the matter with you?" I hissed. He said nothing. "Fine. Talk when you like."

He held his silence a little longer, then spoke so softly I almost didn't hear him say, "Helen—"

"Here you are." One of the ox hides flicked back, showing Hylas's curls haloed by starlight. He shoved a wide-mouthed clay pot inside. It held bread, a ball of hard cheese, and a stoppered flask. "Just water in that," he told us. "I might get in trouble if someone saw me raiding the ship's wine. You can use the bowl for . . . necessities. It won't be pleasant with it under there during the day, but you can empty it out after we beach at sunset and no one's left on board. I can't wait until your master says you can show yourselves. We'll have good times, we three! Sleep well, and the gods favor you." He was gone.

My hands explored the clay pot and carefully set aside its contents. "Well, he thought of everything, didn't he?" I said, joking.

"Of course he did," Milo grumped, and I couldn't get another word out of him.

Milo was just as surly and silent the next morning when the two of us were awakened by the excitement of the *Argo*'s leave-taking, but at least the rocking of the anchored ship hadn't been enough to make him seasick. The shouted commands, the cheers, even the curses from outside our refuge made their own strange music at a feast from which we were excluded. I heard the creak and splash of the oars, the distant snap of the sail when it first snared the wind, the muffled rush and slap of the water against the side of the ship. I stole frequent peeks through the narrow gap at the bottom of the dangling ox hides, but I had to stay low, so all I got for my trouble was flashes of bare, hairy feet pounding past my eyes.

Hylas took good care of us. Whenever I thought I'd go out of my mind from boredom, since Milo wouldn't speak, he'd pop in to bring us something to eat, to drop off a fresh flask of water, or just to see how we were getting on. Milo ignored him, curling up in a ball with his face to the ship's hull. I thought it was the return of his old affliction, seasickness. I was thankful that he wasn't ill enough to need the clay pot to empty his stomach, and I thought he was very brave to hold back any moans of discomfort.

Maybe he's doing so well because he's lying still, I thought, stretching out to take a nap myself. Later, when I woke up hungry and groped around in the shadows for our bread and cheese, I found both half gone. A seasick boy does *not* eat half a sheep's-milk cheese! Milo simply had a fistful of sand up his nose, and I didn't need Athena's wisdom to tell me why: He was mad at

Hylas. But what had Hylas done except welcome us, shelter us, feed us? It made no sense.

I wanted to drag Milo out of his foul mood, yet more than that, I found that I wanted the freedom to speak to Hylas. I wanted to feel closer to him, to have him like me, even to admire me the same way he admired Atalanta, and I wanted it *now*. How could that happen if I was trapped inside this tent, hiding from my brothers? I tried to console myself with thoughts of the voyage ahead. *You'll have lots of time to speak with him soon enough, you goose. Three days at most and Iolaus will be able to give you and Milo the freedom of the ship. Then you can talk to Hylas until your tongue withers. You'll probably be sick of him long before you reach Colchis!* So I told myself, but I knew that wasn't true.

Our first day's voyage ended when I noticed the sunlight fading at the slim gaps in the ox-hide curtains. The ship's planking echoed with heavy, hurrying feet, followed by a series of splashes. I could picture my brothers and the rest of Prince Jason's crew of heroes leaping over the side into shallow water, getting ready to pull the *Argo* aground for the night. I felt the ship's keel scrape the shore as the men, grunting with the effort, used ropes and bare hands to carry the vessel clear of the sea.

"I'm dying to stretch my legs. How long do you think we should wait to go outside?" I whispered to Milo.

"Why ask me? I'm sure *he'll* come back and tell us what to do," he mumbled.

"What's crawled down your neck? When did Hylas insult you, or even treat you badly? He's done nothing but help us, even though we're little more than strangers to him. He's our friend."

" 'Friend'?" Milo repeated bitterly. "Yes, I guess you'll have to be satisfied with that, and *only* that . . . *Glaucus.*" I heard him chuckle in the darkness. It was a joyless sound.

I left him there. I crawled out of our shelter as fast as I could, seething over what he'd said. The worst part was, Milo was right. I couldn't deny I was attracted to Hylas, yet as far as he knew or ever could know, I wasn't Helen but Glaucus, a boy, like himself. We could be friends and nothing more. I was frustrated, but in spite of that, I had to admit I was also just a little relieved. The thought of Hylas made me feel eager and shy at the same time. Though I revered Aphrodite, I still knew very little about love. For the first time, I found myself truly wanting to know more.

Once out in the fresh air, I stayed low, only standing up after I determined that the ship really was deserted. The men had built a cluster of campfires some distance farther along the beach, far enough to keep the *Argo* safe from the threat of an errant spark. The wind carried the mouthwatering smell of meat cooking. With dinner on the fire and the ship safely beached on an uninhabited shore, there was no reason for anyone to come back to the *Argo* soon. I was free to prowl.

I soon learned the mistake of making hasty assumptions. One crewman *did* remain on the ship, curled up fast asleep by the steering oar at the stern of the boat. He had badly thinning white hair and the muscles of a much younger man, but not the same appetite. He'd chosen sleep over dinner. Perhaps I should have returned to my hiding place, but I'd made a choice too: curiosity over caution. I told myself I could walk softly enough to leave the older man's slumbers undisturbed.

I walked forward and stood beside the prow, resting my head against the towering timber. After just a day's sail, the wood smelled more of sun and sea than pitch and paint. It was covered with carvings that told the story of the magical ram whose glittering fleece was the object of our quest. I was idly tracing the patterns all around the prow with both hands, letting my mind wander, when I realized I'd touched a face, a woman's face, carved larger than life-size. It was mounted at the front of the ship's bow, where the painted eyes could gaze out over the unknown waters ahead. The day's sun had left it feeling warm as living flesh. I leaned forward to get a better look at it and sucked in my breath sharply.

Eunike. The Pythia. The knowledge came to me out

of nowhere, strikingly true. How had the sculptor come to make such a perfect image of my friend? I even thought I smelled the heady, spicy aroma of laurel leaves wafting out of the wood. The laurel was Apollo's sacred tree, and the priests of Delphi burned its leaves in the chamber where the Pythia spoke of her visions of the future.

"I wish you *were* here, Eunike," I whispered to the image. "Not to tell me what lies ahead, not even about Hylas and—and me. I need to find that out for myself. Maybe I *would* like you to tell me what's turned Milo so snappish, but most of all, I'd just like to hear another friendly voice. I miss you."

I went back to our hiding place and tried to tell Milo about what I'd seen, hoping he might be interested enough to come with me to see Eunike's face on the prow. He didn't seem to care. While I was in the middle of my story, he took our fouled clay jar outside, as if I hadn't been speaking at all.

"There," he said when he came back, setting it down in front of me. "I emptied the slops and scrubbed it clean. At least you can still find me useful for *that*."

"What are you talking—?" I began. The rest of my protest was lost in the sound of an ox hide being flung back so forcefully that the whole thing tore free of its fastenings. Moonlight flooded my eyes as I stared up at a split-faced monster, a lion's snout above, a man's thickly bearded features below. The whole out-line bristled with hair, with a wild mane tumbling over its shoulders. Strong hands shot out to grasp my wrists and haul me to my feet and higher, until I dangled with my toes barely brushing the *Argo*'s hull.

"By Zeus, Iolaus!" the monster bellowed. "You said you had two weapons bearers, but you never told me you'd robbed Aphrodite's own hearth to find *this* one. Nephew, I envy you. He'd shame Eros himself with those looks. Ah, don't give me that angry stare, lad," it said to me, sending hot breath streaming over my face. "I'm a better friend to you than any you'll meet on this voyage, believe me, and for my nephew's sake I won't ask you for anything more than you'll willingly give, eh?" With that, he planted a rough kiss on my cheek before letting me drop to the planks in a heap. And that was how I met the hero Herakles of Thebes.

I scrambled up as soon as I hit the boards, one hand to the cheek he'd kissed. My skin tingled from the scrape of his whiskers. *Why did he do that?* My thoughts raced anxiously. *A kiss that . . .* forceful *is hardly the way to greet "Glaucus," unless—*

—unless he knows I'm not a boy. Was that his way of telling me he knows my secret?

Now I was used to the moonlight, and saw the reason why I'd mistaken a hero for a monster. All that he wore besides his warrior's kilt was a magnificent lion's skin, taken whole from the animal. The mighty forepaws dangled crisscross on his chest and the maned head rested atop Herakles' own, so that it looked as if the lion were forever trying to devour him and forever choking at the task. If the lion had been alive, it probably *would* have choked on Herakles. He was the mightiest man I'd ever seen, broad-chested and towering.

Iolaus stood in the shadow of his famous uncle. I hoped he could see the startled look on my face. Why had he told us to keep our presence aboard hidden for a few days, only to reveal it this soon? I was so confused by what had happened that I almost missed hearing Iolaus introduce Milo and me to Herakles.

"—and Glaucus, both from Calydon. That's where the problem with the Spartan princes began, Uncle."

" 'Princes,' " Herakles repeated with a sneer. "This ship's crawling with princes, like maggots on old meat. What did the pretty lad do to make *those* two mad? Tell 'em no?" He guffawed and brushed my chin lightly with his knuckles. It wasn't the sort of gesture a man would offer a girl. From the way he spoke and acted toward me, I'd definitely caught the hero's eye, though *not* as Helen. Now I had something new to worry about.

Iolaus sighed. "Does it matter? The fact is, there'll be trouble if Castor or Polydeuces runs into the boy. It won't matter if they see Milo—they've got no quarrel with him—but if they lay eyes on Glaucus, we'll be sailing a hornet's nest to Colchis."

"I see." Herakles stroked his black beard. "Enough chance of that happening anyway, with Acastus aboard. I'm willing to wager five amphorae of the best Theban wine that Jason finds a way to kill his cousin before we even smell the coast of Colchis."

"Prince Jason would never defile himself with a kinsman's blood," Iolaus protested.

"Pay attention when your elders speak, nephew," Herakles replied with a small, crooked smile that wrinkled the bridge of his much-broken nose. "I never said Jason'd kill Acastus *himself*." He stepped forward and rumpled my hair before I could avoid him. "Never fear, Glaucus, my boy. I'll keep you clear of the Spartans, and I'll make sure that the rest of the crew knows to keep their lips sewn shut as well. This ship's not the wide world, but it's large enough to keep a secret."

That night, Milo and I slept ashore beside the same fire as Iolaus, Herakles, Hylas, and three men from the savage northern land of Thrace. It was the campsite farthest from the rest, so there was no danger of anyone catching wind of our conversation. Herakles himself took the Thracians into the plot to keep Castor and Polydeuces ignorant of my presence aboard the

Argo, and he made it plain that he'd be insulted if they didn't consent to work with us. No wise man wanted Herakles for an enemy, though I think those three would have been willing to help even if there hadn't been a threat attached.

Well before dawn the next day, I was shaken gently awake by one of the Thracians, a man named Orpheus. His two countrymen were Zetes and Kalais, brothers who called themselves the sons of Boreas, god of the North Wind. They were rough-spoken men, built like square-cut blocks of stone, while Orpheus was tall and so slender that I wondered why Prince Jason had allowed such a fragile-looking man to join his crew of heroes.

"Glaucus," he murmured. I'd never heard my chosen name pronounced as if it were being tasted to become part of a song. "Did you rest well, child? Did your dreams come to you through the gate of horn?"

"What gate?" I rubbed my eyes, still half asleep, and gave him a puzzled look.

His laughter was soft and musical. "In Thrace we say that the god of sleep sends us false dreams through a gate made of ivory, true ones through a gate of horn. But I suppose that's not what you believe in Sparta."

Sparta! I tensed. Had that been a slip of the tongue, or did he know the truth about me? If so, how had he learned it? I looked steadily at Orpheus. There was something about him that reminded me of Eunike, a hint of forces from beyond the borders of this world, a breath of the gods. "You mean Calydon," I said carefully, watching his face. "It's the princes I've offended who come from Sparta, not me."

"Ah." He gave me a lazy smile. "My mistake. Come with me, Glaucus of Calydon. If you truly must steer clear of those Spartan princes, you'd better get aboard the *Argo* now, before the whole encampment's awake. Zetes and Kalais and I will work with your master and great Herakles today, letting the other Argonauts know your name and your need to avoid Castor and Polydeuces. We'll hide you from them so well that it will seem you've borrowed Hades' own helmet of invisibility."

Orpheus left me to scramble up the *Argo*'s side unaided. Once aboard, I looked over the beached ship's side and watched him stroll away along the tide line. He paused halfway back to our campsite and faced the sea, where the sun was just beginning to show a sliver of rosy light on the horizon. Raising his arms in salutation, he began to sing a hymn of praise to Apollo. The clear, perfect notes climbed the cool morning air like the fragrant smoke of burning incense. I'd never heard a man's voice so blessed by the gods.

I was still lost in Orpheus's song when I sensed that I wasn't alone. I turned to see Hylas at my back, as fascinated by the Thracian's voice as I.

"Beautiful, isn't it?" Hylas spoke softly, with the reverence a pious man might pay to the gods. "They say that Orpheus has the power to calm storms with his songs."

"Is it true?" I could believe it.

"If he can't calm the storm itself, he certainly can calm *our* fears. That's enough of a gift for any man."

"That's too bad." I ran my fingertips along the smooth wood of the rail. "I would have loved to see him sing a storm away."

"So, you've got a taste for wonders?" Hylas smiled at me. "We'll see some marvelous sights together on this voyage."

"Together—?" My breath caught in my throat. It was silly, but no matter how much I told myself that Hylas was a boy like a hundred others, I still couldn't look at him for long without feeling my face grow warm. "I— Yes, that would be— I'd like that," I finished lamely. An awkward stillness fell between us, putting me on edge. "What are you doing up so early?" I asked, wanting to fill the silence.

"No choice," he replied cheerfully. "I had to re-hang the ox hide Herakles tore down last night." He gestured aft to my shelter beneath the steersman's post. "I can't complain about the work. If I hadn't told him about you, I wouldn't have had to—"

"You did *what*?" I don't know how I kept myself

from shouting loud enough to bring the whole crew of the *Argo* running. "Hylas, I *trusted* you to——"

"Glaucus, don't be mad." He was genuinely distressed. "I did it to help you. I kept thinking of you and Milo trapped in that dark place for days to come. That's why I spoke to Herakles, begging him to be your champion. Once he promised me he'd protect you, we fetched Iolaus, not before."

"Oh. Well . . . well, no harm done," I said, my anger fading.

"I'll make it up to you," Hylas said. "Today I *will* bring you some wine, and the best cheese, and——"

If he said he was going to *bring* me food and drink, it could only mean one thing. I glanced aft to my hiding spot under the helmsman's post. "I thought we didn't have to stay there anymore." I'd joined the quest for the Fleece in order to taste freedom. I didn't relish the thought of spending another day as a prisoner.

"Not for much longer, Glaucus, I swear. Just until we've set sail and Herakles has the chance to tell your story to the rest of the crew . . . with two exceptions." His smile glinted with mischief. "If it's any comfort, you'll have the space to yourself. You said the Spartans have no grudge against your sour-faced friend. He's free to come and go as he pleases."

"His *name* is Milo." Even if Hylas was correct

about my friend's bad disposition, I felt he didn't have the right to criticize him.

"From the way he looks at me, you'd think my name was Worm. Did I do something to offend him?"

"It's only a mood," I said. "He'll come around."

"He'd better," Hylas said. "It's going to be a long voyage."

4

BIRDS WITH THE FACES OF WOMEN

Eunike as the Pythia had the gift of prophecy and I suspected that Orpheus did as well, but Herakles too turned out to be an oracle, in his own way. My life aboard the *Argo* worked out just as he'd predicted. Prince Jason's ship was indeed large enough to hold my secret safe. When I emerged from my hiding place the next morning, word of my supposed quarrel with Castor and Polydeuces had spread through the rest of the crew. Herakles made his wishes in the matter clear to everyone. You didn't need the Pythia to predict your future if you crossed him.

From then on, I knew my brothers wouldn't see me unless I allowed it. It was easy enough to avoid them. Each crewman sat on his own sea chest to row. The sole exception was the white-haired man who'd slept on board that first night. He seemed to jump from spot to spot on the ship like a flea. My brothers had the two right-hand places closest to the ship's prow, so I haunted the *Argo*'s stern and never went farther forward than the mast amidships if I could help it.

Of course, the men didn't row all day long. When the winds favored us, my brothers and the rest shipped their oars and gave thanks to the gods, leaving the *Argo*'s fate to Tiphys, who handled the steering oar, and the men who governed the great sail. Even when the winds failed and the crew bent their backs at the oars, there would be times called for them to rest, drink, and wipe the sweat away. I learned to stay alert for those moments. Just because my brothers didn't wander far from their chosen bench didn't mean it would *never* happen.

Keeping an eye on my brothers was a very small part of my days aboard the *Argo*. As far as everyone except Milo and Iolaus knew, I was a weapons bearer and had work to do. Most of it was fetch-and-carry, bringing the rowers watered wine to drink, or a mouthful of bread, dried figs, or wizened olives to silence their stomachs until we beached for the night and ate a real meal. Milo served the men who labored fore of the mast; I worked aft, to keep away from my brothers.

Sometimes we were given a pile of weapons and

told to clean and sharpen them, because even when such things were stowed inside the chests the men used for rowing benches, the sea spray would manage to seep in to damage good bronze subtly but surely. Though Hylas only had Herakles' gear to tend, he always pitched in to help us. After many days of this, Milo began to speak a few words to him. Soon they were trading jokes. I was glad, though I will admit I felt a little jealous. Time Hylas spent talking to Milo was time Hylas didn't spend talking to *me*.

When the sun slid low in the west each day, Tiphys would steer the ship into the most favorable haven he could find. While the crew lowered the mast and jumped overboard to beach the *Argo*, I'd make sure to leap ashore on the opposite side from my brothers. In the nightly commotion of making camp, I gathered firewood and kept my distance from Castor and Polydeuces. At first we were always the same group of eight around our campfire, but after several days we were joined by Prince Jason's cousin, Acastus. He rowed beside Iolaus, who had taken a liking to him.

Herakles teased him about it when Acastus was out of earshot. "Aiming your heart high, nephew, or are you just trying to win that bet of mine? Good luck with that! If Jason's got his mind set on securing his claim to the throne of Iolkos, he'll find a way to get rid of Acastus even if you stick to him like a second skin."

"Acastus and I are *friends*, Uncle," Iolaus replied patiently. "*Only* friends. And I still say that Prince Jason won't raise a hand against his kinsman, neither his own nor another's."

Herakles shook his head. "You believe that? You haven't grown up at all, Iolaus. You're still the same innocent lad who carried my weapons when I fought the Lernian Hydra."

"The Hydra!" I exclaimed. Slaying the Hydra was one of twelve tasks that great Herakles had to perform as penance for a crime he'd committed in a fit of reason-stealing rage. "Were you *there*?" I looked at Iolaus with renewed respect.

"He was," Herakles answered for my master. "The Hydra was a monstrous serpent with nine heads, fangs dripping black venom. Slice off one head and two sprouted in its place! Iolaus was just a boy, but he's the one who came up with the trick that let me slay the beast at last. I chopped off the Hydra's heads; he dashed in with a flaming torch to sear the bleeding necks. The monster never had the chance to grow back so much as a single scale! That was when I knew my nephew was braver than many a full-grown man."

Zetes and Kalais roared their approval of the story. Orpheus spoke soft words of praise. Iolaus should have basked in their admiration, but instead he sat hunched by the fire, his expression grim. Herakles peered closely at his nephew and drawled, "By the way, lad, do *you* ever tell that tale the right way?"

"There's only one right way to tell any story," Iolaus said. "The truth."

"Which is why you've been so swift to tell the Spartan princes about *both* your young servants?" Herakles raised one bushy black eyebrow. Iolaus pursed his lips and the great hero burst into rough laughter. "I'll tell you what, nephew," he said, clapping my master on the back. "If *you* don't go around telling everyone that the Hydra was just a cluster of swamp snakes, *I* won't remind you about how you're stretching the truth thin as a willow leaf for this boy's sake." He nodded at me.

"What difference does it make?" Iolaus grumbled. "The whole world believes *your* version."

"Well, truth or not, it does make the better story," Herakles replied. "And some of them were pretty big snakes!"

We sailed for more days than I knew how to count, sometimes hugging the mainland coast, sometimes passing from one island to another over the waves. The summer weather blessed us with clear skies and tame waters. We did have a couple of times when we had to put in to shore quickly to wait out a thunderstorm.

I think Zeus didn't want our quest to become *too* comfortable.

At first we kept to the western coastline, but when we entered the narrows that marked the last gateway out of the Wavy Sea, we kept the land on our right for a time. As much as I loved the sea, I was happiest when our course took us close to land. I liked to dream about the people who might live there, and wonder whether they looked like us, what strange languages they might speak, and whether or not they knew our gods.

If Zeus sometimes played with our ship just because he had the power to do so, at least his brother Poseidon showed unexpected mercy to my friend Milo, whose old affliction seemed to have vanished. He would run forward even when the sea grew rough, returning aft laughing, his face glowing with health and not a hint of seasickness.

"Tell me your secret," I asked him. "What's changed? Wait, let me guess! You asked Orpheus to offer a prayer to Poseidon for you. Not even a god could resist his voice."

Milo shook his head. "Hylas found out I had a bad stomach for sailing. He does too, if you can believe it, but he's got a remedy that always sets him right. He's been sharing it with me."

"So you've gotten over whatever was bothering you," I said. "I'm glad. I was afraid I'd have to douse you with seawater if you didn't stop treating him like a toothache."

"It was my own fault. Like you said, he's always been a friend to both of us. I was afraid he wanted to be your friend alone, and—and maybe something more. If that happened, I thought you'd have no more time for me." Milo lowered his eyes, embarrassed.

I was just as glad he'd looked away from me when he said that, so he couldn't catch me blushing. "I hope you know that's nonsense," I said.

"Oh, of course I do *now*," Milo said a little too quickly. "I was silly to think Hylas could come between us that way. It's just not possible."

"Why do you say that?" I asked, raising one brow.

"You mean you don't know he's—?" he began, but before he could tell me more, we both heard Iolaus calling him and he dashed away toward the prow, where I couldn't follow.

I was still wondering what Milo had meant to tell me when the air rang with a shout from Lynceus, our lookout at the prow: "Fire to the west! Fire and battle!"

I ran to the mast and stared at the black smoke billowing from the shore. I could just see the walls of a royal citadel on the heights above a harbor in flames. The *Argo's* crew clattered their oars together as they stood at their places, eager to know what Lynceus saw. The word *battle* had transformed them from a well-coordinated crew of oarsmen into a jostling mob of gawkers. Herakles pushed his way forward for the best view. I caught sight of Prince Jason himself at the prow, alternately fighting for a look at what was happening ashore and yelling at his men to return to their seats at the oars.

Iolaus detached himself from the confusion and came to join me at the mast, with Hylas tagging after. Milo remained fore, in the thick of the excitement, and I envied him bitterly.

"I see fire, yes," Iolaus said, shading his eyes. "But battle?"

"Trust Lynceus," Hylas replied. "He sees what he sees. Glaucus, come with me. We've got to give back the weapons we've been tending, and quickly." When I questioned him with a look, he added, "I don't know whose battle that is, but it's going to be ours. Have you ever known a true hero who'd turn his back on a chance to earn glory?"

"Without even knowing who's fighting or why?" I was astounded. "How will the men know which side to take?"

Hylas flashed a quick smile. "The winning side, of course. Herakles is with us."

He sped aft, to his master's stored weapons, and I dashed after. Already the men were throwing back the lids of their sea chests to retrieve the swords stored within. I heard a rumble from the prow and turned in time to see great Herakles working shoulder to shoulder with Milo, trundling out the shields that had been stacked in the space that was twin to my hiding place in the stern. While Hylas readied Herakles' weapons, I crept farther into the space under the steersman's post and found a pile of spears. When I dragged them into the light, there were plenty of hands ready to snatch them up.

"Give me a spear, lad, and be quick!" one man barked at me. "We'll need spears. If my ears are right, they've got horses."

When the last spear had been snatched from my grasp, I crouched with one shoulder braced against the ship's wooden wall and drew my own sword, making sure it cleared the sheath effortlessly. The familiar feel of the hilt comforted me. One blade couldn't win a battle, but as long as it was mine, it could be used to protect me and those I loved.

Everywhere I looked, I saw wolfish grins. Hylas was right, the men were ravenous for a fight. Even Iolaus had caught the battle fever. I saw him stride aft to give Tiphys directions for bringing the *Argo* to the burning shore.

Once the crew had their weapons, they slammed the lids on the wooden chests and sprang back to their places at the oars. Orpheus beat a spear against the ship's rail, marking a quick-time rowing beat for the crew to match stroke for stroke. He raised a powerful paean to Ares, god of war, filling our ears with the promise of the immortal fame that comes to the bravest of the brave, both those who live and those who die. The men answered the end of each verse with a cheer loud enough to shake snow from the peak of Olympus. The ship flew across the water, heading straight for the burning shore.

Abruptly the booming beat of wood on wood stopped. Orpheus swallowed the next line of his blood-stirring song. Without his beat to help them keep time, the overeager men lost control of their oars. The heavy blades clattered against each other loudly, then fell still. Silence rippled over the *Argo* as we stared at the man who'd dared to place himself between a ship of warriors and their desired war.

Prince Jason raised the spear he'd wrested from Orpheus's hands and rammed its haft down hard on the ship's hull. "*Turn*, Tiphys!" he shouted, swinging the spear's point north. "Turn this ship back to her proper course! Have you all forgotten *why* we set sail? We seek the Golden Fleece, not some petty squabble between savages! We'll waste no time and no lives on anything but our true quest."

For a moment it looked as if that would be the end of it. Our helmsman frowned, but he began to lean against the steering oar, turning the ship away from the smoke. The other men grumbled. We were close enough to hear the first faint sounds of fighting, the clash of metal on metal, the crackling of flames.

Then Zetes spoke up: " 'Savages'?" he echoed bitterly. "Is that what you call Thracians? Or haven't you got the brains to know where we are? I know this coastline as well as I know my own sword arm. That's *our* homeland burning!" He clapped one fist to his chest. "If you turn this ship away, I swear by the deadly waters of the river Styx, the oath that binds the gods, that you'll see the last of me, my brother, and Orpheus as well!"

Jason's smile was thin. "Small loyalty, small loss." I didn't like the contemptuous way he looked at his disgruntled crewmen, as if their grievances were hardly worth his time. "I won't risk my ship for anything less than the Fleece."

"*Your* ship, Jason?" Herakles loomed at the mast, his eyes smoldering in the shadow of the lion's jaw. "This vessel was made at the command of Lord Pelias, the *reigning* king of Iolkos. You're king of nothing, and you'll never be king over me. Unless the gods command otherwise, I serve men *worth* serving."

Jason's eyes narrowed. "But the gods *do* command you, Herakles," he said. "If you still claim to be the son of Zeus, they do. I've dedicated this quest to Hera, his wife and queen, because she favors me. But you? Your existence is an insult to her, living proof of her husband's faithlessness. She's got enough reason to hate you already. Do you want to add to her wrath against you by defying me?"

Herakles scowled. "I'll take my chances with Hera. Come closer and take your chances with me!"

No one will win this fight, I thought, every nerve taut, eyes fixed on the two glowering men. I tightened my grip on my blade. I had no idea how much farther we still had to travel to reach Colchis, but I did know that if the quest ended now, the immortal fame Orpheus sang about would become immortal ridicule. The loss would be Jason's doing, but all the Argonauts would suffer for it, including my brothers.

Fame . . . The word trailed through my mind and struck a spark. I sheathed my sword and crawled just far enough to tug at the hem of Orpheus's kilt and draw his notice. He gave me an inquiring look until I motioned for him to bend near. Then I whispered, "How quickly can you remind Prince Jason that fame's more than a word?"

The Thracian poet smiled. "The gods bless you, Glaucus," he whispered back. "You see what I should have seen for myself." With that, he straightened up and began a new song. He didn't need to sing it loudly. The first line was enough to seize everyone's attention. It told of the quest for the Golden Fleece, and how it came to nothing. When the monsters of a hundred unknown seas couldn't sink the *Argo,* foolish quarrels did. The name of Prince Jason would be remembered forever.

I watched closely, with growing admiration, as

Orpheus made the crew understand that they were risking more than their lives with this dispute. Most of all, I watched Jason. I swear by all-seeing Apollo, I could tell the exact moment when he considered killing Orpheus and, the instant after that, when he realized he'd also have to kill every last man aboard the *Argo* if he didn't want to return to Iolkos with a reputation for turning tail. What self-respecting city would have a coward for her king?

His scowl vanished, replaced by a broad smile. I couldn't help wondering if it was sincere or false. "Well sung, Orpheus!" he cried. "I've always said that a man needs a light heart before he goes into battle. We've all had our joke here, eh, Herakles?" He strode forward to slap the astonished hero on the back. "Now let's give this ship wings. To Thrace, and to glory!" He pointed toward the shore.

That's a quick turnabout, I thought. *And calling it all a joke? There's a nimble-witted way to save one's honor. A simpler man would confess that Orpheus's words persuaded him to change his mind.* I wondered if Jason would ever do anything like that, or if he was someone who believed you could never admit you'd been wrong without also admitting you'd lost, you'd failed.

On to Colchis or *On to Thrace,* one of the two was a lie. Jason saw nothing wrong with deceiving his men as long as it saved his pride and let him hold on to his command of the *Argo.* I think I must have been the only one concerned about that, though. The men were too eager to obey Jason's new command, to seize their roles as immortal heroes. They fell back to the oars, Orpheus again set the rowers' beat, and the *Argo* flew arrow-straight to land.

The fighting was strung out all along the shore, between the water and the small, brightly colored houses of those who made their living from the sea. It was thickest at a point two spear-casts north of where the *Argo* came sailing into the shallows. Our sharp-eared crewman was right: There *were* horses, impressive animals bearing warriors clothed in vivid, sleeveless tunics and ankle-length trousers. Flashes of red and blue and green showed beneath the armor covering their chests and shins. Their war cries were the shrill screams of birds of prey.

Zetes and Kalais stood near enough for me to overhear one of them growl, "*Them* again," and the other respond, "Thrice-cursed raiders." Even without their words to confirm it, their grim faces told me that they recognized those mounted fighters and hated them.

Smoke blew across the beach. The *Argo* was the only boat in the harbor that wasn't aflame. The men didn't want to waste time beaching the ship. I heard a loud splash as Prince Jason himself slung the stone anchor overboard; then he took up his sword and shield before jumping into the hip-deep water. His bare legs churned the water to foam as he raced toward the battle. If lying came easily to him, so did courage; I had to give him that.

The other men didn't lose a moment in following their captain's example. As they began leaping over the sides to rush ashore, Iolaus paused long enough to order Milo and me to remain on board. "You're not warriors yet," he said. "You're only weapons bearers with a long way to go before you're ready for something like this."

"Hylas went," I pointed out. He and Herakles were already halfway to where the fighting was most intense. A mob of riders swooped in circles around a core of armed men dressed much like our own Thracians. More smoke rose from within that defensive ring of swords, but it was too thin and pale to come from any great burning.

"Hylas is experienced and can look out for himself. Stay here." With that stern command, he vaulted over the side.

Milo and I ran to the prow to watch. I balanced on the rail and flung my arms around the image of Eunike, leaning so far forward that my shoulders ached. The *Argo*'s crew charged, each man's battle cry loud on his lips. The roaring human wave made many of the circling riders pull back on their reins and turn to meet the unexpected challenge. Some of the riders brandished spears, some flourished short swords. Nearly all carried bows and packed quivers at their backs, but they left those bows unstrung. Instead of keeping their distance, picking off our men from the safety of an arrow flight's distance away, they kicked their heels to their horses' flanks and met the battle head-on.

I couldn't obey Iolaus's command any longer. If I were a *real* weapons bearer, I'd take my rightful place beside my master. I sped to the *Argo*'s stern and lashed an extra sword to my back, then grabbed a spear and leaped over the side, holding it well above my head. I heard Milo shouting after me, then a second splash. He must have jumped into the sun-warmed shallows too, but I didn't waste a moment looking back.

I stumbled when my bare feet met dry land. I was too accustomed to the roll of the ship, but I soon recovered my balance. I ran after Iolaus, taking care to keep just far enough behind him so that he wouldn't know I was there. I'd come to help if needed, not to divert his attention and endanger his life.

I lingered on the borders of the combat between our men and the riders. In the confusion of battle, it was impossible for me to tell whether or not they outnumbered us. I saw Zetes and Kalais plunge into the densest part of the clash, moving so swiftly that perhaps the North Wind *was* their father. The fighting shifted, giving me a clear view of their slashing swords, and my jaw dropped. They weren't challenging the warriors, they were attacking the horses. The beasts shrieked in pain and terror. Their riders were thrown, or else went down in a heap with their wounded steeds. Zetes and Kalais never gave their foes the chance to regain their feet and face a fair contest. Bronze chopped flesh and bone and the coppery smell of blood choked the air. Would the songs to come call these men heroes or butchers?

Those two were the only ones who fought without honor. Herakles moved through the battle armed with a gnarled wooden club big as a young oak. Hylas kept close behind him, carrying sword, spear, and shield, but his master ignored them all. Herakles swung his club left and right, scything a pair of riders from their steeds. Those he missed learned quickly and steered their horses well out of his reach. He bellowed with laughter and pursued them. More riders fell to his club and some didn't rise again. Those who did stood their ground and took on the men who came in Herakles' wake.

Iolaus was fighting one of the warriors Herakles had sent toppling to the ground. My master was being beaten back in a flurry of sword strikes. He took a misstep, slipped, and staggered. As he struggled to keep his balance, his foe's blade licked out lightning-swift, sweeping his shield aside with one swing, knocking his sword from his hand with the other.

"Iolaus! Here!" I dashed to his side. I held the

spear with both hands, using it to fend off my master's adversary until he could draw the spare blade I carried at my belt. I heard the scrape of the sword leaving its sheath, but I never took my eyes away from the eyes of the foe. They shone blue as deep water, and they were all that I could see of that helmet-hidden face except a glimpse of beardless cheek and the hard, small mouth that erupted with a shrieking war cry.

The warrior's sword swung high and fell, splintering the spear in my hands. I danced back a few steps and bared my own blade. It had been too long since I'd last used it. I wished that I'd found time and opportunity during the voyage here to practice the hard-won swordsmanship I'd learned at home in Sparta.

The first clang of my sword against the enemy's blade rang out. The sound shivered through me and kindled an extraordinary transformation. All of my teacher's lessons came back to me not as words, but as knowledge that I carried in my blood. I could do this! Whether or not I'd win, whether or not I'd survive, I could fight. My fate was in my hands alone. So this was why the *Argo*'s crew had thirsted for a fight! I attacked, shouting Ares' name.

My battle joy was short-lived. Iolaus seized the back of my tunic and yanked me back, stepping between me and the other fighter. He'd found his footing and his strength. The fortunes of the skirmish changed and ended with a single stab of Iolaus's borrowed sword. My enemy made a hideous sound and crumpled.

Iolaus turned to me, his face monstrous. "In the name of all the gods, Helen, *what are you doing here?*" He was so enraged he called me by my true name, but it was lost in the chaos of battle. "Get back to the ship now, or I swear by Zeus himself, I'll drag you there by the hair!"

I gave him a sour look. "You'll need both hands free for that. Better give me that sword back first." I nodded at the blade I'd brought him, the one that had saved his life.

Iolaus wasn't in the mood for inconvenient reminders. "I'll thank you later, if you're alive to hear it. Now get back to the ship before something else hap—"

A fresh war cry from one of the remaining riders tore the air, loud and imperious enough to draw everyone's attention. Spear in hand, horse dancing sideways along the tide line, the warrior shouted harsh foreign words. The unmistakable command made the others turn sharply away from battling the *Argo*'s crew and gallop back up the beach to where their comrades still circled that small rising column of smoke. I think there must have been thirty of them still mounted, but I had no time to count them before they were gone. They didn't slow the horses' pace when they leaned over to sweep dismounted fighters up behind them on their steeds. Some of the warriors who'd been un-horsed even managed to sling the bodies of their slain and wounded comrades up and across the horses' backs before saving themselves.

Our men gave chase, as if they had any real hope of overtaking horses. A few of the riders strung their bows and fired off hissing flights of arrows to discourage pursuit. I heard yelps of pain and much cursing, and I saw several men stop short as the darts sliced their flesh. Zetes fell, clutching his thigh. Soon the riders were nothing but a retreating tumult of flying hooves, sand, and stones, and those wild, hawklike war cries.

"You're safe. Thank the gods." Milo appeared at my side, dripping wet, his face scratched and battered. With a shamefaced smile he added, "I fell off the ship."

"*Another* one who won't obey me?" Iolaus growled. He turned his back on us and started up the strand, falling in with the rest of the Argonauts. We followed.

As I walked, I wiped sweat from my eyes and viewed the aftermath of my first battle. Besides the warrior I'd fought and Iolaus had slain, there were seven colorfully clad bodies on the beach. The retreating riders hadn't been able to reclaim all of their dead. We'd lost three of our own, an unexpectedly low price to pay for victory.

We soon reached the place that the riders had

been circling. Now that the chaos of combat was over and the dust settled, I could see that it was an altar, a heap of blood-streaked stones crowned by a small, brightly burning fire. Five more men lay sprawled around it, shields scattered, lifeless fingers still curled around the hilts of their swords. They were none of our crew.

Behind the altar, a company of armed guards stood around an old man whose richly ornamented robes and heavy gold collar, rings, and diadem marked him for a king. He held his head unnaturally high, and kept jerking it from side to side in quick, birdlike movements. "What's happening?" he cried fearfully. "Have they gone? Am I safe? Will they come back? I order you, tell me what's going on!" His eyes were as white as his hair. He was blind.

Jason pushed his way to the king's side. "Greetings, Lord," he said. "I am Prince Jason of Iolkos. I've seen to it that you're safe from those marauding horsemen." He looked as proud as if he'd won the fight single-handed.

The king burst into cackling laughter. "Don't you Iolkans take trophies from your fallen enemies?"

" 'Trophies'——?" Jason was confused.

"My grandfather told me that we Thracians used to take heads." The king's grin revealed half a mouthful of darkly yellowed teeth. "Now we just take helmets."

Frowning, Jason signaled one of the crew to fetch a helmet from among the fallen raiders. The man raced off to obey. His cry of utter shock made the old man laugh until he wheezed. "You didn't fight marauding horse*men*, Jason of Iolkos. You didn't fight men at all."

That night, the fortified citadel above the harbor rang with the sound of celebration as blind Lord Phineas gave us a feast so lavish that even Herakles was satisfied. The great formal chamber in the center of his palace was a sorry, dark, smoky place compared with those I knew, but the food was good. While we ate and drank, the old Thracian king told us all about the women warriors we'd battled.

"Unnatural creatures," he said, holding his silver goblet with both hands. "They live far north of here, on the shores of the Unfriendly Sea, but they come south on raiding parties whenever it suits them. Wild as she-wolves, and their men are worse for not making those mad females behave like proper women. They don't let their daughters marry until after they've drawn a man's blood in battle. After that, they marry anyone they like, as if they didn't have fathers or brothers to find husbands for them! Well, at least you men saw to it that there'd be a few less of them to breed the next generation of Harpies!"

" 'Harpies'?" I whispered the unfamiliar word to

Orpheus. He was seated next to me in the most shadowy part of the hall, far from my brothers. The Thracians didn't waste time seating guests according to their rank or how much the king wanted to honor them. Lord Phineas had commanded Jason to sit to his right, Herakles to his left, and allowed the rest of us to find places that suited us.

"It means someone who snatches things away," he replied. "The way a falcon snatches a rabbit."

Later on, Orpheus stood beside the hearth fire in the center of the hall and sang about the day's adventure. On his lips, the northern raiders were transformed from swift, deadly riders to winged and taloned monsters, part hawk, part woman. Because they could fly so high that spears and arrows couldn't reach them, only men with the blood of the gods in their veins could end the havoc they caused. Luckily, a ship of heroes came ashore to rid the land of the hideous creatures. Zetes and Kalais, the sons of Boreas, had inherited the North Wind's ability to fly and soon defeated the Harpies. They would trouble good Lord Phineas no more.

Orpheus finished his song, and the men cheered and banged their fists on the tables so loudly that it seemed like they'd bring the roof down in pieces. As for me, I kept my mouth shut and my arms folded. Orpheus noticed my frosty look when he sat back down. "You didn't like it," he murmured.

"They deserved better," I replied stiffly. "They were brave fighters."

"I thought I made that clear. Just look at Zetes over there, grinning ear to ear in spite of a nasty arrow wound that probably still burns like Hephaestus's own forge-fires. It might leave him half lame for life, but he won't mind, because in my song, he owns the sky."

"You didn't see the way he fought today," I shot back. "He's not worthy to own a mud puddle. *They* fought well, those women. They were as skilled and courageous as any man, so you turned them into monsters!"

Orpheus was silent for a little while. Then he took a sip of wine and said, "They attacked without warning, they destroyed good ships for the sake of destruction, they violated the sanctity of a sacrifice to the gods, and they would have cut down a blind old man, king or not, if we hadn't come ashore when we did. I won't argue with you about their valor or their mastery of weapons and horses, but see them for what they are, lad. You say I've made them monsters, yet you'd make them gods. They're women, human women, as praiseworthy and as flawed as any fighting men I've ever known, but plain truth makes a poor song."

5

THE CLASHING ROCKS

We sailed the next morning, after tending to the dead. Lord Phineas was a pious man who saw no reason to carry a grudge against fallen enemies. He gave full funeral honors to the northern women who'd died in the fighting. We should have stayed at least one more day to pay fitting tribute to our lost comrades at the funeral games, but Jason was itching to raise sail and be gone. As I hung back in Iolaus's shadow, watching Herakles fulfill the rite of setting the torch to the pyre, I heard our leader telling the king he'd made a vow to Hera never to see more than one sunset from any harbor until we reached Colchis. *Well, that's news to me,* I thought. *Maybe liars do wear only one sandal after all.*

Lord Phineas looked as doubtful of Jason as I felt, but all he said was "And will your vow permit you to accept a few gifts from a grateful king?" Of course it did.

One of the "gifts" came in the form of a captive, a young girl with black braids and dark blue eyes who returned every man's glance with a hate-filled stare hot enough to peel skin from flesh. She wore the ragged remnants of a dress too big for her. Her hands were bound and there was a rope collar and leash around her neck. One of the Thracian guards put the tether's end into the king's hands.

One girl given over to a ship of so many men? I was appalled by Lord Phineas's cruelty. Even if the king meant her to be Jason's possession alone, what guarantee was there that our captain wouldn't tire of her, or just toss her to the crew as a reward someday?

"You are too generous, Lord Phineas," Jason said, his voice flat. "I couldn't possibly accept this—" He waved one hand at the girl. "Not after everything else you've already given us."

The king cackled. "Aren't you the tactful one? Don't be afraid, young man, I'm not asking you to take this little viper into your bed. By Poseidon, I swear that *I* never did. I wouldn't have survived the night! If she was a virgin when I got her, she's a virgin still, and you'd be wise to see that she stays that way. She's the daughter of one of those northern tribes, kin to the raiders your men fought yesterday. One of my soldiers made the mistake of capturing her alive about a year ago. Her people command both sides of the narrow passage you must take to reach the Unfriendly Sea. Hereabouts we call that place the Clashing Rocks, because of how few ships escape without being crushed one way or another. Those savages cling to the cliffs like gulls and watch for prey on the waters below. If you've got a rich cargo, they'll squeeze you for more than half of your trade goods. And if you don't have a bribe big enough to please them, they attack with spears, arrows, even boulders rolled down from above. I've just given you the best bribe of all." He turned his sightless eyes vaguely in the girl's direction and gave her leash a playful twirl. "Haven't I, my pretty dove?"

We sailed away with the pyre still blazing and our ship laden with gifts from the blind king, including his "dove." Orpheus knew a little of the girl's barbaric language. He assured her that no man would lay a hand on her, but her actions made it obvious that she didn't believe him. The Thracian singer made the mistake of removing her leash, as a kindness and a gesture of good faith. She responded by dashing for the ship's rail whenever he turned his back. I would have done the same, in her position. Orpheus literally had his hands full, holding on to her while she struggled to break away from him and plunge into the water, time after time. How the other Argonauts laughed!

Jason was exasperated. He needed Orpheus to keep the rowers working together and he was short by three men since the battle. He couldn't spare anyone else from the crew to keep the girl from killing herself. When he ordered Herakles to grab her and tie her to the mast, our "dove" showed us that she spoke our language well enough to spew blistering curses and threats.

"Listen to that!" Herakles exclaimed with an exaggerated shudder. "She's a witch's daughter, sure enough. She'll put a spell on me if I offend her."

"Stop that nonsense and control the brat," Jason snapped.

"Alas, beloved prince, I can't." Herakles sighed and hung his head with such a pathetic air that Milo, Hylas, and I stuffed our knuckles into our mouths to stifle snickers. "I made a vow to Hera not to touch a woman until we come to Colchis."

That was too much for Hylas. He burst into hoots of laughter, and Milo and I joined in, until we had to clutch one another to keep from falling over.

I was still trying to catch my breath when Jason's foot shot out and dealt me an undeniable kick in the behind. "You think this is funny? *You* watch her!" he barked at me. "If anything happens to the scrawny little bitch, we'll stick *you* in a dress, hand you over to her flea-bitten relatives, and be halfway to Colchis before they figure out they've been duped. If you're lucky, they'll kill you quickly. If not, they might decide to use their knives to turn you into the daughter they lost. See if you can laugh your way out of *that*, boy!" He showed his teeth in a satisfied smirk and didn't understand why I kept on laughing at his threat, even while I walked off to assume my new job as the girl's keeper.

She greeted my approach with wide, fearful eyes, then she spit at me and missed. "Don't do that again," I said calmly. "I know you understand me, so I'm asking you nicely." For her answer, she worked up a fresh mouthful and let it fly. She missed again, but I didn't. She wiped her face, slack-jawed with amazement. "Can we talk now?" I asked.

"What we talk?" she demanded sulkily. Her speech was heavily accented and awkward, but we could communicate well enough. "Of how you use me? How I die?"

"How about how to spit?" I suggested.

She lifted her chin and declared, "You are crazy boy."

"I am Glaucus," I replied. "I'm not crazy, and I'm not a liar either. You're going home. Believe it."

The girl looked away, twisting her fingers together fretfully. "The blind king said that, yes. I heard him. Why should I believe?"

"Not him," I told her, patting her shoulder gently. She didn't pull away. "Me." I felt foolish, asking her to put her faith in me like that. We were strangers. I doubted that I'd do the same if our places were reversed. But it was all I could do.

I was genuinely surprised when she looked up at me again and said, "All right. The good gods are all beautiful, and their words are truth. You are beautiful too, like the young lord who brings springtime, so I will believe you speak the truth, too. But if you lie, the Dark God will take you and the rocks will have your bones."

"Well, that's fair enough," I said. "Now how about something to eat?"

It turned out that Lord Phineas enjoyed making jests. He called the girl his little "dove," and that turned out to be her name, though not her disposition. I made such a mess of trying to pronounce it in her tongue that she finally laughed and told me to just call her "Dove" in my own language. She and I only had a day's voyage together before we reached the Clashing Rocks, but we were friends when we parted.

Jason had Dove and me stand together at the *Argo*'s prow as we approached the narrow waterway. I was ill at ease the whole time, because it put me too close to my brothers. Luckily, Castor and Polydeuces' side of the ship passed closest to a tricky stretch of coast, where every wavelet seemed to reveal the jagged teeth of half-hidden rocks. They paid strict attention to their rowing, not to me.

Just as the blind king had told us, the heights to either side of the narrows swarmed with wild tribesmen. As we sailed into the shadow of the Clashing Rocks, we heard a shout from the left: their leader calling out a challenge in several different tongues. No doubt he'd mastered just enough words in the most common trade languages of the Middle Sea to conduct his people's ill-famed business. All of his demands stopped the instant that Dove shouted back, identifying herself.

Within moments, a group of tribesmen from the leader's side of the narrows had scrambled down the rock face. Those manning the right-hand cliffs vanished from sight, though we knew better than to believe they were really gone. The Argonauts shipped oars and sent a pair of anchor rocks over the side to help hold the ship steady while the manner of Dove's homecoming was settled. Tribesmen still visible on the heights lowered a young tree trunk, shorn of branches, to their kinfolk. Their leader made signs to let us know that they wanted to use the sapling as a bridge to fetch Dove from our ship. When Jason hesitated, Dove rolled her eyes and exclaimed, "What you fear? That my people attack? The tree is narrow. Only one at a time crosses, unarmed! A child could defend that."

"All right," Jason said at last. "But only two of

them can set foot on the *Argo*." He held up two fingers for the bandits to see.

They accepted his terms, and laid the stripped tree trunk from the shore to the prow. I heard a murmur of disappointment from the oarsmen on the right-hand side of the ship, which included my brothers. They wanted a closer look at the marauders of the Clashing Rocks, but they had to stay put, to help steady the ship.

Two nimble bandits crossed the slender span and greeted Dove as joyfully as if she'd come back from the dead. Because I stood beside her, they babbled what must have been thanks to me, embraced me, kissed me, and dropped three of their own necklaces over my head before whisking her away. She raced ahead of them across the sapling and scrambled up the rocks like a young goat. Her waiting kin atop the cliffs disappeared as soon as she and her escorts reached them, and the *Argo* entered the black waters of the Unfriendly Sea.

We sailed on, always keeping the southern shore of the Unfriendly Sea in sight. Those dark waters had a bad reputation for spewing up storms out of nowhere. The farther we traveled from Thrace, the more attention and favor Jason gave to one particular man, strong-limbed and silent, whose few remaining strands of hair were sea-foam white. I'd noticed him many times, both when the ship sailed and when it was beached for the night. He was the one who'd slept aboard that first night out while the rest of the men made camp on the shore. He'd done the same thing from time to time in the course of our voyage, as if he found the ship better company than her crew. He seemed to be forever prowling up and down, examining every part of the *Argo* he could touch. His bench might have been far forward, where I never went, but I never saw him take a turn at the rowing oars, and I never saw him smile.

Beyond the Clashing Rocks, my curiosity finally got the better of me. "Who is that?" I asked Orpheus. The unknown crewman was at the steering oar again, shouting at Jason about how he had no business giving any orders concerning the ship's course. Jason accepted the scolding without a word of argument.

"That's our treasure," Orpheus replied. "If not for him, this voyage never could have happened. Not only does he know the way to Colchis, he saw to it that we've got a ship fit to survive these waters. He designed it, he watched over every step of its birth, and he'd sacrifice his own life sooner than let anything happen to it." The Thracian leaned closer to me and grinned. "Haven't you ever asked yourself why this ship is called 'the *Argo*'? That's Argus, son of Phrixus, the same Phrixus who rode the flying gold-fleeced ram. Nobody knows why Argus left Colchis, nobody knows why he agreed to return, and nobody asks."

"Not even Jason?"

"As long as Argus gives him what he wants—the quickest route to the Golden Fleece and a swift, safe passage back to the throne of Iolkos—Jason doesn't care if the man slit his mother's throat. His own mother's, or Jason's, or both," Orpheus clarified.

The next day, I waited until Argus came aft on his never-ending inspection tour of the ship. As he headed forward again, I stepped into his path and held out a clay cup filled with water. "The sun's strong today," I said pleasantly. "You look thirsty."

His brow furrowed. "What do *you* want? And if you say you only want to give me a drink, save your breath for other lies. I can get my own water when I want it."

"True." I raised the cup to my lips and drained it. "I want to talk with you. There's a question I want you to answer about this ship, that's all."

"That's more than you'll get. I'm busy." He tried to push past me.

"Too busy to repay your debt?" The words flew from my mouth.

Argus stopped and turned back to face me. "What debt?"

"The one you owe me from the Clashing Rocks,

when I saw to it that your ship passed through un-
harmed."

For the first time, I saw Argus's lips lift at the corners. "Don't you mean 'Prince Jason's ship'?"

"I know what I said."

His smile grew a little wider. "You're a funny one.
That's good. Men hunger for entertainment on long
voyages. So I owe you for this ship's well-being, do I?
That's a grand debt for a fingerling like you to hold
over me. How do you figure it's yours to claim?"

"I kept that captive girl from throwing herself
into the waves," I replied. "Without her, the *Argo* never
would have reached the Unfriendly Sea."

Argus snorted, but he was still smiling. "Do you
know who I am, boy?" I nodded. "Then you know
where I'm from, and that our course holds no sur-
prises for me. Don't you think I knew about the
Clashing Rocks and had provided a way for us to pass
through them, even without old Lord Phineas's 'gift'?"

"What did you bring?"

"Much the same thing as you've got right there."
He pointed to the small pouch I carried at my belt.
"I've got five just like that, all stowed away safe in case
of need. If that much gold and silver wasn't enough to
satisfy the bandits, I'd've handed over *your* pitiful little
sack of treasure as well. Hades take those vultures,
I'd've given them *you* to save this ship!"

I cupped my hand around my belt-pouch. "How

do you know I've got anything valuable in here?" I asked.

"My ears are like Lynceus's eyes. I can hear rot in a ship's timbers, and the rumble of a coming storm. Hearing gold and silver jingling in a young sprat's pouch?" He snapped his fingers.

"The jingling could be nothing more than seashells and pebbles," I countered.

Now he laughed. "And why would you want to carry *that* trash? No, you can't fool my ears—" He leaned close and, in a voice for my ears alone, added, "—*lass.*"

My mouth went dry and I could hardly draw a breath. "That's not funny," I rasped.

He threw his arm around my neck as if we were old friends and drew me closer. "Now, now, don't be a fool," he whispered. "I know what you are. A voice like yours gives it away to anyone with the ears to hear it. There's no hint that it'll ever break and deepen, the way a real lad's does."

"That's the flimsiest, most unbelievable—"

"Unbelievable, is it? Yet if I go to Jason, claiming it's so, and telling him there's an old sailor's belief that women bring bad luck to voyages, he won't hesitate to put you to the one test you *can't* bluster your way out of." He savored my distress for five breaths, then cackled and said, "But don't worry, I'm not about to tell a soul."

"What do you want from me?" I muttered. *Because you're not going to get it.* My hand strayed to the hilt of my sword.

He chortled softly. "Look at that stormy face! Don't worry, I don't want you to share my bed. I like my women ripe and plump as pomegranates, not skinny, nor young enough to be my daughter. I told you, long days at sea can be tedious. You've amused me, and you're the first person here who's spoken to me as a man, not a net to snare the Fleece. I've heard you called 'Glaucus,' true?" I nodded. "Well, *Glaucus,* I only want two things from you: one, your promise to do what you can, by choice or chance, to keep me diverted during this voyage."

"Given. And the other?"

He released me from his hold and grinned like a man who needs to practice at it. "Your question. The one I must answer to repay you for saving that girl and our ship. Ask it."

"The carvings on the prow," I said, pointing forward. "There's one that's the face of a young woman. Who's it supposed to be?"

I earned another of Argus's rare smiles for that. "Depends who you ask. Jason ordered me to give him Hera, queen of the gods. But I carved the face of the one who's to blame for me going back to my homeland after all these years." His smile dimmed. "She said if I went home again, I'd die."

"Then why did you agree to—?" I began.

"She said if I *didn't* go home again, I'd live a long life, but a forgotten one, and I'd die without ever having another sight of the sea." Argus scratched a few flakes of sunburned skin from his balding head. "What could I do? I swore I'd go. When the Pythia speaks, only fools don't listen."

6

A SACRIFICE
TO APHRODITE

Argus was right about how a ship's routine made her crew avid for diversion. In the evenings, more and more of the men drifted over to our campfire because Orpheus was there. The god-gifted Thracian was always good for a song, and Herakles was always good for a bragging tale about his own exploits.

I loved listening to those stories, but so did everyone else. More than once I had to creep away from the fire when I saw Castor and Polydeuces coming. I hated crouching in the shadows, waiting for them to have their fill of songs and stories before returning to their own fireside. One night when the moon was bright enough, I took myself far down the beach, along the water's edge, drew my sword, and began dueling an imaginary opponent. I deliberately chose the place where the water lapped the shore, because the sodden ground was unstable. I'd have to pay attention to my footwork as well as how I wielded my blade or risk a tumble. It wasn't the most useful training, but it was exercise, and better than lurking in the dark.

"Want a partner, Glaucus?" Hylas's soft words took me by surprise. I whirled around in a spray of sand and brine. He stepped forward, sword in hand.

My blood pounded in my ears. A chance to practice swordsmanship with Hylas? A chance to match my skills against those of a lad trained by great Herakles himself? The idea thrilled me. Better still, it was an opportunity to win the respect and approval of the one boy I wanted to notice me. Things had gotten to the point where the mere sight of Hylas sent my imagination flying wild. I was convinced that his notice, respect, and approval would *have* to lead to more . . . someday. *Someday when you can let him know that you're a girl,* I told myself.

"I'd love that, Hylas," I blurted. Suddenly a cold wave of reality crashed over my head and I sighed. "But we can't."

"Why not? I'll go easy on you." He chuckled.

I didn't. "If we practice, everyone'll hear the sound of swords clashing and come running up to watch the show."

"So? Let them come."

"Including the Spartan princes?" I reminded him.

"Oh." His face fell. "You're right, I guess." He sheathed his sword reluctantly. I did the same. "Gods above, Glaucus, isn't there any hope that you and the Spartans could settle whatever's bad between you? What did you *do* to them?"

"Don't ask me to talk about that," I said.

"I'll bet Milo knows." I didn't reply, hoping he'd drop the matter, but he went on to say, "You're not denying it. Glaucus, I accept that you and I can never be as close as you and Milo. You two share a homeland and you've traveled together all the way from Calydon. There's a strong bond between you, one I don't want to interfere with, but—but—" He looked up, and moonlight turned his perfect face silver. I wanted to kiss him, then and there. "—but I thought, I *hoped* that we weren't just shipmates. I thought we were friends."

"We are," I murmured.

"Then why can't you *talk* to me? I want to help you! Glaucus, please—" He grabbed my arms and squeezed them hard. I was breathless, all of my romantic dreams flooding over me at his touch.

"Hylas, I—"

"Well, what do we have here?" Thunderous laughter rolled over our heads. Herakles stepped in, threw his mighty arms around our shoulders, and separated us effortlessly. "If I were you lads, I'd pick a more secluded temple to worship Aphrodite."

"That's not what we were doing!" I cried. My face was aflame from hairline to neck.

"We wanted to practice with our swords," Hylas added. His unintended crude joke twisted my stomach with fresh embarrassment and made Herakles laugh so loudly that a crowd of the *Argo*'s crew took notice and started toward us from the campfires. I didn't wait to see if my brothers were among the curious. I ran, and I didn't stop running until I had the bulk of the *Argo* between me and everyone else. After a while, when the noises from shore subsided, I peeked around the ship's prow and watched the men drift back toward their own fires.

"What do you think, Eunike?" I whispered to the starlit face of the carved Pythia looming above my head. "Do you think it's safe for me to go back?" I calmed myself by imagining that my friend was really there to hear me. *Go back, Helen,* Eunike's voice whispered through my mind. *Back, but not to your own campfire, not with Herakles there. You know him, he'll keep making those "jokes" about you and Hylas all night! If you want sleep, find your bed elsewhere.*

As I walked back toward the fires on the beach, I noticed one in particular, far smaller than the others, set apart, with only one man beside it. I approached curiously and recognized the Colchian shipbuilder himself, all alone.

He hadn't lied about those accursed keen ears of his. I thought I'd been moving cautiously beyond the firelight, with a hunter's tread, but he looked in my direction at once and said, "Do you want to talk or do you want to stare out of the darkness like a scruffy little owl?"

"I *want* to sleep." I came into the firelight. "But I wouldn't say no to talk, or to a good story."

"A story?" His grizzled eyebrows rose. "Don't you get enough of those from that muscle-bound Theban?"

"I've had my fill of Herakles' words for the day," I replied, sitting down beside him. "The only tales he tells are about himself."

"What sort of story would you rather hear?"

"Tell me about your home," I said. "Tell me about Colchis and the Fleece."

"Haven't you heard all about it already? The flying ram that saved my father? The unsleeping dragon that guards the Golden Fleece? Jason spins that yarn all the time, as if it belongs to him."

"That's why I'd rather hear it from you, Argus," I said. "I want the truth."

"And you know you'll never get that from Jason, eh? Smart . . . boy." His clumsy grin winked briefly in the firelight before he began his tale. "My father and his sister, Helle, did escape a stepmother who was plotting to kill them, but solely thanks to their old nurse's husband. He was a Phoenician merchant whose ship was called the *Ram*, bound for the gold trade at Aea, chief city of the Colchians. He smuggled the children aboard and that was that. Poor Helle was lost overboard in a storm, but my father arrived safely, dressed like the prince he was. He grew up to marry the king's oldest daughter, who died when I was born."

"So you're a Colchian prince, Argus?" I said.

"Am I?" His face clouded. "Let's just say that my father's troubles with his stepmother taught him nothing. Once we reach Aea, you'll hear rumors about how the royal women worship the dark goddess Hecate, how they're all sorceresses, witches, and expert poisoners. Well, sly words can be poison, too. I was scarcely older than you when Father's second wife tried to have *her* son inherit everything. She ripped her dress, battered herself black and blue, then yowled that I'd ravished her. My father didn't seek proof nor let me defend myself, he just told me to be thankful he was limiting my punishment to exile." Argus gave a humorless chuckle. "He didn't spare my life out of fatherly love. Lord Aetes would kill him if he shed the blood of a royal grandchild."

I gazed into Argus's weathered face and saw

nothing but remembered pain and betrayal in his eyes. "I'm sorry," I said. "I shouldn't have pried."

He gave me a hug so swift that it was over before I realized he'd done it. "Nonsense, friend. Keeping silent about the past won't make it better. All you wanted to hear about was the Fleece."

"But there is no Golden Fleece. Only the *Ram*, bound for gold trade. You said so."

"No *one* Golden Fleece," he responded, shaking a finger at me. "Colchis is rich in gold. It washes down in flakes out of the mountains. Men drop woolly sheepskins into the streams, and when they pull 'em out again, the fleeces glitter like little suns!"

"What about the unsleeping dragon?" I asked.

Before he could reply, we both heard the crunch of approaching footsteps and my brothers lurched into the circle of firelight. I prepared to bolt, but Polydeuces uttered a ground-shaking belch, tripped on nothing, and sprawled forward on top of me. He reeked of unwatered wine.

Castor giggled. "Now look wha' you did," he declared, sweeping his arms wide apart. "We heard Argus tellin' story 'bout the Fleece, all we want's to come listen, an' you crush poor ol'—ol'—whoever that is. I tol' you, you drink too—too—too mush Herakles' wine. Here, I help you up, boy." He took three steps and fell over Polydeuces just when I'd gotten hold of his shoulders and was shoving him away.

Both of my brothers flattened me in a human land-slide. Argus howled with laughter.

"What's going on over there?" Jason's harsh voice cut through the night. I peered through a tangle of my brothers' limbs and saw him burst into Argus's camp-site. I disliked Jason, but he did put effort into main-taining order among the Argonauts, asea or ashore. When he grabbed Castor and hauled him off me, I could have kissed his hands with gratitude.

Polydeuces got to his feet, unaided but wobbling. "Accident," he said. I took advantage of the moment by sidling out of the light crab-fashion, my rump just a finger-span off the ground. I kept a watchful eye on my brothers as I edged away, but my backward retreat ended with a thump as I ran into a massed barricade of legs. The Argonauts had found their evening's en-tertainment.

"You again? This is what comes of letting pretty boys on board an honest ship," Herakles bellowed. He grabbed my arm and pulled me upright. "Nephew, where are you? If you don't know how to keep this weapons bearer of yours from sowing trouble, I might have to take him off your hands."

"Uncle, enough." Iolaus came to my aid, plucking me free of Herakles' grasp. "Run along, lad." I heard the note of urgency in his voice as he gave me a shove away from the fire.

But Herakles wasn't done having his fun. He

lunged after me and dragged me back in two strides. "See, the problem is you go too easy on the boy. No discipline. Hylas! Hylas, fetch my sword." Hylas stayed where he was, but his master didn't seem to notice or care. He returned all his attention to me. "All right, Glaucus, let's see what you can do with that little bee-sting blade you carry."

Gleeful whispers speculated about my chances for survival in a bout against Herakles. Hoarse shouts proposed wagers as to how long I'd last before the Theban hero knocked the sword from my hand and beat me purple with the flat of my own blade. And above all the racket, the words that struck the most fear into my heart came from my brothers.

" 'Glaucus'?" Polydeuces' wine-fuddled voice sounded loud in my ears. "Jus' like our ol' teacher, Castor. Say, that boy . . . He look familiar t' you?"

Castor tried to push in front of the crewmen blocking his view of me, but some of them had been sharing Herakles' wine as well. No one was willing to step aside for Castor, and everyone was more than ready to trade blows with him if he insisted on having his way.

"Stop, I forbid this!" Jason commanded. "Herakles, what have you done to my men, getting them this drunk? They'll be useless in the morning."

Herakles planted his fists on his hips in mock

indignation. "Do I hear you right, Jason? Are you insulting these fine warriors, saying they can't hold their wine? What kind of man can't drink a bellyful by moonset and be ready for battle by sunrise?" The men muttered in tipsy agreement while Jason ground his teeth together and looked ready to bash Herakles' brains out with the hero's own club.

Hylas discreetly stepped between Herakles and me. "Master, I can't find your sword," he said calmly but quickly. "I need Glaucus to come help me look for it."

It was a flimsy attempt at getting me to safety before Herakles' words at Jason's expense stirred things up any further. It failed. The Theban hero sidestepped his weapons bearer and threw an arm around me in a bear hug. "You might have better luck finding my sword if you actually went to look for it," he said. "By my father, Zeus, if you get any lazier, Hylas, we'll have to get you a ship of your own and a quest to go with it!" His rowdy guffaws half deafened me.

"You go too far, Theban," Jason said. The flickering firelight turned his face into a mask of barely restrained rage. The crew cheered, sensing a *real* brawl about to happen.

I faded back into the darkness while the crew formed a ring around the two men. No one stopped me. I popped out of the rowdy mob like a pit from a squashed olive and immediately bumped into Milo.

"Your brothers saw you," he said.

"They saw a *boy*," I answered with forced calm. "And they're drunk. They won't remember *what* they saw, come morning. Milo, listen to me. We have to do something, and do it fast. Jason and Herakles *must not* fight. It'll be the end of the quest if they do."

"Then let it end," Milo said. He seized my arm. I hadn't realized how strong he'd become.

The cheers from the ring were getting louder. I jerked free of Milo's grip and raced around the outside of the human barricade, craning my neck for a glimpse of Argus. When I caught sight of the familiar balding, sun-browned head, I plunged deftly back through the mob to his side.

"Stop them, Argus," I said. "Jason will listen to you."

"Herakles won't, so why should I bother?" He was licking his lips in anticipation. "Let Jason take what's coming to him."

"Jason didn't start this." I spoke rapidly, frantically. "He's no match for Herakles, and when he falls, he'll take the *Argo* with him. A leader who's beaten by one of his own men can't go on commanding the rest. What happens to a ship without a captain, Argus, or without enough men to sail her safely?"

My words touched the one thing truly important

to him. The Colchian strode into the center of the ring and boldly placed himself between Jason and Herakles. "All right, boys, the fun's over," he said jovially. "You gave the men a good show, but you don't want it to be *too* good or they'll be expecting the same every night." He clapped them both on the back, then turned to Herakles and added, "Now listen to me, you ungrateful lout, I built the ship that's hauling your fat behind halfway across the world. What d'you mean, handing out free wine and not offering me a cup? Afraid I've tasted too many *good* vintages to stomach the swill they make in Thebes, or are you just stingy?"

"I'll show you who's stingy, old man!" Herakles roared. But it was a friendly roar. He grabbed Argus, tossed him over one shoulder, and ran back to his own campfire. Grumbling, some of the Argonauts returned to whatever they'd been doing before they were cheated out of their spectacle. Others took off after the Theban hero, most likely in hopes of getting a little more of his wine for themselves. Jason was left behind. The look of surprise and relief on his face was comical, though I didn't waste time laughing. I hurried back to Milo.

Hylas was with him. "Well, *that* was luck," the handsome weapons bearer said. "Good thing Herakles didn't have his heart set on fighting Jason. When he wants something, he's not so easily distracted."

"That had nothing to do with luck," Milo

responded proudly. "That was Glaucus's doing. He went to Argus."

"*Starting* the fight was his doing, too," Hylas said. He sounded serious.

"Me? What did I do?" I demanded. "I was minding my own business when Herakles—"

"He's everywhere that you are, lately." Hylas gave me a shockingly frosty look. "He follows you like a bee follows honey."

"You're imagining things." I did my best to sound casual. "Herakles is a great hero, but he's still a man. He gets as bored as the rest of us. If he is dogging me, it's only to have something to do."

Hylas didn't seem reassured. *Why are you so unhappy?* I wondered.

"Don't worry, Hylas." Milo spoke up. "Even if it's not boredom making Herakles act this way, where's the harm? Glaucus isn't interested."

"That doesn't matter," Hylas replied. "When Herakles wants something, he doesn't stop until he gets it." He left us without another word.

"Poor Hylas," Milo said. "He's in a bad way."

"I wish he wouldn't worry about me so much," I said. "How can I convince him that Herakles is *not* going to get what he wants this time?"

"You think *that's* what's troubling him?" Milo's voice rose sharply. "You mean you don't *know*?"

"Know what? That Herakles is after me and Hylas is afraid I'll be hurt?"

Milo shook his head. "The only person Herakles has hurt by chasing you is Hylas."

"He— What?" My cheeks tingled as though I'd been slapped. I wasn't shocked to learn that Hylas loved Herakles, and Herakles had certainly made it plain that he found other men attractive. The gods themselves were known to do so. There were many tales of how Apollo, Poseidon, and Zeus himself all had become infatuated with beautiful mortal youths. What shook me was how blind I'd been to something that was right before my eyes.

Only because you chose to be blind, I told myself. *Because you'd rather stay blind than let go of your romantic dreams.* Suddenly I felt like a complete fool. I squeezed my eyes shut. *I won't cry,* I thought. *I refuse to cry.*

"Lady Helen . . ." Milo spoke my real name so softly that there was no danger at all of anyone hearing it but me. "Lady Helen, I'm sorry."

"For what?" My voice was a ragged whisper. "You didn't do anything wrong."

"I'm sorry for—for not being a better friend. I could have said something to you about Hylas before, but I didn't, because I envied—"

I silenced him by laying a finger to my own lips. "Instead of an apology, share a promise with me:

that from now on, we *will* be the friends we ought to be."

" 'Friends'?" He smiled sadly, but he gave his word before the gods.

The next morning, the *Argo* set sail amid a chorus of moans and groans from the men who'd shared Herakles' hospitality. I was in my usual place, aft of the mast. I couldn't see how badly my brothers were suffering because of their spree, but I could imagine their pitiful condition after all that unwatered wine.

The crew was in such a sorry state that Argus persuaded Jason to make for land at noontime to give them a rest. They had their conversation by the ship's steering oar, so I heard most of it.

We landed on a small, lovely island with tall cliffs rising behind a narrow arc of beach. Since we weren't going to spend too long there, we left the *Argo* afloat and waded to shore. Everyone sought the shade cast by the rocks and the wind-twisted trees bordering the beach. Some of the men went right to sleep, and others tried to wash the wine out of their brains by dunking themselves in the cool shallows. Herakles strutted up and down the strand, taunting everyone he saw.

"What's wrong, Kalais? Wine and wind don't mix? Hey, Lynceus, how sharp's your sight *now*? Nephew! Yes, *you*, Iolaus! Where's the sour fig you've been nibbling? If you drank straight wine like a man, you wouldn't be looking down your nose at the rest of us; you'd be trying to keep your own head from falling off! Haw!"

Then he caught sight of me. I was lying down in the shade of a pine tree, far from my brothers, nursing a sore stomach. I didn't know what I'd eaten to cause such a bellyache. It had come over me out of nowhere and made me testy. Milo and Hylas were sitting nearby, playing a game of knucklebones. They'd invited me to join them and I'd snapped at them to leave me alone. When I noticed Herakles heading for me, I was in no mood for any of his antics. I got up and tried to evade him by stepping into the trees, but he was too fast.

"Where d'you think you're going, lad?" He caught up with me in the shadows of the beachside grove and snagged the back of my tunic. "If you've got the energy for a hike, maybe you'd like to put it to better use. Tell you what, let's go find a place where none of these fume-headed fools will bother us, and I'll teach you how a real warrior uses his blade."

I tugged my tunic out of his hand and eyed him stonily. "My own master teaches me all I need to know, thank you."

"Oh, I doubt that." Herakles grinned. "Don't frown, Glaucus. The gods will weep if you crease that sweet face with wrinkles. Come on, I'll teach you how to use a club like mine. It's a surprisingly handy weapon, and one I know Iolaus never mastered."

"What else will you teach him?" Hylas appeared from between the pines. He turned a cheerless face to me and added, "Why don't you look happy, Glaucus? It's not every young man who steals a hero's heart." With that he spun on his heel and fled into the trees.

I bolted after him, leaving Herakles calling after the two of us. Hylas and I had the advantage in that race. The trees grew close together, making it easier for us to slip through them than for the broad-shouldered Theban. I saw a clearly marked trail where my friend had broken the thinner pine boughs. It led upward, a steep route that finally ended at the very top of the island.

I emerged into the clearing at the rocky summit and found Hylas kneeling beside a pool of water fed by a bubbling spring. I came closer and saw that the fresh water welled up very near the edge of the cliffs on the island's far side. A glance over the crag showed no narrow curve of beach below, no sign of the *Argo* or her crew. The straight drop down was raw rock, the handiwork of Poseidon when the sea lord earned his title Earthshaker.

"Hylas," I said quietly, not wanting to startle him so close to the precipice.

His eyes were wet. "What do you want?"

"I *don't* want Herakles," I said. I heard the noise of

the Theban hero's pursuit drawing nearer. It sounded like he was tearing down half the forest. I had to speak quickly to have my say before he reached us. "And if he wants Glaucus, he wants a ghost. I'm not what he thinks I am. My name is Helen."

Hylas's perfect mouth fell open. "You're a girl?" He leaped up, grabbed my arms, and stared at me from head to heels, as if seeing me for the first time. "Why tell me this?"

"Because I trust you," I said. "And because I want you to know there's no way I would ever take Herakles from you, even if I could. Hylas, can we *please* step away from this spring? The ground's slippery, and it's too near—"

He wasn't listening. "But why are you here, on the quest for the Fleece? Is Milo your lover? Are you both running away from—?"

"There you are!" Herakles was out of the forest and upon us with astonishing speed. Hylas gasped and let go of me, then took a step back, into the spring. His foot slipped on a moss-covered rock. One moment he was beside me, the next he was plunging down the cliff face to the wave-beaten rocks below.

It was over in a lightning strike. I couldn't even call out his name. It was all I could do to keep my own balance when Herakles shoved me aside to stare aghast into the churning sea. "Where is he?" he howled at the waves, the wind, the sun. "Where is Hylas?"

I ached, speechless with grief. I wanted to say something to comfort him, but I couldn't find the words. It hurt too much to speak my lost friend's name. I admit I was also afraid. Herakles' face was twisted with anguish, and when he abruptly turned to confront me, his eyes burned with a beast's unreasoning rage.

"Where is he?" Herakles repeated. There were little flecks of white at the corners of his mouth. "What did you do with him?"

"I—I didn't—" I forced myself to breathe and cautiously reached for my sword. "You saw what happened, how he stepped into the water and—"

"—they stole him." Herakles' voice dropped to an awestruck whisper. His gaze wandered back to the spring. "They saw how beautiful he was, and they stole him from me." Without warning, he pushed past me, fell to his hands and knees, and began roaring at the water, "Give him back! Give him back to me!" He was still shouting his insane demands and beating the surface of the pool into foam with his fists when I turned and ran back down the trackless hillside to the beach.

I was sobbing when I got to the shore. Milo was the first to reach me, followed closely by Argus, but I felt too wretched to speak to them. Jason and the rest of the *Argo's* crew gathered around us to learn what was wrong. Tears blinded me. I didn't care that my brothers were standing right there, getting a long, close look at me through sober eyes. Iolaus offered me a filled water-skin. I took a deep drink, then choked out an account of what had happened. When I finished, I waited for Jason to give the order for a search party to climb back to the top of the island and fetch Herakles.

I waited for nothing. "We're leaving," Jason said. "Now."

"Leave now?" Iolaus echoed. "You're joking! Abandon my uncle, the best warrior we've got? You're crazy!"

"I'm not," Jason replied evenly. "He is." His gaze swept over the massed crew. "We all know that this isn't the first time Herakles has lost his mind. The same singers who carry the stories of his exploits also tell about how Hera struck him with such an awful attack of madness that when it finally lifted, he found he'd slaughtered his own wife and children."

I was horrified to hear this, and more so when I looked at Iolaus's grim expression and understood it was true. It was old news to all the others, who stood muttering hasty prayers for the gods to keep such dire things far from their own lives.

"Men, I can't deny Herakles' strength any more than I can deny his insanity," Jason went on, his voice smooth as newly churned butter. "He may be a great hero, but I say that so are all of you. I refuse to risk your lives by sending you after him. He's Zeus's son. Once the madness leaves him, he'll find his own way home."

Flattered, the others were eager to agree with Jason's plan. Iolaus was not. "You're dropping flowers on a dunghill, Jason, and you know it. The only reason you're marooning my uncle here is revenge. You can't forgive him for hurting your precious pride last night!"

Jason's lips curved into the smallest sliver of a smile. "Stay with him if you like, Iolaus, you and your servants. I won't stop you."

"I'll stay and look after my uncle until he's well again," Iolaus answered. "I won't ask that of the boys."

"If you stay, they stay. I won't have them on board the *Argo* without you."

My fingers closed around Iolaus's wrist. "We'll stay," I whispered. "Together, maybe we can heal Herakles sooner than—"

"No," Iolaus replied quietly. "This island might have enough food and water to support one person or two, but four? And for how long until my uncle's sane again, and we see another ship?" He shook his head. "I can't do that to you and Milo." He took a deep breath and looked at Jason with pure contempt. "We'll sail."

And so we did, as soon as Iolaus returned to the *Argo* and brought all of Herakles' weapons and belongings to the shore. He also fetched food and a small amphora of wine. When we were all once more on board and the *Argo* pulled away from shore, Iolaus refused to row. Instead, he stood beside our helmsman and watched until the unlucky island was out of sight.

That night, we camped near a fishing village. The women stayed hidden, but the men emerged from their homes and came down to the waterside in a whispering cluster to watch us beach the *Argo*. A ship that big was a novelty to people accustomed to boats only large enough to carry two or three men. The sight of it must have been terrifying and tempting at the same time. They greeted us from a respectful distance and made no move to approach until Argus hailed them in their own tongue.

The next thing we knew, we were being welcomed with bread, salt, meat, drink, and smiles by the entire village. Argus beamed as he told us that we'd finally reached the Colchian lands, though we were still some distance from King Aetes' court at Aea. The crew was jubilant and pitched in to help the fishermen kindle a huge fire on the beach. While Argus proudly showed off the wonders of our ship to the local men, their wives and daughters served us with as much generosity as their lives allowed.

We repaid them with one of our larger amphorae of wine and with Orpheus's gift of song. He sang about how we'd battled the Harpies and cheated the

Clashing Rocks, and how we'd soon overcome any other obstacles that might lie between us and the Golden Fleece. I sat between Milo and Iolaus, staring into the flames.

Then he sang about a young man so handsome that everyone who saw him loved him. One day, when he went to fetch water from a spring, the nymphs who lived in the pool saw him and fell in love with him. They dragged him down into the depths and gave him the gifts of eternal life, youth, and joy, but he could never return to the mortal world again. As I watched the flames and listened to the music, I imagined that Orpheus's sweet song conjured Hylas's spirit back for just a little while. I pictured him the way I best remembered him, happy and kind. *I won't forget you, Hylas,* I thought just as one of the logs on the fire cracked open and my friend's image blew away in a fountain of sparks against the evening sky.

I was still wiping tears from my eyes when my brothers came and planted themselves between me and the fire. "So . . . Glaucus, is it?" Castor said sternly. The two of them were looking right at me, their faces stone. It was over. I stood up to accept my fate.

As I got to my feet, I felt strange. My bellyache was back, worse than before. The heat of the fire must have been greater than I had thought, because I felt a trickle of sweat on my leg.

All at once, one of the fishermen's wives set down her platter of broiled sardines and pointed wildly at me, grinning and calling out to the other women, young and old, in a loud, joyful voice. My brothers were brushed aside as the mothers, daughters, and grandmothers of the village rushed forward and carried me away.

PART III
COLCHIS

7

THE MASK
OF THE HUNTRESS

By the time the women brought me to the large hut at the very edge of their village, I understood what had happened to me. I wasn't a girl anymore. Just before they shoved me through the curtained doorway, I looked up into the night sky and saw the silvery moon that Artemis ruled. Now the moon ruled me.

When my sister, Clytemnestra, first entered womanhood, our mother told us both what to expect, how to deal with our new condition. Clytemnestra was quick to remind Mother that it wasn't "ours," but hers alone. Mother said, "It won't be long before Helen catches up to you. You're twins, after all." But Mother was wrong. I'd spent so long lagging behind my sister that I believed the change would leave me alone until I decided I was ready to accept it. If the gods could read thoughts, how they must have laughed!

Inside the hut, an old woman crouched on a piece of faded blue cloth beside a small fire pit. She was crumbling dried herbs into a painted bowl. While she went about her business, a younger woman came in, handed me a clean wool pad, and spoke to me in a kindly voice. I didn't recognize a single word, but it wasn't hard to figure out her meaning.

By the time I felt clean and comfortable again, the old woman was finished with her task. She raised the bowl of crumbled herbs to the smoke hole in the roof, chanting, and the other woman sang a response. Then she lowered the bowl, poured water into it, and offered it to me.

Just then, there was a commotion outside the hut. I heard many men yelling, and the village women yelling right back at them, unafraid. I recognized my brothers' voices through the tumult. They sounded angry, but scared as well. Over all that loud confusion I heard the voice of Argus, shouting in the local language.

I don't know what he said, but it had the magical effect of silencing the uproar. There was no more yelling from outside, though I still heard plenty of grumbling. The old woman snapped out something that must have been a command. At her words, the young woman who'd helped me earlier went to the door and pulled back the curtain.

"Girl, are you all right?" Argus stood just outside the doorway, speaking barely above a whisper.

"I'm fine," I replied. *For now.*

"So, this women's business of yours——" He sounded ill at ease, speaking about what had just happened to me. "Your new friends here seem to think it's the first time it's happened to you. Are they right?" I nodded. "Ah. Seems like it's something special to them, a great honor to share. This hut you're in, it's the women's shrine, and that crone's a priestess. The only reason they're letting me come this close and talk to you is so I can translate what she's got to say."

"Argus, please tell me what's happening outside," I said. "I know my brothers saw, but the others——?"

"It doesn't matter who saw what, by now everyone's heard all about it. If I were you, lass, I'd stay inside that hut until I had grandchildren."

The old woman said something and thrust the bowl into my hands. I looked to Argus. "What am I supposed to do?"

"You had a mind of your own last time we talked. What do *you* think you're supposed to do?" he countered.

"*You're* helpful." My words were bitter with sarcasm, but nothing on earth was half as bitter as that bowl of herbal brew. The first sip I took made my tongue shrivel. I would have set it aside then and there, but I saw how closely the two women in the hut were watching me, so I closed my eyes, took a deep breath, and gulped the rest of it down. I handed the empty bowl back to the old woman and was rubbing bits of crushed leaves and stems off my teeth when she tilted her head back and burst into wailing song.

"Well, well, isn't that interesting," Argus remarked from the doorway.

"What?" I asked, watching her warily.

"Apparently, our priestess is also the local Pythia. She foretells the future, but only for girls who've just become women."

"Is that what she's doing now?" I asked. "Telling my future?" The old woman was still making noises like those of a hired mourner. I hoped that her woeful tune didn't mean that my life was going to be one long tragedy. "What's she saying?"

"Oh, it's mostly babble. You're brave, you're strong, you're quick-witted, you'll marry a king, find your true love, have lots of babies, kill whole armies with your beauty, and your fame will live forever, yap, yap, yap. If you were one of the local girls, she'd probably say that you attract fish. Don't take any of it seriously, lass. It's just an old woman's way of giving you something to look forward to. That crone knows how hard a woman's life can be, so she's giving you a few dreams to distract you. Hope costs nothing, right?" For once, Argus's smile looked natural.

The old woman ended her song and looked at me expectantly. I wondered how much of it really had been just "babble." Argus was the one to belittle her prophecy, not I. Just because she spoke of the future from a humble village hut instead of from a rich, impressive city shrine didn't mean her gift wasn't genuine. I wished that I could have heard her vision of my future for myself, word for word, without my skeptical friend standing between us. I raised my hands and bowed to the old woman, thanking her even though she didn't speak my language. Argus translated and she smiled. I stood up and took a deep breath. "Time to meet the lion," I said. I started for the door, and the trouble waiting for me beyond the threshold.

The priestess called after me and the young woman attending her laid hold of my arm. "Not so fast, girl," Argus said, his eyes twinkling with amusement. "She's got something for you."

I squatted across the fire from the old woman and watched as she took the bowl from which I'd drunk and smashed it on the stones ringing the little hearth. She chose a small shard, wiped it dry on her skirt, and, from the shadows behind her, produced a palm-sized dish of black paint and a tiny brush. In a few flowing strokes, she drew a design on the shard, then handed it to me. It was a picture of a hunter on horseback, armed with the big spear used to hunt boar. She'd taken care to draw the rider stripped to the waist so that there could be no doubt: The hunter was a woman.

What god had inspired her to give me *this* image? Had her visions shown her my past as well as my future? In such a small number of lines she'd let me see a woman who looked strong and brave, one who rode out to confront the perils of the hunt with confidence and pride, a huntress who chose her own prey and her own weapons.

A huntress . . . The word struck a spark of memory. Suddenly I realized that I had the means to turn the old woman's gift into the perfect weapon. With it at my command, I would face the battle awaiting me outside and come through it victorious. I smiled.

"Argus," I said. "Argus, will you help me?"

"What do you want me to do?" he asked, suspicious. We spoke together so softly that the only people who could overhear our conversation were the two women in the hut with me, and they couldn't understand one word we said.

"Everyone knows I'm a girl now," I replied. "Jason will be afraid to let me back on the ship in case I cause trouble among the men."

"You've got that right," Argus said. "I can't say I wouldn't do the same, in his place."

"You wouldn't," I told him. "You're not like Jason. You're only hard on the outside."

"You make me sound like a beetle, and you still haven't said what you want this old bug to do for you."

"I want you to tell the crew my name."

I waited inside the village women's shrine with the painted shard in my hands. Beyond the door curtain, I heard Argus calling out for the crew's attention. "Men of the *Argo*, you know what you saw!" he cried. "Your eyes didn't lie. The weapons bearer called 'Glaucus' is no lad."

Someone in the crowd made a crude jest. Another man shouted something even worse at Iolaus. I heard the sound of a scuffle and twitched the curtain aside in time to see Iolaus standing over the fallen jokester, cradling the fist he'd bruised on the man's jaw.

"Why tell us what we know?" Jason pushed his way forward, dragging Milo by the arm. He shook my friend viciously. "Who is she, boy? Your bedmate? Or yours?" He glowered at Iolaus.

"Enough!" Argus thundered. "By Poseidon, you'll *hear* me before you start flapping your jaws, sparking quarrels we don't need! This girl is no one's bedmate, young or old. She's as untouched as the holy huntress she serves." He pointed one callused finger at the shining moon, then turned and raised the door curtain. "Come out, Atalanta, and let your shipmates know you at last."

That night, I slept in the old priestess's home. She lived with the younger woman—I supposed they were mother and daughter—and that woman's husband and children. Their house was clean and pleasant, with many bundles of drying herbs and flowers hanging from pegs, covering the smell of fish. They gave me a thick blanket to spread on the ground, more woolen pads in case I needed them during the night, and even a cup of warmed milk with honey to drink before the man snuffed out the lone oil lamp that lit their home. I heard the younger woman crooning to her fretful baby, then silence.

I slept badly. My body was weary, but my thoughts raced over everything that had happened that day. The loss of Hylas, Herakles' madness, the end of my life as Glaucus, the new mask I'd chosen to wear, all of these whirled at dizzying speed through my head. When I did drift into dreams, they were brief, senseless, and horrifying. I woke up clutching my throat, feeling as if I'd nearly drowned. As soon as I saw the hint of dawn beyond the door curtain, I crept out of the house. I had to find my brothers. We needed to talk.

They were awake and waiting for me just six

paces away from the priestess's house. They'd settled themselves on the ground with a clear view of the doorway, and the small space between them was filled with intricate designs they'd scratched into the dirt to pass the time. They stood up together when they saw me, their eyes red and their faces haggard.

"You didn't have to keep watch all night," I said. "I wasn't going to run away, you know."

"We *don't* know," Castor said. "We know nothing about you anymore, Helen. What in the name of all-seeing Apollo were you thinking, coming on this voyage, pretending to be a boy, doing something this—this——" He threw his hands up in frustration and blurted, "You must be as crazy as Herakles!"

"Little sister, you could have died." Polydeuces could hardly get the words out. "All of those days at sea, all the dangers, the raiders in Thrace, the bandits of the Clashing Rocks, even a simple misstep, like the one that killed poor Hylas——" His voice broke. He drew a ragged breath and added, "*Why*, Helen?"

If I answered, would they understand? Their lives were always their own. They never had to fight for their liberty. When Jason came to Delphi seeking heroes, they joined his crew without asking anyone's permission. No one demanded that they justify their choices. If you asked them why they had so much freedom, they'd react as if you wanted to know why the sky is blue.

I'd be queen of Sparta one day. I'd marry because it would be my duty to have children and provide the land with its next ruler. If I was lucky, I'd choose my husband wisely and we'd love one another. But between *You* must *do this because you're a princess* and *You must* never *do that because you're a girl,* there was no time left for *Do what you* like, *because you're Helen.* This quest, this adventure, might be my only chance to.see what it meant to be myself.

What would my brothers say if I told them that?

"Don't call me 'Helen,'" I said firmly, brushing Polydeuces' question aside unanswered. "Helen of Sparta wouldn't be on this ship. I'm Atalanta."

"I was wrong. You're *crazier* than Herakles," Castor said.

I ignored his sarcasm. "When the *Argo* returns to Iolkos, do you want the crewmen scattering to their homes, bearing the tale of how Helen of Sparta threw away her proper role in life to go sailing halfway across the world? What will the lords of Mykenae, Thebes, Iolkos, and all the rest say about us then?"

"That's something you should have thought about *before* you sneaked away from Delphi," Castor said.

"Do you want to argue about how big the fire's grown or do you want to put it *out*?" I countered, hands on hips. "Helen can't be here; Atalanta can!"

Polydeuces shook his head. "It won't work. Castor

and I aren't the only crewmen who were part of the boar hunt. They *saw* Atalanta. They know she's a woman, not a little girl."

"I am *not* a little girl anymore! Atalanta isn't that much older than me. I'm as much a woman as she is, now."

"You're still more convincing as a boy," Castor muttered.

I did my best to fry him with a single look. "I know who was at Calydon as well as you do. Aside from Iolaus and us, I count only three of the boar hunters on this voyage. It'll be your word against theirs if they say I'm not Atalanta."

Polydeuces still looked doubtful. "Even men who weren't on the hunt have heard the songs and know about Atalanta's exploits. Little sister, I love you dearly, but you don't look capable of standing up to a wild boar."

But I did, I thought. *I was there alongside Atalanta. Have the poets told the story as if my part in that great hunt never happened?* Once more I heard Herakles saying, "Truth or not, it does make the better story." At least Atalanta was getting the praise she deserved.

"Listen," I said to my brothers. "You have to believe me, this *can* work. Befriend the other hunters. Tell them I'm not *that* Atalanta, just a girl with the same name. Make up some reason to explain why I slipped aboard this ship. Ask them to help you play a joke on all the crewmen who weren't at Calydon."

"What joke?" Polydeuces asked.

"Convincing them that I *am* that Atalanta." I gave him my most disarming smile.

"Why would they want to be part of such nonsense?" Castor demanded.

"Because they have to be part of it. If this 'nonsense' succeeds, we can return home with no one aware that a Spartan royal princess was ever out of her proper place in the world," I countered. "Besides, they'll be glad to play along, just to keep themselves amused for a while. Iolaus and Milo will help you."

"Iolaus . . ." Castor repeated the name grimly. "He and I are going to have a few words about all this when the *Argo* returns. Or are you going to tell me that he had no idea who 'Glaucus' really was?"

I snorted. "Of course not. He's known me since Calydon, and he recognized me at once when we met in Iolkos. But you can't blame him for bringing me along. I didn't give him any choice." I folded my arms and smiled.

"A little snip like you forced a grown man, a proven hero like Iolaus, to do your bidding?" Castor said. He grimaced. "Unfortunately, I can almost believe it."

"Well? Will you do things my way, too?"

My brothers exchanged an uncertain look. Polydeuces sighed. "I guess it's better than the alternative."
"What alternative?" Castor asked.

By the time our ship pulled away from that Colchian
fishing village, my new identity was established. I was
Atalanta to the crew of the *Argo*, though for some of
the men I was merely an ordinary girl with the same
name as the famous huntress.

Jason himself invited me to join him at the prow
of the *Argo* when we sailed. It was as if my new identity had created a new Jason, one who was all charm
and compliments. He made such a show of welcoming me as *that* Atalanta in front of the whole crew that
my relief became suspicion. *Not even one question to test
me?* I wondered. *What's he up to?*

I had my answer a little while later, from Orpheus. Jason's effusive words were still ringing false in
my ears when I went aft to the helm in time to overhear the Thracian singer tell Milo, "What luck for
Jason. He's lost Herakles, but Atalanta's fame will do
something to make up for that. Even if he never per-
forms a heroic act himself, he'll be renowned as the
man who commanded heroes. Her name alone will be
enough to make people remember his." Then he saw
me. "Hail, great huntress," he murmured with a faint,
knowing smile.

So that was it. Jason treated me as if I truly were

Atalanta the huntress because it served his own purposes, not because I'd fooled him for an instant. I wouldn't be surprised to learn that many of the other crewmen were acting the same way just so they could go home someday and say, "There she was, the same Atalanta who helped Meleager bring down the Calydonian boar, the huntress whose beauty destroyed heroes! She always fought at my side, you know. The poor girl was crazy in love with me, but I like *real* women."

I wondered what Atalanta herself would do if she ever heard such nonsense. *But what* could *she do, once the stories spread far enough?* I thought. *Even if she swears the holiest oath that she was never on the* Argo, *who'll believe her? If the songs are more exciting than the truth, they'll become the truth that everyone remembers. Atalanta, my friend, forgive me. I promise you that whatever happens, I'll bring no dishonor to your name.*

8

THE KING'S DAUGHTER

As the day went on, I discovered that being Atalanta had its privileges. No one expected me to continue my duties as Iolaus's weapons bearer, and they didn't expect me to take a place at the oars with the rest of the crew either. I was free to stroll the length of the *Argo*, to watch the passing shoreline, to eat and drink whenever I liked. I took advantage of it all without a second thought, and anyone who claims he'd never have done the same thing, given the chance, is probably lying. I only wished that the real Atalanta had been treated with such honor in Calydon. *Still, better a heroine than a princess*, I thought gaily.

Iolaus, and Milo too, benefited from my new fame. Many of the other Argonauts had decided that the only possible reason for a woman to volunteer for a perilous voyage was to be with the man she loved. They just couldn't agree on which of my friends was the irresistible fellow. Some argued that Milo's youth put him out of the running; others countered that he was old enough, and called attention to his first shadowy growth of whiskers as proof. Some said it *must* be Iolaus, who wasn't just a hero in his own right but shared Herakles' glory for his part in slaying the Hydra. Some played it safe and took both sides. At first the whispers made Iolaus and Milo uncomfortable, but it didn't last long. When a man stops looking embarrassed and starts wearing a preening little smile, I'd say he's gotten used to his new reputation.

There was a good wind and a calm sea with us that morning. Everyone knew Argus had proclaimed that Aea was only a day's sail away, so the rowers worked harder than ever, energized by the thought of reaching our voyage's goal. I took my place at the prow so that I could enjoy the sensation of skimming across the waves like a white-winged gull.

Argus joined me, resting his hand on the carved scene showing Helle falling to her death from the back of the flying ram. We didn't speak at first, both of us captured by the spell of the sea. When I stole a glance at him, his face was blissful and serene. I was happy to see him so contented until I remembered how this voyage was fated to end for him. He'd told me the Pythia's prediction: "She said if I went home again, I'd die. She said if I *didn't* go home again, I'd live a long life, but a forgotten one, and I'd die without ever having another sight of the sea."

"Lovely, isn't she?" he said to me, speaking of the sea. "Look there!" He pointed at a scattering of dark shapes on the horizon. "Those are the first ships besides ours that I've seen since we left Thrace. They must be merchant craft. I wonder where they're bound? Even when I was a boy, not a day went by without ships from at least twenty kingdoms sailing into port at Aea."

"Are we almost there?" I asked.

"You won't be sleeping on the beach tonight," he replied. "Not unless you're fool enough to insist on it."

"I don't mind sleeping under the stars."

"Well, isn't that what a legendary huntress always does?" He winked at me. "Or have you become someone else already?" He kept his teasing to a whisper.

"Very funny."

"Put your quills down, little hedgehog, I'm not your enemy," Argus replied. "I owe you plenty for what you've brought to this voyage. Thanks to you, I only felt like throttling Jason every *second* day. I wish I knew your true name so when I die, I can tell Hades, 'See that girl? She's sharp as a shark's tooth, brave enough to battle the worst storm Poseidon could throw at her, and one of these days she'll be as beautiful as a sunrise on a summer sea. So you tell the Fates to spin the thread of her life good and long, or you'll have Argus to answer to!' " He chuckled.

I placed my hand over his on the prow. "I hope the Pythia was wrong," I told him. "Not because I like you, but so Hades doesn't have to put up with you too soon."

"Land! Aea!" Argus was still at the ship's prow when we came into sight of the Colchian royal city. He even beat keen-eyed Lynceus to the announcement. "There she is! By the gods, she's as magnificent as I remember her." A loud cheer went up from the crew. The men shipped their oars and raced to the rails, avid for their first look at the city of the Fleece.

Milo and I were aft, near the steering oar. We hadn't had the chance to speak more than ten words to one another since the moment I'd swapped "Glaucus" for "Atalanta." I was hoping to amend that, but once Aea was on the horizon, the opportunity fled. The *Argo's* helmsman was as excited as the rest of the crew. He barked a command at Milo, and my friend suddenly found himself holding on to the steering oar while Tiphys hurried forward to gape at the great port.

"You must've left your weak stomach on the shore at Iolkos. Look at you!" I told Milo proudly. "You're a born sailor. You should become a seagoing merchant's apprentice when we go home again. You could even have your own ship someday."

"If I do, will you sail in her?" Milo asked.

"If you set her course, I will."

He grinned. "You'll have to run away again. Once you return to Sparta and your parents find out what you've been doing, they'll lock you up."

"And draw attention to the whole scandalous business?" I responded, pretending to be shocked at the very thought. "How would they manage to find any man willing to marry me then?"

"The man who won't marry you because you chose this adventure doesn't deserve you," Milo said. "A man who truly loves you will understand why you ran away. He'll know who you really are." His smile was gone. "And if you can't love him as much as he loves you, he'll understand that, too."

"Milo . . ." I reached out to touch his arm, but just then Tiphys came running up to take back the steering oar. Argus was hot on his tail, calling him and all his ancestors so many foul names that I didn't know whether to duck out of sight or start memorizing the most impressive ones.

"Is *this* how you treat my beautiful ship?" Argus yelled, bright red in the face. "Trusting her to an inexperienced boy is bad enough, but at this time?" He gestured to the west, where the sun was already beginning to dip below the sea. "Count yourself lucky that I don't give you a fine view of Aea from the bottom of her harbor!"

"Gods above, calm yourself," Tiphys muttered. "It was only for a moment. No harm was done."

"Why don't I take you to the roof of the Sun Temple, once we're ashore, and push you off? You can keep repeating, 'No harm done, no harm done,' up to the instant you hit the ground! Of all the miserable, ignorant—!" Argus choked on his own fury. I don't know how long he would have gone on if a call from the prow hadn't distracted him.

The port of Aea was like nothing I'd ever seen before. Even in the fading daylight, it was a splendid spectacle. The waterfront teemed with gaily painted buildings, all dwarfed by the high citadel with its thick stone walls, red as old blood. As our vessel came closer, I saw bustling hordes of people, most of them richly dressed in the brightest hues, skin and hair also in a stunning variety of colors. Ships of all sizes crowded the shore, and the shore itself was strangely formed, with many narrow stone fingers stretching out into the water. Argus smirked to see the whole ship's crew so dumbfounded by our first sight of his homeland.

"What's wrong, lads?" he demanded. "Never seen a dock before? Trust me, you'll come to love it. No need to break your backs hauling the ship onto dry land, and she'll be happier too, left cradled on the water." He gave orders to everyone manning the oars, the helm, and the sail. Soon the *Argo* was safely berthed at the very end of the dock farthest from the citadel, tied to several of the pillars bristling from the stone.

The crewmen were used to dropping over the sides of the *Argo* into shallow water. Leaping from the gently bobbing ship to the dock was a new experience, even more difficult to master in the dusk. Many of them stumbled and fell to hoots of delighted laughter from their comrades. I watched closely to learn from the mistakes that others made, then jumped and landed firmly on my feet. The men cheered, and I even saw my brothers smiling their approval.

Only half the crew was off the ship when a group of six spearmen came trotting down the length of the dock to intercept us. Their tunics were as red as the royal stronghold walls, and their shields and helmets glinted in the dying daylight. Their leader was a short, swarthy man with a boarhound's face half covered by a sooty beard. He hailed us in the local tongue and then, to my surprise, in several more languages, including our own.

"If you come in peace, be welcome to Colchis," he said. "What is your business here?" As he spoke, he cast a canny, expert eye over the *Argo*. His thoughts were as plain as if he spoke them aloud: *If you're a merchant vessel, where are the goods you've brought to trade?*

Argus would have answered, but Jason hurried to plant himself between the shipbuilder and the spearmen. "I am Prince Jason of Iolkos, and my business here is with your king."

"Iolkos?" The lead spearman repeated the name in a way that showed he'd never heard of it. "What would my lord Aetes have to do with Iolkos, wherever that is? If that's your only claim to an audience with the king—"

Argus made an impatient noise. "Since when does Lord Aetes need the likes of you to decide who he'll want to see? Or has his kingdom become so poor that he can no longer afford a little bread and salt for his own kin?"

The spearman goggled at Argus. "Are *you* claiming kinship to Lord Aetes, old man?"

"I look older than I am, fool, just as you'll look the worse for wear when my grandfather finds out you insulted me. I'm Argus, son of Phrixus and the royal lady Nera, Lord Aetes' eldest daughter by his chief wife. Do you recognize my name, or were you whelped yesterday, pup?"

The spearman's mouth flattened. "You were banished."

"So I was. Yet here I am. Now *use* the mind the

gods gave you. Ask yourself why any sane man would risk his life by defying an order of exile. What could be so crucial that I'd be willing to put my own blood in the balance for it, eh?" He clapped the spearman on the back before the man could react and concluded, "Don't you think Lord Aetes might want to know the answer to that, too?"

Night enveloped the port of Aea and still we stood on the dock. The leader of the spearmen left his troops to watch us while he carried the news of our arrival to Lord Aetes. The men still aboard the *Argo* kindled a few oil lamps to chase away the shadows.

I sidled up to Argus. "What do you think will happen?"

He made a dismissive gesture. "It's going to take my grandfather some time to chew over the news, then to decide what he wants to do about it. Don't worry. I remember him being a reasonable man. If there's a price to pay for my return, I'll be the only one who'll have to pay it."

"We won't allow that," I said staunchly. "We'll stand by you."

His laugh was short. "You can't speak for anyone but yourself, O huntress. The other men *might* defend me, if only to add to their fame as fighters, but Jason himself would skin me alive with his own knife if

Lord Aetes offered to swap the Golden Fleece for my old pelt."

"What are you saying, Argus?" Jason came out of the darkness like a murdered man's ghost. "I heard you mention my name."

"Only telling Atalanta here about your own exploits as a hunter," Argus said as naturally as if it were true. "You ought to show her that leopard-skin trophy of yours. It's a beauty."

"There'll be time enough to show her that later." Jason tried to look annoyed, but I could tell that Argus's smooth talk had flattered him. "When I choose to do it, not when you try to send me off on an errand. I still lead this venture, not you."

I hated his arrogant attitude toward Argus, to whom he owed so much, but there was little I could do about it. The best I could manage was a ruse to divert him. "A leopard skin?" I put the proper note of awe into my voice. "You should wear it when Lord Aetes summons us to his hall. One look at such a prize and he'll know who our leader is without asking!"

"You think that will be necessary?" Jason growled, giving Argus a hard, resentful stare.

I pretended I hadn't heard that. "A leopard! Not even Herakles could boast such a kill. He wore a lion's pelt, but brute strength's all you need to slay one of those beasts. You need strength *and* brains to overcome a leopard."

"Would you really like to see the pelt?" Jason asked eagerly. I nodded. "For you, then, honored huntress," he said in a low, honeyed voice. He leaped back aboard the *Argo* with so much vigor that Argus had to bite his lips to hold back the laughter.

"I'll never call you 'girl' again," Argus said to me. "A woman twice your age would envy your cunning!"

"If I were still 'Glaucus,' you'd say I was smart or clever, not cunning," I chided him.

"Pfff! What does one little word matter?"

"So you won't mind if I call the *Argo* a ferryboat?" I replied sweetly.

Jason returned with the leopard skin draped over his shoulders. I noticed that he'd also taken the time to put on a clean blue and green Mykenaean-style kilt and to bind his long, dark curls back with a white cord shot with gold. Rock-crystal earrings caught the lamp-light as well. He smiled warmly at me, and I heard Argus snort behind my back.

"What do you think, Atalanta?" Jason purred. "Do I look more to your liking now?"

"Never mind me," I said, taking a step closer to Argus. "It's Lord Aetes you want to impress."

"Not just Lord Aetes," Jason said.

He looked at me like a hound looks at a tasty piece of meat. I wanted to get away from him, but I knew if I did that, he'd only follow. Instead I sprang toward him and grabbed the leopard pelt by one tufted ear. "Tell me about how you caught this marvelous animal!" I exclaimed. Jason would never pass up the chance to talk about the one person dearest to him. He was still gabbling about his prowess as a hunter when the leader of the Colchian spearmen returned with the news that Lord Aetes awaited us.

We didn't make a very impressive showing as we marched from the *Argo* into the heart of Lord Aetes' stronghold. By order of the king, only ten of the *Argo*'s crew were invited into his presence. Besides Jason and Argus, our group consisted of Acastus, Orpheus, my brothers, Iolaus, Zetes, Kalais, and me. The rest of our men were forbidden to leave the dock until Lord Aetes said otherwise. Milo was miserable.

Argus's attendance was essential. Aside from that, it was Jason who decided who would come to the palace. There was cool calculation behind every choice he made. Orpheus, Iolaus, Zetes, Kalais, and "Atalanta" were part of the group because we were all famous, in our own ways. The divinely gifted singer, the nephew of great Herakles, the twin Harpy-hunters, and the legendary huntress were easy choices. Castor and Polydeuces accompanied us at my request. I wasn't afraid to meet Lord Aetes, but I didn't want my brothers to worry, having me out of their sight for so long.

They'd become so protective of me that I feared they might do something foolish, like breaking the Colchian king's ban on leaving the *Argo*. I was willing to sacrifice a little independence if it meant keeping my brothers safe. As for Acastus, he was chosen even though he was Jason's rival for the throne of Iolkos. What better way to throw off any suspicions that Jason might be plotting against Lord Pelias's son than by making sure to include him?

To his credit, the Colchian king saw to it that a wagon laden with fresh provisions was brought down to the ship by the same company of torchbearers assigned to escort us up to the palace. Every one of them was dressed just as richly as the spearmen, many wearing heavy gold studs in their ears. If they were servants, they were well paid. If they were slaves, then gold must be as common as pebbles in Colchis. Their appearance put ours to shame. Only Jason was dressed in something better than travel-worn garments.

The citadel gate was far more massive and imposing than the one that guarded Mykenae. The archway into the palace grounds was flanked by titanic winged beasts with writhing serpents' bodies, taloned paws, and fangs like scythes. Watch fires burned in footed bronze pots at either side of the gate, making the creatures' painted scales blaze blue, green, red, and gold in the flickering light. I stopped and marveled at the monsters.

"Never seen a dragon before?" Castor whispered mischievously in my ear.

"Is that what they look like?" I whistled in admiration. "I heard that a dragon guards the Fleece, but I didn't know what sort of animal it was. Are those carvings life-size?"

"How would I know?" my brother said as we passed between the awesome guardians of the gate.

Lord Aetes' palace was larger and more luxurious than any I'd ever known. Wherever I looked, I caught the wink and gleam of gold, the flash of brilliant colors. In spite of the wealth on display all around me, I saw that there were a few things about Lord Aetes' palace that reminded me of home. We were brought to a waiting room just outside of the king's great hall and offered wine, the same treatment my own father gave to ambassadors. After that, a dour, hawk-faced man came to lead us before Lord Aetes.

The king of Colchis sat on a painted stone throne, its high back crowned with the image of a dragon's head. There was a wide fire pit between him and us, a grander version of the hearth that burned in my father's hall. Many attendants stood against the walls, minding the lights of countless clay lamps. I peered through the smoke and dancing flames. The king was a dark-skinned man dressed in robes of dazzling splendor, a tall gold crown atop his long white hair. He looked old enough to be Argus's grandfather, but when he gestured for his servants to bring him the bread and salt, his movements were strong and sure.

There was a second, smaller throne next to his, but it was empty. I guessed that either Lord Aetes' queen was dead or it wasn't the custom for her to be part of this ceremony. Then I saw a flare of scarlet and a sparkle of gold just behind the smaller throne.

"Daughter, why are you acting like a little mouse again? Come here and help me welcome our guests!" He spoke our language, out of courtesy. His command boomed like a breaking storm wave, and the lurker stepped into the light. She looked a little older than my brothers, with pale skin and dull black hair, though her eyes were remarkable, a deep, radiant amber that lit up her face. She cringed under the weight of her gorgeous robes and golden ornaments, as if she wanted nothing more than to disappear.

Still, she obeyed her father, taking the bread and salt from him and serving each of us. Her hands trembled, and when I thanked her, the only response I got was a tiny gasp before she fled to the next guest. Lord Aetes watched her every move.

When we'd been properly welcomed, the king stood up and opened his arms to Argus. "My beloved grandson, I thank the gods for the joy of seeing your face again before I die. I wish with all my heart that you'd come back to us sooner."

Argus smiled, but made no move to approach his

grandfather. "You'll have to forgive me for staying away so long, Lord Aetes. As dearly as I love you, the idea of being put to death on my return to Aea kept me away. It's a trivial thing, the fear of losing one's life, but it means a lot to me."

Lord Aetes scowled. "Your father, Phrixus, was wrong to exile you, but every man has the right to rule his own family. I thought Phrixus was unjust, but I couldn't intercede. I had a good reason." He didn't elaborate.

"A very good one, no doubt," Argus drawled. "Is it going to be good enough to justify executing me now that I'm back?"

The king shook his head. "Your father and step-mother are both dead. Any quarrel you had with them is over. Your innocence and honor are not to be ques-tioned by any man who owes me allegiance. All of your rights as a royal prince of Colchis are hereby re-stored."

"All of my rights?" Argus echoed. "You mean my stepbrother, Karos, is dead, too?" Lord Aetes didn't answer. Argus stroked his beard. "I see. Well, won't *he* be thrilled to learn that he's going to have to share his inheritance."

"There will be peace between my grandsons," Lord Aetes stated, gritting his teeth. "I will not have it otherwise. Did you come here to vex me, or to rejoin your family?"

Argus's laughter danced with the smoke and sparks rising from the fire pit. He strode around the hearth and embraced the king. "My apologies, Grandfather, but can you blame me for snapping? Look at the two of us. My years of exile have aged me so that we could pass for brothers!"

Lord Aetes smiled and returned Argus's hug. "That's over now. We'll soon have you looking your proper age. Medea! Come here and greet your nephew." He waved for the shy young woman to approach. When he threw one arm over her shoulder and forced her to face Argus, she shuddered and shrank so that even at a distance, I couldn't miss it. "Argus, this is my last-born daughter, Medea. She has a remarkable gift for herbal lore. I'm almost thankful that she hasn't yet been able to attract a worthy husband, for who'd take her place, making brews to ease the pains of my old bones? Maybe one day she'll perfect a potion to restore your lost youth, eh?"

He patted Argus on the back, then gave his attention to the rest of us. "My friends, thank you for fetching Argus home. The gods have not been kind to me. I have had four queens and many concubines, yet Medea and her younger brother, Apsyrtus, are my only surviving children, just as Argus and Karos are all the grandchildren I have left. You've brought me a great treasure. You are welcome here, you and the rest of your men."

Lord Aetes summoned the same hawk-faced servant who'd guided us into his hall. "These men are my sacred guests. Send word to their ship, call all of the crewmen here at once, and prepare food, drink, and the best sleeping quarters in the palace for them. Tomorrow night we'll give them a worthy feast. See to it!" The servant's glum expression never changed, though he pressed his palms together in a gesture of obedience before leaving to fulfill the king's orders.

"There! That's done." Aetes sat down and slapped his thighs, satisfied. "Now, my honored guests, tell me all about yourselves. I have heard that your ship carries no cargo, so I know you're not traders. Surely you didn't undertake a voyage solely to restore my grandson to his family?"

It was Jason's moment to shine, and he seized it. He introduced each of us, somehow making it sound as if we owed some part of our fame to him. When he presented me as "Atalanta, the heroine of the Calydonian boar hunt," he took pride in describing my initial masquerade as a weapons bearer. "That was all my idea. I wanted the great huntress to share in this adventure, but she was afraid of what would happen if the crew knew she was a woman." If the real Atalanta had been there to hear it, she would have taught him a hard lesson at the point of a boar spear.

"Is that so?" Lord Aetes studied me where I stood. "She doesn't look like the fearful type."

"I'm not," I said firmly. "But you know how it is with sailors, Lord Aetes: The truth never gets in the way of a good story." I ignored Jason's dark scowl.

The Colchian king laughed out loud. "You look very young to be so bold. Medea! Take Atalanta to your own quarters and see to her comfort."

Lord Aetes' daughter looked stricken. "Now?" Her glance darted from her father, to me, to Jason, where I was surprised to see it linger.

The king glowered at her. "What's wrong with you? You heard me!"

"I—I only wanted to hear more of our honored guests, Father. They haven't told you why they've come to Colchis yet." Her voice sounded strained, as if she weren't used to putting up the mildest argument.

"If that turns out to be any business of yours, you'll be told. Now go, before you shame yourself in front of our guests any further."

He might as well have slapped her face. Medea quailed, then moved quickly toward me, made an awkward bow, mumbled something in her own tongue, and escaped from the king's hall. I presumed I was supposed to follow her. It wasn't easy. She ran as if fleeing a pack of hunting hounds, outdistancing me until she reached a small courtyard where a fountain bubbled. I didn't need to see her face to know she was crying. Her body shook, but the few sounds she made were smothered, as if she didn't have the right to weep.

I approached her carefully, not wanting to add to her distress. "You don't have to look after me if you don't want to," I said gently. "I'm used to taking care of myself. Just show me where I'm supposed to sleep, and—"

She looked up at me suddenly, her face streaming tears, and grabbed my hands. "How did you do it?" she asked urgently. "How did you make him love you?"

I jumped back, taken by surprise, and jerked out of her grip, so that her fingernails left long red tracks on my hands. "What are you talking about?"

"The prince of Iolkos. If I were blind, I could still see how hotly he burns for you!"

"The prince of— You mean Jason?" She had to. "Lady Medea, he doesn't love me."

"Why wouldn't he love you? You're so beautiful, and so young! He brought you on this voyage, helped shield you from the other men. How did you do it? Was it enough just to let him see your face, how gracefully you move, or did he fall in love with you after he heard about your fame as a huntress? Is that what he wants from a woman? It isn't fair. You have so much to draw his heart to you, and I have nothing." She wrung her hands.

I was speechless. *She must be mad, thinking she loves him! How is it possible? She just set eyes on him.* Suddenly Hylas's image flashed through my mind, and the memory of my own reaction at the first sight of his handsome face. *But that was different!* I protested to myself. *Hylas wasn't just handsome; he was kind, and thoughtful. Jason thinks of no one but himself. I don't care how handsome he is, it's a thin coating for an ugly core.*

"Listen," I said to Medea. "Take me to the shrine of whichever god you worship most faithfully and I'll swear on the altar that I don't love Jason and Jason doesn't love me. As far as I know, he loves no one." *Except himself.*

Medea's eyes lit up with a blazing hunger. She was no longer the same girl who'd cowered at Lord Aetes' stern words. The change was so abrupt, so complete, that I felt a stab of fear, for her sake. *It's like she's got two spirits living in one skin,* I thought. *How does she keep them from tearing her apart?*

She dragged me back into the palace and through many hallways until we came to a door painted with jewel-bright dragons and studded with polished bronze. A boy dozed against one of the doorposts. Medea gave him a kick to rouse him and said something sharp to him in her own language. White-faced, he flung the door open before us, then bolted away as if he'd caught fire. We entered a high-ceilinged chamber, sumptuously furnished, lit by a forest of tall braziers. Three harried serving women were hastening to kindle the last of these. When they saw Medea, they bowed so low, so swiftly that I thought they'd snap in two at the waist. She gave another command and they fled the room in an instant. I could almost smell their terror as they flew past me.

Does Lord Aetes know his little mouse can wear a wolf's skin when she wants to? I wondered. *Or is this other self something beyond even her control?* I had no answer to that, only a growing sense of misgiving.

Medea pulled me over to an elaborately painted couch and made me sit beside her. She undid one of her necklaces and forced it into my hands. "I owe you a better gift than this for what you've just given me," she said passionately. "From this moment, you are more sacred to me than any guest. You will be my beloved sister."

"Lady Medea, I've only told you the truth. I've done nothing to merit this." I tried to give her back the necklace.

She wouldn't have it back. "Then take it as a reward for what you *will* do for me." A thoughtful look came into her eyes. "You come from *his* lands. You know what women there do to attract a man. You will teach me."

I didn't like the way our conversation was going. Even though she kept her voice soft and coaxing, she wasn't asking for my help, she was demanding it. "Lady Medea, I don't know about such things."

"You wouldn't need to, would you?" Now her expression was hard and bitter. Her moods shifted at a frightening rate, and my apprehension grew with each change. "You don't need to do anything but breathe and the men flock to you, ready to die for your sake."

"That's not true. You heard how I came here. No one questioned my disguise for an instant." *Except Argus,* I reminded myself. *And perhaps Orpheus too, though he never came out and said anything about it directly. But she doesn't need to hear that.* "Besides, I have other things to occupy my days: hunting, riding, racing, practicing. . . ."

"I can't learn how to do all that before Jason leaves!" she wailed.

"I'm not saying you should," I told her. "I doubt such skills matter to Jason, or any other prince, when it comes to choosing a bride."

"Is that why he's come here?" Medea's dramatic despair became wild-eyed hope. I wished I could get away from her. I didn't want to come face to face with whatever lay at the core of so many abrupt transformations. "He wants to marry? But that's wonderful! I'm the only one left. He'll have to choose me!"

I hesitated. I dreaded her reaction once I told her the true purpose of Jason's voyage to Colchis. *Best to get it over with.* "He hasn't come to Colchis for a bride," I said. "He's still a prince without a throne. That's why he's here, to bring back one of the famous gold-filled fleeces of Colchis. Lord Pelias of Iolkos has promised to set aside his own son, Acastus, and make Jason his heir if he fulfills that quest."

To my relief, Medea didn't burst into tears, curses, or worse. Instead her expression turned thoughtful again, and then she actually lifted one corner of her mouth in a half-smile. It was like watching a serpent raise its head to strike. "A golden fleece? I can give him that," she said. "I can give him the best of them all."

"He'll be happy to hear that," I said. "You can tell him so in the morning."

"Oh, I couldn't!" Medea hid her face in her hands and giggled. "You must be there with me, Atalanta. I wouldn't be able to say a word if I was alone with him. And we must see him secretly. If my father knew, he'd lock me up again."

Again? I wanted to ask what she meant, but with Medea, perhaps there were some riddles better left unanswered. I assured her that I would do whatever I could to help her. She gave me a ferocious hug, then ran to the doorway and shouted for her servants.

I was given a small room in Medea's apartments and soon I settled comfortably into the thickest, most sweetly perfumed bed I'd ever known. I should have fallen asleep at once, but my thoughts kept me awake. I was haunted by the memory of the harsh, critical way her father had treated her before us all.

Is there anything *about her that pleases him? He praised her skill with herbs and potions, but otherwise he made it plain that she's a disappointment.* I recalled the immeasurable affection my own father had always given me and felt deeply sorry for Medea. I'd heard stories of famine years, and how starvation could deform the body. *If you starve the heart, do you deform the mind?* That might explain why she'd attached herself to Jason with such an intense, all-devouring passion, but suspecting the cause behind Medea's behavior didn't make it any less alarming.

I'd better try to get some sleep, I thought. *I've got the feeling that I'll want to stay alert as long as I'm anywhere near Medea.*

I shifted onto my side, facing the wall, and was just beginning to drift off when I got the abrupt, startling sensation that I wasn't alone. I turned over quickly just in time to catch sight of a shape clinging to the doorpost. It fled with a gasp when I started up from my bed. It might have been no more than one of the servants, but I had the disturbing feeling it was their royal mistress. I wasn't able to fall asleep again until just before dawn.

9

THE GIFT OF HECATE

I had barely dozed off when Medea shook me awake much too early the next morning. Her face was drawn, her eyes feverish. "Can you fetch him now? Now, before my father finds out? I'll show you where I'll be waiting, then you can bring him to me."

I sat up, rubbing my weary eyes. "I don't know where to look for Jason," I replied.

She ground her teeth so hard that I could hear it. "Don't lie to me. You're wasting my time with your excuses. Come!" She dug her fingers into my wrist and would have yanked me from the bed onto the floor if I hadn't braced myself.

"Stop that!" I ordered her, pulling my hand away. "What's the matter with you? One moment I'm your sacred guest, your beloved sister, and the next you're acting like I'm one of your slaves. I won't let you treat me like this." I was too sleepy to worry if my bluntness might send her into a rage.

I was lucky. Instead of storming at me, Medea was immediately sorry, though I knew her heartfelt apology might turn into a fresh spate of false accusations at any moment. I got up and dressed as fast as I could. She'd done everything but grovel, yet I'd caught an icy glimpse of malice in her eyes. *The less I thwart this girl, the healthier I'll stay,* I thought. *How does she manage to make my heart break and my skin crawl at the same time? O gods, grant me some way to escape her "hospitality"!* She took me out of the palace and past humble outbuildings protected by the citadel enclosure. The smell of cookfires was already on the fresh morning air. Slaves and servants trotted busily to and fro as Lord Aetes' stronghold stirred itself from sleep. None of them seemed to regard it as strange to see their princess roaming the grounds outside the palace. The building she sought looked like a potter's shed, with the oven for baking the clay pots beside it. There was a scattering of broken crockery in front of the doorsill. Medea stooped and examined it keenly, then stood up and smiled at me as if I understood all her secrets. "No one has been here. We can enter."

She opened the door and urged me to follow her. I did so, and soon found myself deep in stench-haunted shadows. I groped behind my back and was reassured to feel the door. Just then, a spark flared in the darkness. Medea had kindled a fat wick stuck into a cup of tallow. It burned with more smoke and stink than lamps fed with olive oil, but she didn't seem to mind.

"You will bring him here," she said. "Hecate herself will stand witness to all we say to one another. But not yet. First I must worship the goddess who has answered my prayers."

She gestured with the flame and I saw a waisthigh block of stone at the rear of the little hut. The image resting on it was made from rock so black it seemed to gulp down any light that fell on it. It was a carving of a three-headed goddess, though only one head was human. The other two were those of a wild horse and a viciously snarling dog. A serpent encircled the goddess's waist. One of Hecate's hands held a torch, the other a sword.

I knew Hecate's name. I'd known it long before Argus mentioned her to me when speaking about his stepmother. Even if we didn't worship the goddess willingly in Sparta, my parents still made the occasional sacrifice at her shrine to protect us from her anger. Some believed she was only another side of Artemis, who changed her appearance and entered the underworld on nights when the moon was dark and dead. Others said she was a goddess in her own right, the ruler of wild and haunted places. Even Zeus feared her powers, for she was the mistress of magic strong enough to undo the normal order of the world. As I gazed at the image, Medea placed the burning cup at its feet and took a small, covered pot from among dozens crowding the top of a table propped against the sidewall. A knife lay there as well, its leaf-shaped blade mottled with stains. I tried not to think about what might have made them.

Medea removed the lid of the little pot and a cloying sweet smell fought the stink of burning tallow. She held it out to Hecate's image and chanted words I didn't understand, then set it down and turned to me. "Hecate is pleased. You can go now. Bring Jason. I'll be waiting."

I couldn't get out of that hut fast enough. I shut the door behind me and stumbled over Medea's tell-tale pottery shards in my haste to flee. I had no intention of fulfilling her command. I'd fallen in love with Hylas at first sight, but now I saw how different those feelings of mine were from Medea's unhealthy fascination with Jason. She and I had both been attracted to a handsome face, but I'd seen Hylas as human, not as something I had to *own*. Which god had twisted her mind so badly? Not gentle Aphrodite, surely! I didn't know much about love, but I was willing to wager all I had that Medea's passion was something else. It was all-consuming, terrifying, and utterly unwilling to hear the word *no*. I wondered if her cold father had somehow taught her that the only way to hold on to what you loved was to embrace it so tightly that you crushed it.

I ran to find Jason. He had to be warned. I didn't know where to start looking for him. Lord Aetes' palace was huge. It was no use asking the servants for help, since none of them were likely to speak our language. I wandered through courtyards and passageways until I heard the faint sound of familiar voices, familiar words. I followed them to a large room strewn with bedding and the remains of breakfast. My own stomach rumbled as I watched some of the *Argo's* crew picking over bits of bread and cheese while they talked.

I was overjoyed to spy Milo among them. He caught sight of me and came running to the doorway. "Glau— I mean, Hel— *Atalanta*, there you are! I—" He dropped his voice sharply so that no one else could hear him say, "I've missed you."

"I've missed you, too," I said as I led him off. The other men catcalled after us, but we ignored them. "Listen, do you know where Jason is? I have to find him."

"Lord Aetes gave him a fine room on the upper floor," Milo said. "I'm not sure where, exactly. Let me help you."

We had no better luck working together than I'd had on my own. When we finally agreed to give up the search, I told Milo about the night I'd spent in

Medea's disturbing company, and about the strange shrine to Hecate that was her den. "I guess I'd better let her know I failed to find Jason," I said as we left the palace and walked past the outbuildings.

Milo tapped my arm. "It looks like she found him herself." He motioned with his eyes.

Arm in arm, Jason and Medea came strolling along, laughing and talking as though they were old friends. Slaves and servants ignored them, but four Colchian guards shot disapproving stares. Medea noticed and spoke a few sharp words to one of them. The man turned white and ran.

"Ah! Atalanta!" Jason saw Milo and me standing there and waved us near. "You must see the marvel that Lady Medea's just shown me."

He gave her an adoring look so overdone that it wouldn't have fooled a child. She devoured it. I'd done much the same thing to him earlier, when I'd diverted his attention with flattery about that leopard-skin trophy of his. Still, there was an important difference: I'd acted to divert his anger from my friend Argus. He was acting for no one's benefit but his own.

"Of course she shall see it, if that's what you want, Lord Jason," she said, indulging him with a king's title. "Follow me." She released his arm reluctantly. There were little white finger marks where she'd clutched his flesh. In one agile maneuver, she shunted

Milo aside, got a painful grip on my wrist, and raced away with me.

"I didn't need you after all," she whispered triumphantly, keeping us well ahead of the others. Her eyes sparkled with a wild light. "As soon as you were gone, Hecate spoke to me. She told me not to trust any other girl when a man's love is the prize. You can save the rest of your lies. I left the shrine and found him walking toward me, a gift from Hecate herself! He's mine now, mine always. Remember that."

Well, that was fast, I thought. *I wonder if Jason knows. I almost feel sorry for him. Medea might have the power to terrify the palace underlings with a few words, but Jason's a free man, able to look out for himself. What's the worst she could ever do to him?*

Medea led us to another part of the citadel enclosure, a space set aside by a low stone wall. Three small shrines stood inside the little barrier. Two were no more than four pillars supporting the roof over a god's image. The third boasted sturdy walls, gorgeous decoration, and everything it took to declare that this was the home of the king's favored god.

An ancient priest dozed in the shade of the building as Medea led us inside. She dropped my hand and reattached herself to Jason before announcing, "This is Ares' shrine. My father worships the war god above all others. Every year, when the spring rains bring the gold down from the mountains, he dedicates one

fleece to every shrine in Aea, but Ares alone has *that.*"
She pointed dramatically.

I looked up at the wall behind the statue of Ares
and saw a masterpiece of solid gold. It was the perfect
life-size image of a ram's pelt, including the head,
horns, and hooves of the beast. Every detail, down to
the smallest strand of wool, was etched into the soft,
glowing metal.

So the Golden Fleece exists after all, I thought, breathless with wonder. The ram gazed back at me with
enameled eyes the color of the sea.

"It was a gift from Phrixus, to thank my father for
giving him refuge, a home, and a royal bride," Medea
said. She squeezed Jason's arm. "Now it will be a gift
of thanks *from* a bride to her beloved husband."

Jason looked down at the Colchian princess and
smiled. "Are you certain your father will part with it?
After all, I'm already taking his best treasure with me
when I go." Medea giggled.

As promised, that night, Lord Aetes lavished a fine
feast on us to welcome back his grandson Argus.
Jason, of course, behaved as if it were all to glorify
him. Though Colchis was a foreign land, they followed some of our customs. The closer you were
seated to the king, the more respect he meant to show
you. Argus and Jason were placed to either side of
Lord Aetes, which left Jason sour-faced over having to

share the highest honor. His expression grew even more resentful when he glanced at his cousin, Acastus, seated next to Argus.

I noticed other customs that were purely Colchian. As each dish was brought to the table, a group of handsomely dressed men stepped in to taste the food. They also tasted the wine, and examined the knives and spoons used to serve the meal. I wondered what it must feel like, knowing that your life could end with the next mouthful you swallowed. And what sort of mind could be both so clever and so cowardly as to kill by tainting the good gifts of Demeter and Dionysos? If the stories were true, Colchis did harbor monsters.

Medea and I were seated together, among the other palace women. She hardly ate a bite all evening, her eyes fixed on Jason. I tried to talk with her, but she refused to be distracted from him.

When the banqueting was finished, Lord Aetes called for silence. "My friends, it's thanks to you that I've been reunited with my beloved grandson Argus. It's not my way to ask the true purpose of guests who come to me in peace until they've had ample time to rest and refresh themselves. I believe that moment has come. I invite you to share the reason that's brought you to Aea. If I have the power to help you, I'll do it freely."

Jason was on his feet at once. He launched into a

long-winded, self-exalting history. He took credit for every successful adventure we'd experienced on the voyage to Colchis. He did toss a few crumbs of praise to some of the men, granting them minor parts in his own fabricated triumphs. Zetes and Kalais were credited with driving off the Harpies, but only after Jason commanded them to do it! When he saw that Lord Aetes and the Colchian nobles were thoroughly fascinated by his wild tale, he finally revealed the object of his quest.

"A golden fleece?" Lord Aetes was all smiles. "Only one? That's hardly a fitting reward for your accomplishments. You and your men shall have one apiece, I insist!"

Jason lowered his eyes. "You are gracious, Lord Aetes, and you give me more than I ever dreamed of asking." He sat down in silence, and the king called for more wine.

I felt a sharp pain in my left hand. Medea had dug her fingernails into the skin. Her jaw was clenched, her face ashen, and her eyes blazing with unholy rage. "Not a word about me?" she whispered. "Not one to ask my father for permission to marry me?"

"Lady Medea, maybe Jason didn't want to talk about that now, in front of everyone," I murmured, trying to calm her. "He'd look too greedy if he asked Lord Aetes for his only daughter after the king just gave him not one golden fleece but fifty."

Medea sucked in her breath with an eerie hissing sound. "You know nothing about love," she said coldly. "Don't speak to me again until you do." She rose from her place, her scowl instantly becoming a look of utter meekness when she addressed Lord Aetes. "Father, may I go?" she asked, eyes downcast but voice raised to bridge the distance between the women's table and the king's. "So much wine . . . it's given me a headache."

Lord Aetes dismissed her without a second glance. I finished the banquet blissfully free of her presence, though I wasn't looking forward to returning to my bed in her rooms. Fortunately, when the time to retire came, Lord Aetes' chief servant appeared at my elbow and let me know that I'd be sleeping elsewhere that night. "The lady Medea is too ill for company," he intoned. "You are welcome to use the queen's apartments."

A maidservant bearing an oil lamp guided me to my new rooms. The queen's apartments encircled a private garden, where flowers drowsed in the moonlight. Lord Aetes had outlived all of his wives, old and young, so the royal rooms were vast and empty, but clean. Even if they teemed with ghosts, I preferred them to Medea's company.

The maid used her lamp to light another that sat on the floor beside my bed. Since she didn't speak my language, I had to use signs to request a jug of water and a basin for washing. Luckily, she was quick-witted and brought me everything I needed, then left.

I awoke with my fist clenching a wad of soft, supple cloth. It was the hem of a fine crimson gown adorned with an intricate pattern of leopards and grapevines. I could see every stitch of the gold thread outlining the fruit and leaves. The leopards' eyes were tiny amber beads. I saw every detail clearly by the light of the dozen lamps surrounding my bed.

I'd gone to sleep with only one lamp, and I'd extinguished its flame myself. No matter how costly the gift, stealing into my room while I slept was an invasion, and it had Medea's mark all over it. I traced the embroidered outline of a grapevine with one fingertip. The divine Dionysos gave us the gift of vines, grapes, and wine, but there were stories of men and women driven into violent frenzies by the god as punishment for offending him. Medea's extreme, unpredictable passions didn't come from wine. Perhaps it would have been better if they had. At least then I might be able to catch sight of her with a goblet to her lips and brace myself for her next eruption.

I shook out the fabric, and a strange, heavy perfume wafted from its folds. It wasn't unpleasant, but it was overpowering. I brought the cloth closer to my nose and sniffed. There was a second smell lurking beneath the thick, flowery scent. Its sour harshness refused to be smothered completely, and only a few breaths of it made me queasy. So much for the beautiful dress. I wasn't going to wear it. Maybe that disturbing scent meant nothing, but I mistrusted the giver too much to embrace the gift. I folded it and laid it across the foot of my bed, then put out all the lamps except one.

When I woke up the next morning, the crowd of dead oil lamps around my bed was still there, though the crimson and gold dress was gone. In its place was a simple blue gown that carried no suspicious scent. Why had Medea crept back to exchange one dress for another? Had she even done this herself, or had she sent a servant to fulfill her whim? In either case, I should have sensed the presence of my midnight visitor. I'd have to be more vigilant in the future.

The new dress was very tempting. I hadn't had fresh clothes to wear for days and I longed for the feel of clean cloth against my skin, but wariness made me hesitate. I was still holding the dress up, debating whether or not to put it on, when I heard a deliberate cough from the doorway.

"*Milo!*" I was so happy to see him that I nearly knocked him off his feet. "You probably know your way around the palace already. Can you help me find breakfast? I'm starving."

"That's why I'm here." There was a small basket at his feet. It held bread, cheese, figs, and some smoked meat.

I sent Milo into the corridor while I cleaned up and put on the new dress. I made sure to fasten my sword at my waist. The weathered belt looked out of place against the fine blue fabric, but after the double invasion of my room the night before, I wasn't going to take chances.

We ate in the queen's garden. I was halfway through my second chunk of bread when I said, "You forgot to bring—"

"—something to drink," Milo finished. "Sorry. Do you have anything in there?" He pointed at the doorway to my room.

I shook my head. "I used all my water for washing."

He stood up and stretched. His time aboard the *Argo* had been good to him. He'd put on healthy weight and gained a sense of confidence. He no longer looked as if he feared to wake up one day and find that his freedom was only a dream. "I'll see what I can find, then," he said. "There were plenty of amphorae in the crew's sleeping chambers this morning, wine and water both."

"Do you think there's any left?"

"Water or wine?" He grinned.

"By the way, where are all the men?" I asked.

"The ones who aren't busy bothering the serving girls are practicing their battle skills with Lord Aetes' guards. There's a training ground, but it's a fair distance from the citadel. I think the palace weapons bearers get more exercise than the men, carrying their gear there and back."

"Except for *one* lazybones who's hiding in the queen's garden instead of doing his proper work. Poor Iolaus! This is the thanks he gets for hiring you." I was teasing, and Milo knew it.

"And what about a weapons bearer so lazy that he'd rather turn into a girl than do his job?" Milo countered, laughing.

I stood up. "A girl who can carry two amphorae of wine to your one," I said.

"One to my three, you mean!" Milo declared, getting into the spirit. "But you'll have to find them first." He made a taunting face at me and darted into the palace.

I raced after him gladly, our laughter echoing through the halls. We had a few near collisions with Lord Aetes' slaves and servants, and drew our fair share of outraged curses from stuffy palace officials, but it felt so *good* to run! Milo soon forgot all about going back to the crew's chambers to search for those amphorae. He ran right past the doorway and didn't give it a glance. Though my dress hindered me and my sword slapped against my left leg at every stride, I was enjoying myself.

When we'd exhausted the maze of corridors on the lower floor of the palace, Milo took our wild chase up a flight of stairs to the second level. Here the passageways were mostly narrow walkways leading to the sleeping chambers around the palace's many courtyards. Because of my skirt, Milo outdistanced me just as we burst out of a dark corridor and into one of the open spaces. My eyes were dazzled by the sudden sunlight, but I could still see him putting even more space between us. *Oh no you don't!* I thought, and paused to hike up the hem of my dress and jam it into my sword belt before taking off after him again.

I ran headfirst into Medea. In the scant few moments I'd paused to adjust my dress, she'd stepped out of one of the upper-level rooms and right into my path. The impact sent both of us tumbling backward onto our rumps. She yelped indignantly.

"What's the matter with you, woman?" came a male voice. "Do you *want* your father to have me killed?" Jason strode out of the same room Medea had just left.

"It's her fault!" Medea whined, jabbing a finger at me. "She was spying on us!"

"Why would I want to waste my time doing that?" I replied tartly.

Medea glared at me. Jason helped her to her feet and kissed her in front of me as if I were nothing but a piece of furniture. When she finally unhooked her fingers from the front of his tunic, she was smiling.

"Running around my father's palace like this, not caring if you tear your pretty new dress! Really, Atalanta, you *are* uncivilized." She giggled and gazed up at Jason. "See how badly she treats my gift!"

"Then isn't it a good thing that you didn't give her the other dress?" Jason said. "I told you she didn't deserve it." He turned to me, and for a moment I saw something different in his eyes. It wasn't his usual smugness or arrogance. I might have been wrong, but it looked like a warning.

"I suppose I should thank you both, then," I said. "This dress suits me much better than the crimson one."

"That's what my Jason said," Medea replied, simpering sidelong at him. I couldn't be certain, but I thought I saw him cringe just a little. "I wanted you to keep the first one, but he said no. I'd die before I'd disagree with him. He even insisted on coming with me, to make sure you found the right gift waiting for you when you woke up."

I gave Medea a hard stare. "I might not be as civilized as you, Lady, but I've slept under more than one king's roof. Last night was the first time my room was entered secretly, not once, but twice. You treat the sacred trust between host and guest differently here in Colchis."

She tittered. Either she was going to ignore my

accusations or she simply didn't believe she'd done anything wrong. "You sleep very soundly, for such a famous huntress," she said.

"I'll do better about that in future," I told her. "Count on it."

Just then, Milo appeared at one end of the walkway. He must have realized he'd lost me entirely and was now backtracking. Medea's sharp eyes spotted him at once.

"You mustn't waste any more time on us, dear Atalanta," she cooed. "I see your precious *friend* has come seeking you. Better hurry to his side, before he loses interest."

I didn't like her insinuating tone, but before I could react, Jason spoke. "My beloved princess is right, Atalanta. There's nothing to hold you here, in our company. In fact, I've got work for you." He ducked back into his room and returned holding a pile of blankets, which he shoved at me. "Take these to the *Argo*."

I wanted to object, but whatever else Jason was, he was still our leader. It would be childish to defy him over such a trivial command. I bowed my head and started for the stairs. "Come on, Milo!" I called back over one shoulder.

Milo tried to scamper after me, only to have Jason's hand fall to his shoulder. "You can manage a few blankets on your own. Milo will accompany me to the training ground. I'm sure Iolaus will be happy to see that at least one of his weapons bearers is still doing his proper job."

I had no choice. I left Milo standing there between Jason and his wild-eyed lady. *I couldn't save Hylas,* I thought bitterly as I descended the stairs. *I can't let anything happen to Milo.*

10

A FEAST FOR THE FURIES

Three days passed before I was able to talk to Milo again. No matter how early I woke up and went to the room my friend shared with some of the other crewmen, he was never there. To my disappointment, I also failed to encounter my brothers and those Argonauts I knew and liked best. Jason, however, seemed to show up everywhere I turned, Medea clinging to him like a wet olive leaf. It was all I could do to dodge them before they spied me.

I did run into Orpheus, late in the afternoon of the second day, and asked him about the others. "I only see them at the evening meal, when I'm stuck at the women's table," I complained. "They *look* well, but we don't get to exchange a single word, and afterward everyone goes to bed."

"Argus spends his time renewing ties with his family," the singer replied. "Iolaus and your brothers are probably exercising on the royal training ground."

"Where is it?" I asked eagerly.

He shook his head. "I wouldn't know. I've been going elsewhere to do my own sort of exercise." He held up his lyre. "Care for a lesson?" He soon discovered I had a voice fit to frighten crows and no real interest in learning to pluck anything but a bowstring, but it was kind of him to offer.

On the morning of the third day, I was sitting on a rock just outside the citadel gate, lazily wondering whether I should explore the city below or spend the day down by the waterside, when luck let me find Milo. He was heading out with Iolaus and my brothers, his arms filled with javelins. The men all carried swords, and Polydeuces had a bow and quiver on his back.

"No need to ask where you're going," I said, overjoyed to see them. "I've been wanting to visit a good training ground for weeks, since before we left Iolkos. Give me just a moment to put on something better than this and I'll come with you!" I tugged at the blue dress.

"The training ground's not the place for you, Helllllanta," Castor declared. He cast a quick glance at the guards on duty at the gate behind us.

"That's not your decision to make, is it?" I replied sweetly.

Polydeuces laughed. "It never was. Come on, then."

"Are you insane?" Castor spoke in an anxious whisper that only we five could hear. "She's *supposed* to be Atalanta. You think the other men know nothing about that woman's reputation for strength and speed, for excellence with the spear and the bow?"

"Helen's smart," Iolaus murmured. "She wouldn't come to the training ground if she thought it would endanger her disguise."

"You know I'm good with the bow and the light javelin," I reminded Castor. "And if I can't outpace any man on the crew in a footrace, I'll——"

"And what if they challenge you to a sword match?" he interrupted. "You could never hope to beat any of them."

"Oh really," I said, planting my hands on my hips. "I seem to remember beating *you* a time or two."

"That was different." Castor dismissed my words with a wave of his hand. "We were children. You can't come to the training ground just because you're bored. You stand to lose too much if your true identity is discovered—and you're not the only one."

"I know all that." I stiffened my spine. "I'm not doing this on a whim. I *need* to practice my weaponry. It's been too long since I've had the chance. If fear makes me lose the skills I fought so hard to learn, then I'm the worst coward in the world. Castor, I swear by the all-seeing eye of Apollo, I have a way to use the training ground safely, without risk of discovery." I raised my hands to the sun.

Castor still looked dubious, but Polydeuces came forward and said, "I don't need Iolaus to tell me how quick-witted you are, little sister. If you say you've got a plan in mind, I trust you."

"Thank you, Polydeuces," I said. I wanted to embrace him, but it would have looked suspicious to the guards at the citadel gate if the aloof huntress Atalanta suddenly hugged anyone. Instead I turned a questioning look to my other brother.

Castor shrugged. "Go change your clothes," he grumbled.

As Orpheus had said, most of the other Argonauts were on the royal training ground. I saw all our crew except for Jason, Argus, and the Thracian singer himself. Even Zetes was there, wounded leg and all, watching his shipmates show off their skills with weapons. Milo was soon busy, doing a weapons bearer's job of fetching the javelins and arrows the men sent flying.

I soon set Castor's mind at ease about how I'd protect my borrowed identity. To stave off any challenges I couldn't handle, the first thing I did was issue a challenge of my own against any man who wanted to try his luck besting me in a footrace. I beat five men, including Kalais, a so-called son of Boreas, the North

Wind. No one else challenged me for the rest of the morning. What man wanted to risk losing to a woman in front of all his friends?

I should've given some time to sword work, but I had my misgivings about that. If I made too poor a showing, the men might suspect something. I owed it to my brothers to preserve the illusion that I was Atalanta. I'd find my own time and place to practice using my blade. *Maybe I can get Iolaus to work with me later,* I thought as I went off to borrow Polydeuces' bow.

"Come with me!" I called out to Milo. I headed for the far side of the training ground, where Lord Aetes' guards had set up a row of straw targets. A desolate hillside rose beyond it. It was a safe place for any private conversation. "I need you to fetch my arrows."

Milo trotted dutifully after me and stood by my side while I strung my brother's bow. It wasn't easy, bending a strong piece of wood that had been made for a grown man's use, but I had to do it. It cost me a lot of sweat and a lick or two of blood when I lost my grip on the bowstring and it slashed my palm, but I won in the end.

I glanced around casually as I chose my first arrow. No one else had a taste for archery that morning. "Where have you been, Milo?" I asked quietly. "It's been three days."

"Working for Jason," Milo replied, his voice low.

I frowned, setting the arrow to the bow. Anyone watching us would think I was the world's most cautious archer, to spend so much time preparing to make my first shot. "Doing what?" My muscles strained as I pulled the bowstring back.

"Protecting you."

The bowstring released with a loud twang, and the arrow arced through the air, barely grazing the top of the target before falling to the earth beyond it. A few of the men practicing with javelins saw my miss and called out that I'd find a spindle easier to manage than a bow. I snatched up a second arrow and buried it fletch-deep in the core of the target. The jeering stopped. Only then did I return my attention to Milo.

"That makes no sense," I muttered. "In the first place, what protection do I need? And since when does Jason care about anyone's skin but his own?"

"There may be more to Jason than you think," Milo said softly. "That day in the palace when Jason made me stay behind, he told the lady Medea he had to go down to the *Argo* to make sure that the ship was being well kept while she was in port. The gods have mercy on us, you should have seen Medea's eyes when he said that!"

"What, now she's jealous of a *ship*?" I said. I shot another arrow. It hit the top of the target.

"He'd just sent *you* down to the *Argo*, remember? With those blankets?"

"Oh, yes." I pretended to study the shaft of my fourth arrow for straightness. "I was grateful to him for giving me an excuse to escape Medea. She makes me nervous, Milo, even while I'm feeling sorry for her. Her mind's badly wounded, and the gods alone know why. The gods alone can heal it."

"Well, she was sure Jason was going to check on the ship just to have a chance to run after *you*. He swore that wasn't so, and finally told her that he wouldn't go to the *Argo* that day, just to please her. Then she became all honey cakes and nectar, draping herself over him like a vine. I wanted to get away, but Jason forced me to wait there until she decided she'd better go. That was when he turned to me and said, '*Now* do you see the danger? Your friend's too busy pretending to be Atalanta to admit how bad it is.'"

I set aside the fourth arrow as if I'd found a flaw in it, and reached for a fifth. My hands were shaking. "He knows who I am?"

"He knows who you're *not*," Milo replied. "He told me, 'I don't care who that girl really is, runaway slave or the bastard daughter of a king. Thanks to her, I can count Atalanta among my crew, but I don't want to count her corpse. She's a brave young woman. I admire that. I was raised by strangers, with nothing but my own wits and nerve to get me through some hard times. I can appreciate boldness, and when I see it in a girl, of all things—! That's a miracle worthy of the gods themselves. But it's a miracle that will end badly if she doesn't watch her step.' "

I fired the fifth arrow, but Milo's revelation about Jason shook me so deeply that it went wide of the target. The Argonauts were too busy with their own exercises to notice. "That's the last one," I said, and Milo ran to gather up my arrows for me, leaving me a little time to ponder what he'd told me. *I've misjudged you, Jason,* I thought. *I don't know what you endured, growing up the way you did, but at least you've let me see there's more to you than self-preservation turned to selfishness. I wonder if I'll ever be able to thank you for it?*

When Milo came running back with my arrows, I said, "Was there anything else Jason wanted me to know?"

"That he's going to keep his distance, for your sake, and that you should do the same. He said that the less chance there is for Medea to catch him in the company of a beautiful girl, the better for everyone."

"If you ask me, he's been staring into the sun too long." A wry smile curved my mouth. "Or else he's as mad as she is." While I took aim, I told Milo briefly about Medea's first "gift" to me, the crimson dress with its suspicious smell. "Jason told her I didn't deserve it," I said as I loosed the arrow. It was a hit, but a poor one. The memory of that uncanny gown made me shiver and had thrown off my aim. "Now I understand what he meant. I don't know much about poison, Milo. In Sparta, the word means certain serpents that carry death in their bite, certain plants that have the power to kill with a taste." I shaded my eyes, as if evaluating my shot. "In Colchis, *poison* means slaves who risk their lives daily to shield their masters from tainted food and drink, ordinary things that carry hidden death, and cowards who kill without giving their victims the chance to defend themselves. Jason must know that Medea is . . . not quite right." I glanced at Milo and saw him nod. "Then why is he courting her? Is he afraid to turn her away? Or does he dream he'll win all Colchis if he marries Lord Aetes' mad daughter?"

"Not that," Milo replied. "Her brother is Lord Aetes' heir."

I sniffed. "If Jason even *hinted* that he wanted the throne, Medea would destroy anyone who stood between him and his heart's desire, even her own brother."

"Well, he doesn't want that," Milo said. "All he wants is the Golden Fleece."

"He's getting it," I said, firing the next arrow. "*Fifty*, in fact. He doesn't need her to—"

"He thinks he does," Milo said. "He's going to take her with us when the *Argo* sails home."

I lowered the bow and stared at him. "He's doing *what?*"

I don't remember much more about the rest of

that morning at the training ground. It all became a
blur of arrows in flight, and the repeated thud of
Milo's feet on the earth as he ran back and forth,
fetching my darts from the targets. It was amazing
that I managed to score so many hits. I was trying to
keep my eyes on the target and at the same time be on
the lookout for any sign that my brothers were preparing to head back to the palace.

I could have spared myself the effort. When they
were done exercising, they hailed Milo to pick up the
javelins. I went with him under the pretense of giving
back Polydeuces' bow.

"I have to talk to you and Castor," I said. "Now."

"There's a pine grove on the seaward side of the
path back," Polydeuces said, keeping his voice pitched
low. While he spoke, he pretended to examine his bow
and arrows for any wear and tear. "You can't mistake
it. A ruined shrine lies under the trees. Go there and
wait for us behind the fallen stones, out of sight of
the road." I could tell that he was dying to know what
was troubling me, but he'd wait until we were safe
from any prying eyes.

"Will Iolaus be with you?" I asked. "You all came
down here together."

Polydeuces glanced across the field to where Iolaus stood chatting with Tiphys, then shook his head.
"If too many of us vanish into the pine grove on the
way back to the palace, the others will get curious." I

saw his point and agreed. "Good," he said. "Now let's get you out of here."

He began testing the sharpness of an arrowhead with the ball of his thumb. All at once, he glared at me and shouted, "Look at what you've done to my arrows! This thing couldn't pierce cheese now. It serves me right for lending a man's weapons to a clumsy woman. You may be able to handle a boar spear, Atalanta, but next time I'll loan my gear to a cow sooner than to you!"

"Better a cow than a jackass!" I shouted back, and raced away from the training ground, blessing my brother for giving me the perfect excuse to avoid the crowd of guards and crewmen.

I found the remains of the shrine in the pine grove and settled myself down behind the weed-grown altar and waited. I saw Iolaus go by, with a laden Milo behind him earning his keep as a weapons bearer. The sound of clattering javelins, marching feet, and deep voices soon faded in the distance. Only then did my brothers arrive.

I told them everything that had happened between Medea and me. I let them know all about the message Milo had brought from Jason, and about Jason's intention to bring the mad princess back to Iolkos. Their faces paled when I spoke about Medea's shrine to dark Hecate.

"Hecate's followers are all expert poisoners," Castor

said. "I've heard that they can make *anything* deadly to taste or touch."

Polydeuces shook his head. "There's more to her worshippers than that. Those who serve Hecate do learn how to make countless salves and potions, but only a few can kill. Most are blessings. Some even have the power to control love."

"*Only* a few can kill?" Castor repeated. "One is all it takes."

"Do you think Medea gave Jason a love potion?" Polydeuces asked.

"More like she drank one herself," I said. "A bad one."

"It sounds like it hit her brain as well as her heart," Castor said. "If she still thinks you want Jason, then you're in grave danger, Helen. It'll only get worse if she's coming back on the *Argo* with us."

The thought made my mouth taste sour. "She won't believe me, even if I swear by the river Styx that I don't want Jason. She's too used to listening to her own madness to try listening to the truth, and I won't be able to avoid her forever aboard the *Argo*." All the pity I'd ever felt for Medea was overwhelmed by how deeply I'd come to fear her. I couldn't keep my voice from breaking. "What am I going to do?"

My brothers put their arms around me and held me tight. "It's all right, Helen," Polydeuces said. "She won't harm you."

"Not while we're here," Castor added.

"But what can we do to keep her off the *Argo*?" I asked. "What if I warned Lord Aetes about Jason's plan to—?" I stopped myself. "No. If the king believes Jason's going to run off with his daughter, he'll kill him."

"Maybe us, too." Castor looked troubled. "When you hear mice in the grain, you don't kill only one."

"We can't stop Medea from boarding the *Argo*," I said. "And I can't be safe on the same ship with her. There's only one way around this." I looked at my brothers. "I have to go home."

"You mean on some other ship?" Castor shook his head emphatically. "That's impossible."

"Why? The harbor here is filled with ships," I said.

"That doesn't mean that any of them are bound for Iolkos."

"I don't have to go back to Iolkos." *But I do have to return to Delphi*, I thought. *I can't simply go home and leave the fisherman's daughter pretending to be me. And Eunike will want to know that I'm all right.* "Any port on the far side of the Hellespont will do. I can find another ship from there, or travel the roads."

"It's much too dangerous."

"Not as dangerous as traveling with Medea," I replied sharply.

Polydeuces intervened. "You're both right. I'd say

that of the two choices, Helen will be safest if she finds her own way back."

"A girl traveling alone on a voyage *that* long?" Castor protested.

"I've done it before," I reminded him. "Not as a girl."

"Yes, well, er, a few things have *changed* about you since then." His face turned a little red.

"I know how to count days and watch the changing of the moon," I replied. "I won't be taken by surprise again, even if I have to spend every day of the voyage wearing a——"

"All right, all right, I believe you!" Poor Castor couldn't wait to drop the subject. "You'll travel as a boy again. Fine."

"And Milo will come with me, so I won't be making the journey alone," I said.

My brothers exchanged a doubtful look. "She does insist that they're only friends," Polydeuces said.

"So far," Castor remarked. "The boy's young, but not *that* young. Have you looked at him lately? I wager that by the time he reaches Sparta, he'll have a thicker beard than Father's."

"Why are you talking about Milo and me as if I weren't here?" I asked angrily. "What are you afraid will happen between us? Half the Argonauts believe it already did, but that doesn't make it so."

"Not yet," Castor said. "People change, especially on a long voyage."

"Why does this matter so much to you?"

"Because now, Helen, you can have a child," Polydeuces replied. He lifted my chin gently. "You are the next ruler of Sparta. The man you marry will be Sparta's king, and your children will rule our land after you. If you have a baby now, that child could grow up to challenge your other children for the throne. Sparta's enemies would be only too happy to help that child raise an army, then swoop down on our lands in the wake of the war and devour anything that remains. When you're dead, do you want to leave your people peace or chaos?"

I didn't have to give him an answer. We both knew it.

"Now, Polydeuces, let her be," Castor said, hugging me again. "Look at that face! Her brow's all creased with worry, and for nothing. As if our little sister would ever give her heart to anyone less than a prince! As if a slave's child could ever raise an army to take Sparta!"

I whirled out from under Castor's arm. "Milo is no slave, and he's worth *ten* princes!"

Castor sucked in his breath sharply and looked to Polydeuces. "All right, *now* I'm worried," he said.

"Either you trust me or you don't," I said. "That's

your only worry. I've made my decision. I'm going to the waterfront, I'm praying to Poseidon that I'll find the ship I need, and I'm going home. As a boy. With Milo."

My brothers smiled. "It's good to see you so confident again," Polydeuces said. "But not *too* confident to reject some help from your devoted brothers?"

I threw my arms around their necks. "Never."

As soon as we returned to the palace, we took Iolaus into our confidence. He agreed that the best course for me to take was one that carried me far from Medea, and the sooner, the better. He even volunteered to help us seek out the right ship for the task.

Poseidon must have heard my prayers. The very next day, Castor and Polydeuces found a Phoenician trading vessel set to sail for Athens the following dawn. That afternoon, they had me follow them into a small, disused storeroom and gave me the news that the ship's captain stood ready to accept two passengers, "Prince Glaucus" of Sparta and "his" devoted servant.

"And never fear, you'll both be properly dressed for your new roles," Polydeuces said, handing me a cloth bundle. "We came back here through the marketplace. Hermes helped us trade well for these new tunics and sandals."

I accepted the gift gratefully, then said, "I hope I can hide this well enough, in case Medea decides to prowl my room again."

Castor grinned. "She'll be too busy making herself pretty for the feast."

"What feast?" I asked.

"Word has it that Lord Aetes wants to give us our gold-laden fleeces tonight."

When the sun was down and the moon climbed the sky, the king of Colchis offered us a banquet more spectacular than any I'd ever seen. The room was lit with oil lamps as numerous as the stars in the sky, and there were also torches held by patient slaves, flooding every crevice and corner of the place with flickering light. I smelled incense, and delighted in the songs Orpheus gave us so freely. He performed accompanied by the music of flute, lyre, hand drum, and sistrum, all ably played by young girls crowned with flowers.

The flowers were everywhere. Their fragrance mingled with the scent of burning incense and the aroma of roasted meat. Their bright colors glowed like embers in the firelight. Garlands spiraled their way up stone pillars and snaked down the length of the tables. Red, yellow, blue, and white petals drifted across the painted floor. Wherever I looked, I saw scattered wreaths of violets, ivy, and roses.

My brother Polydeuces came by to speak with me at the women's table. "I've told Milo the plan," he said softly. "He knows that he's supposed to slip out of the palace before the gates shut at midnight and meet you on board the Phoenician ship. I still don't like the idea of your making your way through Aea in the dark, alone."

"I'll be fine. But I'm going to miss you and Castor terribly."

"And we'll miss you. At least we'll sail off with a memory of how happy you look tonight."

"I am happy. You-know-who isn't here." I rolled my eyes in the direction of Medea's empty chair. "I hear she's got a headache. It must be a big one, to keep her away from seeing Lord Aetes honor her precious hero."

"Orpheus tells me she approached him about making a praise-song recounting how Jason won the Golden Fleece. You should have heard the wild ideas she wanted him to include! Fire-breathing oxen with bronze hooves, dragon's teeth that sprout into hosts of fully armed men, an unsleeping monster guarding the Fleece—"

"As if he needs *her* help with making imaginary monsters!" I smiled. "The closest thing I saw to a sleeping monster was one old priest, napping near the temple to Ares, where—" I caught my breath. All at once I realized exactly what Jason was planning to do and why he needed Medea so much that he was willing to woo someone so dangerously unpredictable. "The Fleece," I muttered. "He's going to steal the real Fleece."

"What are you talking about?" Polydeuces asked.

I whispered the answer, telling him all about the glorious golden masterwork that hung above the war god's altar. His eyes filled with dread. "Oh, no. *No*. He can't even consider doing something like that. It's worse than thievery. It's blasphemy, desecration of Ares' shrine, a violation of the sacred trust between host and guest. The gods will destroy him, if Lord Aetes doesn't do it first."

"Can you stop him?"

Polydeuces shook his head. "I've taken an oath of my own. On the night before we sailed from Iolkos, Jason made all of us stand before the altar of almighty Zeus and swear to follow him until the *Argo* either sank into Poseidon's arms or returned successful. You know the fate of oath breakers."

The Furies, I thought. I didn't want to speak their name aloud. Terrifying goddesses who wielded whips made of snakes and scorpions, they punished crimes that lay beyond the reach of mortal justice, and they were merciless.

I clasped my brother's hand. "If Jason violates Lord Aetes' trust, he'll be the oath breaker," I said. "I pray that when the Furies punish him for it, they'll spare the innocent."

"Hey! Why the long faces? Tired of waiting for the food tasters to finish their work?" Argus burst in on our muted conversation in a gust of wine and a storm of falling flower petals. He tore the wreath from his balding head and tossed it at Polydeuces. "Here, put this on while you're waiting. Or fill your belly with wine. Don't worry, Grandfather makes sure that the wine's safe long before he pays any attention to the food. By the gods, how I love that man!" He belched loudly and gave us both a huge, lopsided grin. The other women at the table squealed and tittered at him behind their hands.

"Better take it easy, Argus," Polydeuces said in a friendly manner. "You drink any more and you'll miss the rest of the banquet."

"So what?" Argus shot back, sticking out his chin. "If I miss this one, there'll be plenty more in my future. I'm finally in a safe harbor, and here I'll stay. *That* for the Pythia's prediction!" He snapped his fingers.

His words filled me with unease. This was the same man who'd resigned himself to death because he was convinced that the Pythia was never wrong. I didn't know why he'd cast away his faith in Eunike's infallibility, but why did he have to flaunt his new belief this way? Scorning the Pythia's gift of prophecy was too close to scorning the powers of the god she served, and that could be dangerous. *Apollo, pardon him,* I prayed. *That's not Argus talking, but the wine.*

Argus plowed on, unconcerned. "That babbling child claimed that if I came home, I'd die. I believed her at first, especially once I heard my stepbrother, Karos, still lived. I figured she'd had a vision of him killing me so he could hold on to his inheritance, but you know what? She was wrong. Karos is a good man. S'matter of fact, he says he's glad to have some family back after all these years. Not like that vicious mother of his, not at all. Here's to my brother!"

Argus grabbed the goblet from my place and tried to pour out a small libation to the gods before drinking the rest. He gaped to find it was empty. "Lady," he said, turning his head ponderously in my direction. "Lovely lady, it breaks my heart to tell you this, but some rotten thief's stolen your wine."

He staggered forward and nearly fell. Polydeuces and I hastened to lay hold of Argus's arms and help him sit beside me at the women's table. He leered happily at every woman and soon a small island of isolation separated the three of us from the rest of the table.

"Look at you," Argus said to me, his voice fuzzy. "If you don't put all these pretty flowers to shame, I don't know sun from moon. Is that why you're not wearing your wreath?" He prodded the ring of roses on the table before me. "Afraid the poor blossoms'll die of envy?"

"I didn't know I was supposed to wear it," I said. "I thought it was to decorate the table." I reached for the roses, but he snatched them away.

"Ah-ah-ah! No you don't." He wagged one finger in my face while holding the wreath high above his head. "You don't need to wear something like this, not with that thick, lovely hair you've got, shining bright as morning. My head shines too, y'know." He bowed a little, showing off his balding scalp. "Better let me have this to cover it up before the glint blinds some-one." We were all laughing together when he jammed the roses down onto his head.

"Ow! Curse it, that hurt." Argus shifted the wreath and touched his right temple. He fingers came away smeared with blood. "Stupid slaves, don't know enough to cut off the thorns before they make a rose wreath. Hunh! Well, at least I spared you the pain, pretty one. I'd say you owe me thanks."

"I agree," I said gaily, and gave him a kiss on the cheek. "That's for saving my life from a bloodthirsty bunch of flowers. And for being my friend and ship-mate, too. I'll never forget you, Argus."

He got to his feet shakily. "See that you don't, whoever you are." Polydeuces caught him when he lurched to one side, and helped him back to his place at the king's table.

The food tasters finished their business and a troop of servants brought heaping platters of meat, bread, roasted fowl, cheese, and olives to the tables. I was savoring a tiny, crisp quail's leg when a clamor from the king's table drew all eyes. Lord Aetes himself was on his feet, shouting for aid. I caught sight of Jason and my brothers in the crowd around Lord Aetes, but with so many people surrounding the king, I couldn't discern the reason.

Then someone shouted, "He's dead!" The women at my table broke into shrieks and sobs, though they had no more idea than I did about who "he" might be. They leaped up and fled from the hall. I ran too, but I rushed into the thick of the mob, my heart choking me as I pushed and shoved my way forward. I had to see. I had to know.

Argus lay slumped on the floor, his head lolling in the ruin of the wreath he'd taken from me. His skin was ghastly white and there was a trickle of dark blood at the corner of his mouth. I stared at him for a moment, his words a mocking echo in my ears: "*That for the Pythia's prediction!*"

I have to get out now, or the Phoenician ship will sail without me, I realized suddenly. *Lord Aetes will seal the palace. He won't let a flea escape until he learns who killed his grandson. O gods, who could have done such a thing?* As I flew through the halls, I remembered how happy Argus was, bragging about his stepbrother's generosity and affection.

Somehow I made my way from that awful feast to the docks. I thanked the gods for giving me the presence of mind to retrieve the things I'd need for the voyage and the speed to escape the citadel before the great gates closed. Once in the streets, I found a dark, deserted alley, where I changed clothes, transforming Atalanta the huntress into Glaucus the prince. From there, I walked to the Phoenician ship. It would have seemed suspicious if I'd arrived at a dead run. The watchman on board the trading vessel greeted me sleepily and showed me to the small pavilion that awaited me.

"Can I help you, young lord?" he asked, watching me while I stowed my bag of belongings. "The master told us you'd be traveling with a servant. Perhaps he was mistaken?"

"What, the boy's not here yet? That miserable dog, he said he'd come before me and make sure everything was ready!" I spoke with bluster worthy of the haughtiest nobleman, though I was worried. Milo knew the plan, but Argus's death changed everything. Would my friend be able to escape in time? I ranted even more loudly to drown out my fears. "He thought I wouldn't board this ship until dawn, when she sails, so off he goes to some tavern. May the gods make me strong enough to give him the whipping he deserves!"

"My lord, perhaps you misjudge the boy," the watchman said. "This might be all a simple misunderstanding. I hope you'll find it in your heart to listen to the lad's excuses once he gets here."

I couldn't let him suspect how deeply I appreciated his compassion for my so-called servant. I grumbled a few vague words and let him know that I wasn't in the mood for company. He left me alone, and I settled down to wait and worry.

I must have fallen asleep. The next thing I knew, Milo was rocking my shoulder gently and whispering, "Helen?" I awoke at once and lunged toward the sound of his voice, wildly thanking all the gods I could name that he was safe. He'd been squatting beside me, and my unexpected enthusiasm pitched him backward onto the ship's planking.

"Careful there," he said, righting himself. "Do you want the crew to think I'm more than just your servant?"

"Don't flatter yourself," I said, joking back. "I was afraid you wouldn't be able to get out of the palace." I heard raised voices outside the pavilion, heard the creak of timbers and the groan of ropes. "What's going on?"

"It's dawn. We're sailing."

"So you nearly *were* left behind." I shivered.

Milo's hand touched mine in the dark. "But I'm here now."

I made a fist and pulled my hand away from him. "He'll pay for what he's done," I said, my jaw tight.

"Who?"

"Karos, Argus's accursed stepbrother. Even if he is Aetes' grandson, he must be punished for murdering—"

"Karos is innocent, Helen," Milo said gravely.

"What? Argus was drinking a lot of wine. Karos must have slipped some poison into his goblet."

"No. Listen. I was in the kitchens when Argus died. We all ran as soon as we heard the news, but I was the only one headed for the palace gates. I was going so fast, I ran right into her, a little slave girl, bruised and crying in the dark like a wild thing. I spoke kindly to her, and that set her tongue loose. She had to tell *someone* the reason for her misery. She was supposed to bring a gift to the king's feast, a gift for an honored guest. But she failed to fulfill her mistress's orders. She just left the gift at the guest's place and ran away without making sure that it reached the person who was supposed to have it."

"A gift . . ."

"A wreath of roses woven by the lady Medea's own hands."

PART IV
ATHENS

MEN AND MONSTERS

The ship that carried us back toward the setting sun covered the distance in far less time than the *Argo*. It was thanks to the Phoenicians' skill and experience at navigating by night as well as by day, in all weather except outright sea-churning storms. We reached the port that served Athens on a chilly day. Summer was gone.

Once ashore, I gave Milo several of my remaining gold charms and asked him to find us another ship, one bound for Delphi.

"And what will you be doing?" he asked.

I lifted my eyes toward the heights of the nearby city. "I'm going to make a thanksgiving sacrifice to Poseidon. I owe something to Apollo as well, and Aphrodite, who's always been good to me, and it's never wise to ignore almighty Zeus. Above all, I need to make offerings to Hades."

When I mentioned the lord of the Underworld, Milo made a small sign meant to ward off bad luck. "Why *him*?"

"For Hylas. For him, and for Argus, too."

I picked up two amphorae of wine at the nearest tavern and began seeking the gods. They'd all receive libations, but I'd have to offer Hades more than a sip of wine. The lord of the dead had to have meat and honey cakes as well, to sweeten his temper and make him treat Hylas's and Argus's ghosts with kindness.

Poseidon's shrine was near the water, but I had to turn my footsteps uphill, into the heart of Athens, to find the other gods. Rather than haul two heavy amphorae around while I wandered the city, I found an old man loitering beside one of the public fountains, told him where I wanted to go, and asked him to be my guide to the temples.

"Ah, you're a pious young fellow," he said, pleased, and soon led me from Zeus's temple to Apollo's, then on to Aphrodite's, and finally Athena's. He told me how the goddess of wisdom had earned her place as patron of Athens by giving mortals the olive tree. It would have been a serious mistake to visit her city and not honor her.

Athena's temple stood at the very top of the tall, rocky hill, where the city clung, the doorway guarded by a pair of carved owls, her sacred bird. As we left the sanctuary, I turned to the old man and said, "Just one last shrine for me to visit and then I hope you'll let me reward you with a good meal and a few cups of wine."

His eyes twinkled. "Well, it wouldn't be polite to say no. So, where is it you want to go?"

"The temple of Hades," I replied. "But first I need to get more wine for the offering."

The old man edged away from me and made a warding-off sign when I named the lord of the Underworld, but after that he brought me to the house of a gray-haired woman who was happy to provide me with wine, honey cakes, a fistful of black rooster feathers, and a bright red pomegranate as gifts most likely to please Hades. She packed all this into a basket and I gave her a large amber bead and two bits of silver in trade, then looked around for my guide.

"Oh, he's gone," she told me, smiling as she led me back onto the dusty street. "Slipped away on the quiet. He whispered to me that at his age, the farther he keeps from the lord of the Underworld, the easier he breathes. Don't worry, the shrine's not far. Go past the temple of Athena toward the palace gate and when you've taken thirty steps or so, you'll see a cypress tree to your left. Go behind it, out of sight of the gateway, and seek the place where the earth slopes down sharply, as if a god had pressed his finger deep into wet clay. Look for it well or you'll miss it. A freshwater spring bubbles up at the bottom of that notch in the earth, and there's a flat stone with a carving of Cerberus, Lord Hades' three-headed watchdog, with the monster's feet hidden in the mint plants that grow all around the water's edge."

"Why would anyone dedicate a god's shrine in such a hidden spot?" I wondered. "Is that place sacred to Hades for some reason?"

She shook her head and looked sad. "It's sacred to our king. He built it after his father died, so that it would be convenient for him to make daily sacrifices for the comfort of Lord Aegeus's spirit."

Theseus as a devoted son? I thought as I set off in search of the shrine. It wasn't an image that matched the braggart of Calydon and the bully of Delphi. *Well, it's possible. I thought Jason was all selfish ambition until he warned me about the crimson dress.*

I found Hades' hidden spring, a pretty, peaceful place. The cypress tree's spreading crown cast a cool shadow over the spring, and the thick growth of mint plants at the water's edge filled the air with a refreshing fragrance. There was a flat black stone just across the pool from the carving of Cerberus. When I ran my fingertips over it, they came away stained with blood, wine, and a smear of cake crumbs. All were fresh. Were they gifts from Theseus, or some other worshipper?

I knelt to unpack my basket beside the flat rock, setting out my own offerings of sweet cakes and figs. I held the pomegranate in both hands and smashed it open, sending the juicy, glittering seeds spilling across the altar stone like blood drops. Then I stood up and raised my hands to hail the god.

"O dread Lord Hades, hear me. Look with kindness on the shades of Hylas and Argus, my beloved friends. Don't let them wander lost among the hopeless ghosts, but grant that they find their way to the gardens of the blessed dead, the peaceful groves and fields of Elysium. If you will hear my prayer, I promise that I'll give you a generous sacrifice every year of my life, and that when I rule Sparta, I'll build a temple to honor you. Lord Hades, ruler of the dead, give comfort to Hylas and Argus, and let them know that while I live, they will never be forgotten."

I stooped to pick up the last part of my sacrifice, a small clay flask of wine. I pulled out the beeswax stopper and was about to pour the libation when a sharp voice shouted, "Hey! What do you think you're doing there?"

I turned slowly, the wine unpoured, and saw a young man glowering at me like a dog protecting a meaty bone. His skin was scarred with pockmarks, and mud-colored hair straggled down over his shoulders from beneath a bronze helmet too big for him.

He was having some trouble holding fast to the tall spear he carried. He'd draped a cloak over his shoulders, because of the cold, and the thick blue cloth kept snaring his arms.

"I'm making a sacrifice," I replied. "I'm almost done."

"You're done *now*," he snapped. I glimpsed small, watery green eyes under the outsized helmet's brim. "Get out of here. This is the king's shrine!"

"This is the shrine the king built," I replied, striving to keep my voice even. I hadn't come for an argument. All I wanted was to complete my offering to Hades, go back to Milo, and leave Athens as soon as possible. "It belongs to the god."

"Well, you don't look like a god to me," my tormentor jibed. He waved his spear at me vaguely. "I'm one of Lord Theseus's guardsmen, and I'm telling you to move *now*."

With one twist of my wrist, I upended the flask and sent the wine splashing over the offerings on the black stone. I'd wanted to pour it out in a slow, graceful stream, the way I remembered my father doing it whenever he brought the gods a gift of wine, but this wasn't the time for that. As the last drop fell, I let the empty flask tumble into the basket. "All right," I said to the meddling guard. "*Now* I'll go."

I started up out of the little hollow holding

Hades' shrine. "Stop!" the guard ordered. He took a wide-legged stance, barring the narrow way out. "You disobeyed me."

"I'm doing what you asked," I replied, feeling my own temper rising. "You said you wanted me to go. Step aside and let me pass."

"You should have left when I told you to." He readjusted his grip on the tall spear. I heard a loud, moist squeak from the wood. His hands must have been sweating badly. "You've defied Lord Theseus's authority *and* you desecrated the offering he made to his royal father's ghost. You'll have to answer to him for that. Come with me."

That was enough. I dropped the basket and drew my sword. "No."

He lowered his spear, let out a guttural yell that cracked midway through, and attacked. He had the advantage of the high ground. He should have held it rather than rushing down at me like that. He also had a heavy spear, like the one Atalanta had used to hunt the Calydonian boar. It was impressive to look at, but intended to stop a charge, not lead one. He didn't have the strength to keep the massive bronze spearhead from dipping low as he ran. By the time he reached me, it was a simple thing for me to sidestep his clumsy onslaught, leap aside, spin around, and stamp my foot down on the wooden shaft. My teacher, Glaucus, was right when he taught me that sometimes a

warrior's best weapon is her opponent's worst judg-
ment.

The young guard sprawled on his belly. I jumped astride his back, yanked off his helmet, and grabbed a fistful of his hair, jerking his head back and letting the flat of my blade just touch the side of his neck.

"I'm going to leave now," I said. My words were calm, but my heart was beating wildly. "And you're going to let me go in peace." He cursed, so I gave his hair a second tug to recapture his attention. "Look, I didn't come here seeking trouble. I'm no Athenian. I was told that anyone could visit this shrine. If I've done something wrong, it wasn't deliberate. I've just completed a long, dangerous voyage, but a friend of mine wasn't so lucky. He wasn't much older than you. Show a little pity for the dead, all right? I promise you, you'll never have to see me again."

"Fine," my captive grumbled between gritted teeth. "Let me up and get out of my sight."

I sprang to my feet and sheathed my sword, but before I left the seething guard, I seized his fallen spear and shouldered it. It didn't matter how heavy and unwieldy it was, I had no choice but to deal with it. How smart would it be to turn my back on an angry enemy and leave him armed? I thanked the gods when I saw that the only other weapon he bore was a dagger, much too small to be any danger to me now.

"I'll leave this spear for you at the temple of Zeus,

behind the altar stone," I told him. I walked away at a smart pace, but I didn't run, no matter how much I wanted to turn my feet into wings.

I left the spear where I'd promised I would, then I *did* run all the rest of the way back to the waterfront. I found Milo on the shore near the Phoenician ship. He reported that he'd gotten us a room at a clean inn, and that, by a wonderful piece of luck, the young widow who ran the place was the biggest gossip in Athens. She knew the destination of every ship in the harbor.

"There's a Corinthian merchant who'll be home-ward bound the day after tomorrow," he told me glee-fully. "I got him to agree to take us with him for just three small amphorae of olive oil apiece, as long as we bring our own food and drink. I took care of that, too. It's all stowed safely in our hostess's care already."

"Thanks, Milo. That was quick work."

"And all for just *one* of the charms you gave me." Milo proudly puffed out his chest. "You wait and see, I'll make a fine merchant myself one day. I bet I'll strike us an even better bargain once we reach Corinth and take ship for Delphi!"

We enjoyed a good, simple meal at the inn, then found our beds in the small room behind the hostess's own sleeping quarters. There was only a tattered blanket between the two rooms. The widow made a great point of letting us know this, making cow-eyes at both of us and stomping off in a snit when I assured her that we would respect her privacy. Milo collapsed laughing.

The room was so small that it must have been a storage chamber formerly. We were crammed into it like bales of cloth, sharing the small space with our possessions, our provisions, and the six amphorae. Still, it was comfortable enough, and the cold weather favored us. It discouraged fleas and kept the windowless cubicle from being oppressively hot. I wrapped myself in my cloak and fell into a deep slumber filled with hazy, pleasant dreams.

The widow's shriek tore me out of sleep. I sat up to see the curtain ripped down as two broad-shouldered shapes burst into the room. An oil lamp flared near the ceiling, then dove to blaze a thumb-span from my nose.

"Well, is *this* the one?" came the gruff demand from the darkness behind the flame.

"Yes, yes, that's him!" a vaguely familiar voice answered from beyond the doorway.

"That's what you said last time, fool, and it wasn't. You can't even *see* him from there. Gods, Telys, did he scare you that badly? He's hardly more than a child, not even the ghost of a beard on him. Look!"

A strong hand clamped itself to my arm and hauled me upright. I didn't have the chance to grab my sword. I yelled wild threats, swinging fists and feet. I struck the walls and our piled-up belongings more than I hit the man holding me. The oil lamp's flame streaked crazily through the air.

"Hunh! He's a fierce one. Hood him for me," my captor said. Someone else dropped a cloak over my head. Though my ears were muffled, I heard Milo's voice rise up in protest and challenge, and the sound of further struggles. Then I heard the cold, unmistakable scrape of a sword being drawn from its sheath, a blow struck, and my friend crying out in pain. Something heavy hit the floor. I shrieked Milo's name again and again, though the thick wool cloak covered my face and choked off half my breath. I was still screaming, "Milo! Milo! Milo!" as I was slung over one man's shoulder and carried away.

They took the cloak off my head and set me back down on my own feet when we were about halfway up the city hill. Dawn was breaking, and by the first faint light I clearly saw the three men who'd burst into the widow's house. Two were new faces. The third was the bumbling young guard who'd challenged my presence at Hades' shrine and lost.

No need for me to wonder what had happened. *Fool,* I thought. *You're so hungry to punish me for humiliating you, you don't see that you're bringing even worse humiliation on yourself. Good. You deserve every joke and jeer your fellow guards will heap on your head from now on.*

"How dare you?" I said, all ice. "You coward, how

dare you do this? If you wanted to reclaim your honor, you should have come to me alone, like a man."

The young guard bit his lips, his thickly blemished face going red, but his helpers roared with laughter. "Hey, Telys, you said this pup was a stranger, but it sounds like he knows *you* well enough!" one of them exclaimed.

"I *am* a stranger to Athens," I said. "I come from Sparta. I didn't know that Hades' shrine was the king's alone. I did no harm."

"You attacked one of Lord Theseus's guards," one of the brawny men said. "Not a very good one, but you still have to answer for it. Move." He spun me around facing uphill and gave me a rough shove.

I trudged along with scrawny Telys ahead and both of the big men behind. I wished it had been the other way around. My hands were free. One quick pivot, a kick or a sudden push, and that pock-faced wretch would be flat on his back and I'd be racing downhill, dust in the distance, well on my way back to Milo. I wasn't about to try my luck escaping from the others, though. They had the look of seasoned warriors. They'd catch me and give me reason to regret my escape attempt.

Glaucus had taught me to choose my battles, and to choose them wisely. I chose not to fight this one. Not yet. *Great Apollo,* I prayed, *let your healing powers help and sustain Milo until I can be with him again.*

We entered the royal stronghold, greeted by loud catcalls. Apparently all of the guards knew about what had happened to Telys. As soon as they laid eyes on me, he found himself walking through a gauntlet of hecklers.

"*That's* who took your spear? He's an infant!"

"How'd he beat you, Telys? Trip you with his cradle?"

"Hey, for all you know, the baby didn't *take* the spear. Telys probably loaned it to him so he'd have something to teethe on."

With every step we took, the young guard drew his shoulders up higher and higher, like a turtle taking refuge in its shell. As much as I despised him for what he'd done, I was relieved when we entered the palace itself and left his tormentors behind.

I was herded into a small reception room and told to wait. The two big men took up positions flanking the doorway outside, but Telys waited with me. He avoided my eyes, pretending to be fascinated by the wall paintings. They showed a powerfully built man defeating a series of opponents, some by the sword, some with his bare hands. The most spectacular picture had him locked in combat with a bull-headed man, the Cretan Minotaur. *I hope you rewarded the artist well, Theseus,* I thought. *He's drawn you as if slaying monsters were as easy as swatting flies.*

By the time I was summoned from the waiting

room, I'd had enough time to memorize every curl of
hair between the Minotaur's painted horns. A well-
dressed servant came to announce that Lord Theseus
would see me. I walked with my head down, not because I was ashamed, but in hopes that Lord Theseus
would *not* see me. I pretended to scratch my head so
that I could pull a tangle of hair down over my face. If
he shared his soldiers' contempt for Telys, perhaps
he'd dismiss the whole matter without giving me so
much as a glance. *The gods grant it!*

I also gave thanks to the gods that the previous
night had been cool enough for me to wear a loose,
shabby tunic for additional warmth under my blanket.
The looser, the better, I thought. My body had changed in
more ways than one since the *Argo* sailed from Colchis,
changed outwardly as well as within. I hunched my
shoulders forward, trying to conceal the telltale curves.

The Athenian king's throne room was very much
like the others I'd seen in my life, including my own father's. I tried hiding in the shadow of one of the big
guardsmen. It proved to be a useless tactic. Theseus sat
on a high-back stone seat. A regal, gray-haired woman
occupied the smaller throne at his right hand. They
were sharing a joke when we entered, but the smile on
his face was nothing compared to the ear-to-ear grin
he wore the moment he caught sight of me.

"I don't believe it!" he exclaimed. "What wonderful, generous, beloved god has brought me *this* prize? I

swear I'll build him a temple, the likes of which Athens has never seen, as a thanks offering!"

Foolish Telys stepped forward. "I brought him here," he said, eager to claim credit for whatever had so overjoyed his king. "I caught him making a sacrifice to Lord Hades at your shrine, my lord Theseus, and when I tried to stop him—"

Theseus's laughter crushed Telys's weak attempt at boasting. "We all *know* what happened when you tried to stop him, you clown," he said, wiping his eyes. "The whole palace is talking about how you were bested by a mere boy. Well, the truth is even better."

He was off the throne and across the floor in an instant, scattering everyone who stood between him and me. He bounded behind me, grabbed the waist of my tunic with both hands, and yanked it back, hard. I'd relied on the looseness of my clothing to hide my breasts, small as they were, but now the thin cloth pulled taut against every line of my body. I might as well have been wearing nothing at all. I heard the on-lookers gasp.

"Why aren't you smiling, Telys?" Theseus leered as he confronted the horror-struck young guard. "You ought to be glad. You weren't beaten by a boy after all." He scowled at his subjects, which scared up a few half-hearted titters, but most of the people present were too jolted by their king's crude behavior to react at all, except with silence.

Maybe Athens is civilized after all, I thought. When I twitched my tunic out of his grasp, looking at him as if he were a mouse-dropping in a bowl of milk, he appealed for sympathy from the woman on the queen's throne.

"Mother, what's the matter with this girl? Don't Spartans have a sense of humor?" he asked, completely ignoring the fact that his own people hadn't found anything funny in what he'd done. "Or perhaps it's just their royalty who can't take a joke."

" 'Royalty,' my dear?" Theseus's mother raised her eyebrows and looked at me doubtfully. I couldn't blame her.

"This is the princess of Sparta, Helen, daughter of Lord Tyndareus and his queen," Theseus proclaimed. He caressed me with a slow, sidelong look. "Lady Helen of Sparta, my lovely bride."

For a moment, shock snatched the breath from my lips. When I could speak again, I said, "If that's another of your 'jokes,' Theseus, it's not funny."

He laughed at me. "It's not supposed to be. Mother, look after my sweet queen-to-be. She seems weary."

The older woman came toward me and rested one soft, slim hand on my arm. "I am Lady Aithra of Troezen, my dear. Please come with me." Her voice was warm and kind. "You'll stay in my quarters."

I drew away stiffly. "I'm not staying with you, *or*

your son, *or* in this city," I declared. "This is ridiculous, a disgrace! I demand to be set free at once."

"And then what, my sweetest one?" Theseus drawled, amused. "Where will you go? I doubt that your royal parents know you're here alone, so far from home."

"I'm not alone," I countered. "I'm traveling with—with an escort."

"Yet here you are. Not very good at their work, are they?" Theseus said.

One of Telys's hulking comrades spoke up. "*He,* not *they*. She was sharing lodgings with a youth when we found her." Theseus grimaced in displeasure. The guard went on hastily, as if trying to distance himself from his king's wrath. "They weren't sharing a blanket. He was probably just her servant, nothing more. When he drew a sword against us, it was easy to kill him."

To kill him . . . The words hit me like stones. A howl of sorrow stripped my throat raw as I sank to my knees. I'd feared Milo had been hurt, but this? *This?* I wailed until my voice shattered and all I could do was rasp air.

I let the lady Aithra help me to my feet and lead me away. I didn't care where I was going or what would become of me. I was walking through a black tunnel, and the only light I could see in the distance burned red as blood.

I lay on a flower-scented bed for four days, not rising except when I had to. I slept without dreams, ate nothing, and only took a sip of water now and then because Lady Aithra wouldn't leave me alone until I did. I didn't want to die, but I didn't want to live either. I wasn't sure what I wanted, unless it was to escape from the unmoving thought *Milo is dead.*

When Hylas died, I'd mourned. I'd felt pain and loss, but this—this was different. It was a headlong plunge into darkness. *Did I love Milo so dearly?* The question wandered through my mind like a wisp of smoke, and the answer followed: *Yes. I loved him, but not with the flare of love I felt for Hylas, or the steady-burning love my parents know, or Medea's devastating blaze. O Aphrodite, will I ever understand all the forms your gift can take? My brothers were afraid Milo and I would share a bed. How to tell them that we shared a different bond of love? And now . . . he's gone.*

On the fifth day, my stomach creased with hunger so painfully that I ate the meal a slave brought for me. This was the first time I did more than stare dully all day at the filled cup and platter. The first nibble soon turned to a frenzy of gobbling, until my belly revolted and I threw up every mouthful. I fell back groaning onto the bed and the frightened slave ran to fetch Lady Aithra.

The king's mother quickly saw to it that I was

given some vegetable broth to drink, which soon settled my stomach. She watched with genuine concern while I made a second try at eating. It was the first time I'd received such care since I'd left Sparta, my mother, and my nurse, Ione. Warm memories of home mingled with the pain of losing Milo and turned into tears. I sobbed myself to sleep with Lady Aithra cradling me as if I were her own child.

The next time I woke up, I felt more like myself. I sat up and saw that Theseus's mother was seated beside my bed, working on a piece of embroidery. She smiled when she saw me. "Better now?"

I got out of bed and knelt before her, embracing her knees. I didn't know the custom in Athens, but when a Spartan petitioner was desperate to have his plea granted, this was how he approached the king.

"Child, what's the matter?" the old queen cried, dropping her cloth.

"Lady Aithra, I beg of you, tell me that your son was only jesting about my being his bride. It can't happen. Surely he realizes that? Please, speak with him. Tell him that he's had his fun, but now it's time to let me leave Athens. The gods will reward him for his kindness."

"But, my dear, it's all true," Lady Aithra said, stroking my hair. "He loves you, you know. Even before you came to us, he spoke to me of how you'd met in Calydon and again at Delphi. 'It's a sign that she and I are fated to be together,' he told me. You're a very fortunate girl to have a man like my son in love with you."

"If he loves me that much, am I free to go?"

The question bewildered her. "But—but if you go, how can you marry him?"

"I won't," I replied hotly, pushing myself away from her and standing tall. "Your son isn't in love with me. He loves the Spartan throne. He thinks he'll win it if he forces me to marry him, but all he'll get is war. My father won't allow—"

She interrupted me with a wistful little laugh. "Listen to you, you little firebrand! I used to turn the smallest thing into a big uproar when I was your age, too. Stop being silly. Royal marriages make peace, not war. Both of our peoples will benefit from that. Lord Tyndareus won't raise a hand against Athens. What sane man goes to war against his own kin?"

"Marriage won't make me kin to Theseus."

"Your child will." Her face was utterly serene. "My boy explained everything to me. He's so very clever! No one knows you're here. Well, no one but the people who were in the throne room five days ago, but they're loyal Athenians, and the slaves know better than to speak out of turn. You'll marry Theseus, I'll pray to the gods that you're blessed with a baby as soon as possible, and *then* we can send the good news to your parents. Think of how pleased they'll be, to learn their daughter will be queen of *two* great cities!"

I felt cold. "Your son's cruel, not clever. To wait until I have a baby . . . You know how long that can take!" I thought of Delphi, and the fisherman's daughter. My friend Eunike had used her position as the holy Pythia to enable my adventures by saying it would be a year or more before I came home. Yes, but how much more? My parents wouldn't wait forever. "My family will think I'm *dead*! And may the gods forbid it, but what if my father were to die before your son achieves his 'brilliant' plan? My sister, Clytemnestra, would take the throne. She's a princess of Mykenae now. Do you think her husband would hand back Sparta without a fight? You *will* have war!"

Lady Aithra was unperturbed. "Then we'll let your parents share our joy as soon as you're pregnant. *That* won't take long at all. You *have* become a woman already, haven't you?"

"No," I said. I had no second thoughts about that lie.

"Lady Helen, I didn't mean that as an actual question. Your belongings were brought to the palace four days ago. A *girl* doesn't need those woolen pads." She shook her head sadly. "Really, my dear, you'll have to trust me. I'm going to be your second mother."

Not if I can help it, I thought.

I made four escape attempts that very day. I didn't expect them to succeed. What I wanted to do was learn as much about the ins and outs of the palace as I could as quickly as possible. Theseus was no fool. He knew I wasn't about to submit docilely to his plan to wed me.

My technique was simple: hike up my skirt and take flight the instant my keepers' attention wandered—simple, but it wasn't easy. By Lady Aithra's order, my boy's clothing had been taken away and replaced by dresses suitable for her son's intended bride. They were pretty enough, and they provided warmth against the chilly weather, but they were cumbersome. It was like running with a blanket tangling my legs. I was caught every time, though not before I managed to add to my familiarity with the palace.

And it felt so *good* to run, even clumsily, after all of those miserable days in bed! I couldn't help grinning every time I slipped away from my escorts and dashed off. I did it without thinking, though once I realized how thoughtlessly happy I felt, reality hit.

Forgive me, Milo, I thought as my smiling mouth shrank to a grim line. *I haven't forgotten you, I swear it by almighty Zeus. You died trying to save me from my captors. If I don't get out of this prison, you died for nothing.*

By my third try, Lady Aithra had lost her patience and brought me to stand before her son while he was

in conference with a group of hard-faced Athenian
nobles. I smiled unashamedly when she called me will-
ful, wild, and ungrateful, which provoked her so much
that she actually dared to declare, "My son, you must
not marry this girl. I don't care how beautiful she is,
she'll bring us nothing but grief and leave Athens in
flames!"

Theseus's brow furrowed. "If I don't ask for your
opinion, I don't want it. Be silent, Mother. You sound
like a fool." The men with him looked at one another
unhappily to hear their king speak so coldly to his
own mother. One of them must have mumbled words
to that effect, because Theseus whirled fiercely on the
imprudent counselor and shouted in his face, "While
I rule here, no one rules me!"

"But, my lord, she's your mother," the man persisted. I admired his courage, no matter how badly it
would serve him against Theseus. "You should respect
her enough to let her have her say."

Oh, *that* was a mistake. I recognized the callous
look that came into Theseus's eyes. I'd seen it at close
range on a street in Delphi when he'd grabbed my
wrist and twisted it painfully because I wouldn't bend
to his will. *May the gods have mercy on you*, I thought, looking with pity at the counselor. *Theseus won't.*

I was right. The young Athenian king moved with
a panther's speed, knocking the outspoken man off
his feet with a blow that split his lip and drew blood.

"Since when do I answer to *you?*" he bellowed. "Poseidon is my witness that I treat the lady Aithra with more respect than my father, Lord Aegeus, ever did. *I* brought her to Athens, to sit on the throne he denied her! She's usually smart enough to remember that and to mind how she speaks to me. You'd do well to learn from her." Grudgingly, he helped the bleeding man to his feet again. The assaulted counselor retreated swiftly.

Theseus returned to his throne and raised a hand for silence. "The lady Helen of Sparta will become my bride ten days from now. Mother, see to the preparations for the feast. Men, you and all the rest of Athens's noblest families will celebrate my good fortune in having such a beautiful young woman for my wife, but if one whisper of my plans reaches the ears of anyone else, I promise I'll find out whose lips betrayed."

"Why all this secrecy?" I spoke up clearly. "You're *terrified* that my father will hear that you've taken me prisoner. No Spartan woman marries a coward!"

"Watch your tongue," Theseus growled, his hands clenched. If he hit me, I'd hit him back, no matter how bad a beating I got for it. I would not surrender.

"Or what? Will you kill *me?* Go ahead and try. If you succeed, you lose what you really want to gain from this marriage. If I die, I take the Spartan crown with me into Hades' kingdom. Better that than let you get your filthy hands on it!"

He took a step forward. I held my ground, shifting my weight just a bit and grabbing hold of my skirt. I'd changed my mind. If he gave the slightest sign that he intended to strike me, I wouldn't wait for the blow to land. I'd jerk up the hem of my gown and kick him so hard that——!

Suddenly the hall rang with Theseus's laughter. He held his sides, threw back his head, and brayed. "Ah, Lady Helen, the gods have been more than good to you. The three Graces gave you a face to outshine the sun, then filled your lovely mouth with these bursts of comical nonsense. We should be grateful to them. It's all that keeps us poor mortal men from mistaking you for a goddess."

He turned his back on me and returned to his throne. From there he proclaimed, "As a reward for amusing me so well, I'm going to give the lady Helen her own lodging in the palace and her very own attendant to be responsible for her every wish, her every whim, and above all, her every movement. Now who deserves such a prize?" His eyes closed and a mean smile twisted his lips. "Telys."

12

QUEEN'S SON,
SLAVE'S SON

I was moved out of Lady Aithra's quarters and into a windowless room so narrow that if I stretched my arms sideways as far as I could, my fingertips brushed the walls. The mat on which I slept took up most of the space, and a small, square table occupied what little was left. A few pieces of clothing were stuffed into a small box kept beneath the table, though most of my garments remained in Lady Aithra's room. She was overseeing preparations for the wedding, which included collecting gowns and ornaments Theseus would want to see me wear. My dresses were being treated better than I was.

I did my best to keep idleness from filling my mind with worries over things I couldn't control. I was concerned about what would happen when my parents finally learned my fate, and I did fret over where my brothers might be by now, but I couldn't let such thoughts dominate my days. Hardest of all was cherishing my best memories of Milo without letting them drag me back into despair.

The only privacy I had was a curtain across the doorway, and it ended about a hand-span from the floor. I didn't care. I had enough blankets to keep out the cold, and a door would have held in the smell from the night-soil pot in the corner. Theseus had rewarded my defiance by thrusting me into a storeroom, like the amphorae of wine that were also waiting for the king's wedding day.

Telys stood on watch outside my doorway, never leaving his post except when Lady Aithra came with a group of attendants to escort me to meals. I suppose he used those times to gobble a little food himself. Sometimes I heard him hail any other guard who happened to be passing by in the hall, begging for a chance to take care of his body's needs.

One night, four days before the wedding, I woke up from a dream in which I was sinking into a pit filled with smoke, choking on shadows. I woke up shaking, my mouth dry with fear. I'd pinched out my lamp before going to sleep and had no way to rekindle the wick, so my miserable excuse for a room was dark. My eyes were drawn to the space between the bottom of my door curtain and the floor, where a band of torchlight from the hallway danced and flickered.

"Telys!" I called out. "Telys, I want water! And here, light this." I fumbled for the dead lamp and stuck it out under the curtain. My guard had been instructed to obey my wishes and serve me as well as he could without abandoning his post. If I needed something fetched, he managed to obey by shouting for one of the palace slaves. He had a thin, bleating voice like a frightened goat's. After six days, I'd know it anywhere.

The voice that boomed the command "Water for Lady Helen!" was deep, strong, and most definitely did not belong to Telys. I crept to the doorway, flicked back the curtain, and peered out to see a strange face. He answered my puzzled look with a broad, self-assured grin.

"Where's Telys?" I asked.

His grin got wider. "He's got to sleep sometime, Lady Helen. Besides, Lord Theseus doesn't trust him to stand guard at night. He said you'd probably be able to convince that scrawny goose-brain that you were dying, and when he ran to bring help, you'd vanish into the dark."

"I didn't know Theseus thought I was so clever," I said.

The guard laughed. "More like he thinks Telys is so stupid. On the day he says one good word about

that dolt, the sky will rain wine and honey. Lord Theseus despises him."

"Then why doesn't he get rid of him?"

"He would if he could." The guard scratched the
back of his head and spit on the floor. "But too many
folks would say it was a poor way for any man to treat
his brother."

"What?"

The guard chuckled. "Oh, yes, you heard me
right, Lady Helen. Telys is Lord Aegeus's son. His
mother was a slave, and not even a pretty, young one.
She's the reason he didn't bring Lady Aithra to Athens."

"He loved that slave woman so much that he kept
his own wife away?" I could hardly believe it.

" 'Wife'?" the guard echoed. "Lord Aegeus never
married Lady Aithra, though none say that where
Lord Theseus might hear." He shrugged. "Anyway,
she's the daughter of Troezen's king, so it's her boy
who rules this land now. When Lord Theseus first
showed up in Athens, Lord Aegeus had no choice but
to send the slave girl away. He set her free and gave
their child a place of honor in the palace as one of the
guards. So here Telys stays, because Lord Aegeus
wanted to provide for his son and Lord Theseus wants
to keep a close eye on his brother. A *very* close eye," he
added meaningly.

"Does he think Telys will try to take the throne
from him someday?" I asked.

I got a scornful snort for an answer. "He hasn't got the grit for it."

I didn't like his tone. "Maybe he's simply faithful to his half brother. Does betrayal count as a virtue in Athens? You make it sound like treachery's the same as courage."

A worried look flashed across the guard's face. "That's not what I meant," he said quickly. "I'm loyal to my king! I felt sorry for you, up at this lonely hour, so I talked to you, all friendly, and for what? So you could twist my words and get me in trouble, carrying lies to Lord Theseus?"

I shook my head. "All I wanted was water and a light for my lamp. You haven't gotten me either one yet. Telys always manages to fulfill my requests *at once*. Maybe he's not so worthless after all."

The guard grumbled and lit my lamp from one of the torches, then bawled for water so ferociously that a sleepy slave came running, stumbling under the weight of a painted jug. I returned to my mat satisfied, but I couldn't get back to sleep. My mind was buzzing.

Milo's dead because of Telys, I told myself. So why did I take his side against that guard? I loathe Theseus. Is that why I spoke up for Telys? Because Theseus hates him and I hate Theseus? Or because maybe, just maybe Telys is as much a prisoner in this palace as I am? His mother was a slave. No one asked her if she wanted to share Lord Aegeus's bed, and no one asked Telys if he wanted to be a royal guard. He had to take what he was given. I feel sorry for him, and yet— I shook my head, trying to make sense out of everything. *And yet if it weren't for him, Milo would be alive and I'd be free.*

I was still trying to sort things out when I heard the guard in the hall growl, "There you are, you snail-dropping. It's about time you got here!" Telys muttered an apology. I lay on my belly and peeked out under the doorway curtain just in time to see the other guard give him a nasty smack before shouting, "Keep me waiting here again and you'll get worse!" and stomping away. Telys settled his back against one of the doorposts and sighed.

"Why did you do it?" I asked.

The abruptness of my question made the poor thing jump. "Wha—wha— Lady Helen, did you speak to *me?*"

It was a silly question, so I ignored it and pressed on. "Why did you let him hit you? You didn't even try to strike back."

Telys sighed again, more deeply. "And give him an excuse to beat my bones to dust on the training field? If I keep my head down, he goes easy on me. That's worth a slap or two."

"And what's your honor worth?" I got to my feet and pulled the doorway curtain all the way aside. "Four slaps? Seven? Spartan warriors don't bargain with our opponents. We beat them." I rested my hands on my hips. "Why am I surprised? You're a coward. When I beat you at Hades' shrine, you came sneaking after me by night, with two real men to do what you couldn't. And you killed my friend."

"I—" Telys began, then stopped and looked away. "No. If I say anything now, you'll only claim I'm even more of a coward, making excuses."

"Go on," I said, on guard. "I'll listen."

"I didn't want your friend to die, Lady Helen. I wouldn't have gone after you that night, but just my luck, Lord Theseus saw me when I returned to the palace. He demanded to know where I'd been. I thought he'd be pleased that I'd tried to protect Hades' shrine, but he made fun of me for failing. Then he said he wanted to meet the man who'd given me what I deserved. He ordered me to take two comrades and go from one lodging house to the next, searching for him—I mean, for you. I didn't know they were going to treat you so roughly, and when your friend grabbed that sword and drew it—"

"Enough." I felt the sting of fresh tears. Telys's tale rang true, but that didn't mean I'd let him see me cry. I bit my lip to regain control of myself, then said, "Swear that what you've told me is true."

"I swear it," he said without hesitation. "I swear by my life. If I'm lying, may the Kindly Ones hunt me down."

"I believe you." No man would draw the attention of the Furies heedlessly, even if he called on them by their less terrifying name.

Later that morning, a maidservant arrived with my breakfast and a message from Lady Aithra: "The queen requests your presence at the palace training ground after you've eaten."

"Finally, some exercise," I said with a half-smile.

The girl took me seriously and was suitably shocked. "Oh, no, Lady Helen! The queen would never expect you to go anywhere near something as dangerous as swordplay, even if it's only done for practice. She wants you to sit beside her and observe how well our soldiers fight."

"Now where's the fun in that?" I drawled. "No, thank you. I'd rather stay here, in my spacious quarters."

The girl became more and more flustered. "But you *can't*," she blurted. "All the royal guards are expected to participate. Even him." She cast a belittling look at Telys. "No one will be free to keep an eye on you."

"In that case, let's go now," I said. "I've lost my appetite."

"You *must* eat, Lady Helen," the girl cried in alarm. "If you don't eat, Lady Aithra'll blame everyone from the cook to—"

"—to you?" I finished for her. "I didn't know I was so closely watched, or that you all cared so much about my welfare. If that's so, learn this: Needless cruelty, no matter how petty, makes me sick. I saw how you looked at Telys. He might not be Theseus's most skilled warrior, but he's still young. Someday he might surprise everyone. Now why don't you surprise him with an apology?" The girl lowered her head and muttered a few insincere words, but it was enough for Telys. He cheered up on the spot.

I ate up every last bit of my breakfast, then let Telys lead me to the training ground. It lay in a little hollow just below the royal citadel walls, out of sight of the city. I paid close attention to the terrain. In the meantime, I was looking forward to watching the men practice. I felt strange, being there in a dress. If I couldn't hone my swordsmanship firsthand, I still hoped to learn a new trick or two from observing others in action. Alas, my eagerness was doused the moment I saw who was waiting for me.

"There's my lovely bride!" Theseus called out, spreading his arms wide.

I stood my ground, arms folded, and glared at him until he mumbled something to Lady Aithra. She came to my side, linked her arm in mine, and pulled me to the seat she'd abandoned. If I'd resisted, I was sure that Theseus would have found some way to use my rebellion as an excuse to punish Telys.

The king's half brother certainly got enough punishment that day. He lost every bout, and when it was a matter of hitting a straw target with spear or javelin, his attempts always flew wide. I began to wonder whether he was being given crooked missiles.

"Are you trying to make me jealous, my pretty bird?" Theseus asked, teasing. He took one of the filled wine goblets from the cupbearer attending him and tried to give it to me. I turned my shoulder to him deliberately. "You can't seem to take your eyes off Telys. What will it take to make you spare just one of those sweet glances for me? Shall I step onto the training ground myself?"

"Only if you'll let me be the one to fight you, sword against sword," I replied. "I'm willing to stake my freedom on the match."

His lips twisted into a mocking smile. "And risk damaging that face? In four days' time, we'll be married. I intend to have a queen whose beauty makes me the envy of all." He tried to stroke my cheek. I jerked my head back.

"Don't worry, Theseus," I said. "If we fight, I won't be the one who'll take away a scar. But if you're afraid, name one of your men to match swords with me." I swept the training ground with my eyes and in a loud, carrying voice added: "Or are all the men of Athens scared to fight a Spartan girl?"

A grumbling ran through the ranks of the assembled guardsmen. My barb had hit the target and sunk in deep. Theseus didn't like the way things were going. He tried to pull the fangs from my challenge by turning it into a joke.

"Ha! I know what you're after, Helen. You're hoping I'll say yes to this mad proposal of yours, then you'll find some sly, womanly way to fix it so that you fight Telys. There's an easy win for anyone!"

I looked into his leering face and decided I'd seen enough of the cold malice everyone in the palace inflicted on Telys. The soldiers, the servants, and even the slaves were all a yapping pack of hounds following the lead of Theseus, the nastiest cur of them all. I leaped to my feet and shouted, "You *worm*! If you're too scared to fight me yourself, then say so!"

Theseus jerked away involuntarily, tipping his cup into his lap. Wine splattered over his tunic, dyeing the white wool crimson. He was up in an instant, looming over me. Lady Aithra called out for her son to be merciful, to mind his temper. I knew he wasn't going to listen. I heard a scuffle from the training ground and Telys's bleating voice, but I couldn't tell what it was all about. I looked Theseus in the eye, unflinching, and braced myself for what would come.

"Lord Theseus! Lord Theseus!" A man came scrambling down the path from the citadel, his half-clothed body thick with the dust of the road. He carried the small forked staff made of bronze that marked him as a herald. Only the most lawless, impious outlaws would dare interfere with him.

The herald's arrival shifted Theseus's attention at once. He demanded to know the man's purpose. The herald collapsed at the king's feet, breathing hard. Theseus gave him what was left of his wine from his own cup, then asked for the news a second time.

"My lord, I come from Thessaly, from the kingdom of the Lapiths in the shadow of Mount Pelion."

"Where Pirithous rules?" Theseus tensed. When I'd first encountered him in Calydon, Pirithous had been with him. Their friendship was like the bond between loving brothers. "What's wrong? Is he—?"

"He's well, my lord, but he needs your help. Horsemen have been raiding his lands. They grow bolder with each successful assault. He lacks the troops to do more than defend his stronghold. I would have come to you sooner, but the ship that was bringing me here ran aground at Marathon. I had to come the rest of the way on foot."

The herald had scarcely finished his report when Theseus burst into action. Orders flew, soldiers ran, slaves raced back to the citadel. Theseus dispatched his best men to the port to do whatever might be necessary to get ships to carry him and his troops to Pirithous's aid. I was hustled back to the palace with the other women and soon found myself standing beside

Lady Aithra, watching the king's ship sail away. No matter what else I thought of Theseus, I had to admire his competence as a leader of men and his loyalty to his friend.

"We must go to the temple of Ares," the queen said solemnly once the ships were gone. "We must pray for my son's victory."

"Don't forget to make a sacrifice to Zeus as well," I said lightly. My mind was echoing with happy thoughts. *He's gone! He's gone! There won't be any wedding! I have time to escape it! Thank all the gods, he's gone!* I felt in the mood for jesting. "And Athena, while you're at it. Sometimes cleverness wins wars when troops can't. Oh! And you shouldn't overlook Poseidon. I've heard Theseus claim to be his son more than once, and he *will* be sailing to Thessaly. If he neglects his own father—"

Lady Aithra slapped my face hard, twice. While I was still reeling from the blows, she turned to Telys and barked, "Take her to her room and keep her there. Your life still answers for hers, even though my son's no longer here. I promise you, I'm *much* less likely than he is to allow you any mistakes."

Telys swallowed and gently urged me back to my narrow room. Once there, I sank down onto my sleeping mat, nursing my tingling cheeks. "I didn't know Lady Aithra was so devoted to the gods that she can't even hear a joke about them," I grumbled.

"It wasn't what you said about the gods," Telys replied. "It was what you said about Theseus's father."

"Poseidon or Aegeus?"

"Lord Aegeus, my lady."

"Then why don't you say '*my* father' when you speak of him? Don't look so shocked, Telys. I know the truth. Palace secrets swarm and fly everywhere, like bees."

Telys looked downcast. "It would've been better for me if Lord Aegeus—if my father had denied I was his. I could have made a different life for myself somehow. I'm not fit to be a guard. Besides, I hate it."

"Then leave." I didn't see the problem. "That's what I'd do, if I could."

He shook his head. "If I left the palace, Lord Theseus would worry that I was plotting something against him. I'd have to leave Athens itself to be free of him, and I can't do that."

"Why not?"

"My mother. If I left, they'd take it out on her."

"Well, then take her *with* you!" It all seemed so simple to me.

Telys shook his head again, more vigorously. "She's too old to leave on foot, and we're too poor to get passage on a ship."

Now I understood, and I felt even worse for Telys than before. I decided it was best to divert him from dwelling on his unlucky situation. "I still don't see what I said that was so wrong," I remarked. "Did Lady Aithra think I was insulting *her* by giving Theseus two fathers?"

"That wasn't it," Telys replied. "It was what you said about him neglecting his father. Do you know about his first bride, the lady Ariadne?"

"I heard he was sent to Crete to seal an alliance by marrying her, but that he came home alone. That's all."

"There's more to it than that. Lord Theseus loved her dearly, chosen for him or not, but a plague struck Crete before they could sail."

"She died?" I felt a pang of sympathy.

Telys nodded. "A ship from Crete carried rumors here of a royal death, but none aboard knew more than that. Lord Theseus was too grief-stricken to think of sending word that he was alive and well. Lord Aegeus—my father—was out of his mind with worry." Telys sighed deeply. "Lord Theseus came home under a black sail to honor his lost bride. A lookout recognized the prince's ship and brought word of the black sail to the palace. All Athens heard of how wildly my father wailed, 'He's dead! He's dead!' and ran to the edge of a cliff above the sea. No one could stop him. He jumped to his death."

"Horrible," I murmured. "May Hades be good to his spirit."

"And to the spirit of the slave they forced to give the tragic news to Lord Theseus," Telys said with a shudder. "That's why he built that shrine to the lord of the Underworld, the one where we met. He wanted to atone for what he'd done, and what he'd neglected to do."

Theseus was gone and I enjoyed a breath of freedom. The wedding no longer haunted me. The first night after he sailed north to help Pirithous, I stood before the oil lamp in my room and raised my hands in prayer to all the gods. They'd given me the precious gift of time to think, and I was grateful. Then I murmured a special prayer to Athena. "Goddess of wisdom, make me wise enough to escape from Athens before Theseus comes back, wise enough so my guard Telys won't have to pay for my freedom with his blood. Even though my hands are clean, I feel accountable for how Hylas, Argus, and Milo died. How can I bear another death? So help me, great Athena. Once I'm free, I'll make you any sacrifice you ask for, but not Telys's life."

I lowered my hands, extinguished my lamp, and lay down under my blanket. Just before I fell asleep, I thought I heard a voice whisper, "Thank you, Lady Helen," but I was so drowsy that it might have been only the herald of my dreams.

13

LESSONS TAUGHT, LESSONS LEARNED

In the days that followed Theseus's departure, life in the palace changed. Theseus had taken many of his soldiers with him, but he couldn't take all of them, leaving his city undefended. The men he'd left behind resented the king's choice. Every day, I had to spend some time in Lady Aithra's company, and every day, I heard the guards grumbling. They soon found a defenseless target for their bile. Telys was still assigned to keep an eye on me through most of the day, so I heard every nasty jibe they tossed his way.

"You ought to teach them some manners," I murmured to Telys one morning as we passed a trio of those ugly bullies.

"I can't," he replied unhappily. "They'll use it as an excuse to mob me." He gave a little sigh. "Even if they would fight me one to one, I'd still lose. You saw how useless I am with weapons."

"I know what I saw," I replied as we walked on. "I was wondering about it. I know your father made you a guard when Theseus first came to Athens. That must have been years ago."

"Ten years, I think. I was fifteen."

"Telys, it's just not possible for someone to serve as a man-at-arms for so long and still be as—as— well, as *bad* as you are with weapons. It makes no sense."

For the first time, I saw a flinty look of resentment on Telys's face. "It wouldn't be if I were given decent weapons and real training. I had both when I first started, but my father died too soon, and when Lord Theseus took the throne—"

"I can imagine. If you'd had the proper equipment, your story would be different."

He smiled shyly. "I don't think so. Having the right weapons isn't all it takes to be a good warrior. You've actually had training, Lady Helen. I still would have lost to you."

His words hit me in the same way that the Muses' divine inspiration is supposed to strike their most beloved singers and poets. I stopped and poor Telys stumbled into me, but I didn't care. In one beautiful instant, my eyes had opened to a way for me to flee

Athens without having to worry that Telys or his mother would suffer for it afterward.

"Oh, Telys, this is *wonderful!*" I exclaimed, turning a beaming face to him.

I suspect that my unexplained joy must have looked like an attack of madness to him. "Lady Helen, is something the matter?" he asked, genuinely concerned.

"That . . . depends," I said, growing thoughtful again. "Telys, how badly do you want to leave Athens?"

"Shh!" He darted nervous glances all around, then whispered, "With all my heart. But you know I can't."

"No, I think you can, you and your mother both, safely. All you lack to do it is the means to buy passage on a ship bound far from here."

A dreamy look came into his eyes. "Mykenae. I'd like to go there. I've heard it's a finer realm than Athens, and that the king has a taste for beautiful things. My mother was no ordinary slave. She had a gift for painting pottery and images of the gods. She taught me her skills when I was little, and I loved it. I think I could recapture the art if I had the chance."

The two of us were standing still, talking like the friends we'd become instead of like the future queen and the despised guardsman. Suddenly I was aware that there were too many eyes on us, too many tongues keen to carry false tales to Lady Aithra's ears, and Lady Aithra was much too eager herself to hear bad things about Telys.

I turned and doubled back the way we'd come, walking briskly. Telys fell into step in a guard's proper place, right behind me.

"Lady Helen, where are you going?" he asked, flustered. "The queen's waiting for you with her women."

"The queen can wait. All she ever wants to do is force a spindle into my hands, then *tsk-tsk-tsk* over how badly I tangle the wool." I widened my eyes and tuned my voice to imitate Lady Aithra's. " 'My goodness, child, how *do* they raise girls in Sparta?' " I wrinkled my nose in disgust.

"Then where—?"

"Somewhere we won't attract notice," I said. "Around people who've got too much honest work to do to bother listening to conversations that don't concern them. We're going to the kitchen." Telys looked doubtful, but he trusted me.

The palace kitchen was bustling. Kitchens that need to feed many people always are. As soon as we walked in, I asked for food to give us a reason to be there, then settled myself in one corner of the busy room. The head cook himself brought me a plate of broiled quail, but hurried back to his work almost before I could thank him. Telys and I were left entirely to ourselves.

"Just the way you said it would be," Telys remarked. "Amazing!"

I flashed him a smile and bit into one of the crisp-skinned quail on my plate. "I just hope I'll be able to come up with some equally amazing way to find us a safe place for your lessons. I'm going to teach you how to fight, Telys."

He brightened at once. "My lady, I've got just the place, if you don't mind a bit of a climb. There's a part of the citadel walls that encloses older stonework. No one's sure if it's a ruined tower, or a shrine, or just the last remnant of the fortress built by Lord Kekrops, the first king of Athens. An ancient oak stands there too, a huge one, and between that and the old wall there's a small, well-hidden space that might do."

"Is it big enough to swing a sword?"

Telys smiled. "We can find out."

I nibbled the last bit of meat off a quail's tiny leg bone. "When the night guard comes to take your place at my door, you'll have to find us a pair of wooden swords to practice with and bring them to that place. You can't let anyone catch you, Telys."

"The place I have in mind is always deserted. No one likes to go there. They think the place is haunted by the old king's spirit."

"Theseus's warriors fear ghosts?" I wanted to laugh.

"Lord Kekrops's ghost is different. He was a dragon from the waist down."

I raised my eyebrows. "Better that than from the waist up, I suppose."

I decided that the best course to take would be spending two days in Lady Aithra's tedious company for every one that I'd spend teaching Telys, so that she wouldn't be too quick to suspect anything odd about my absences. I put this plan into effect at once.

When those first two spindle-cursed days passed and Telys and I were finally able to begin our lessons, I couldn't tell which of us was happier. I knew I'd never seen him walk with such a light step as when he led me to the hidden place he'd spoken of, between the old walls and the new. He ducked behind the great oak tree and brought out a cloth bundle.

"I couldn't find wooden practice swords," he said. "You'll have to teach me using this." With a surprisingly graceful move, he whipped the cloth away, revealing my own sword, which my teacher, Glaucus, had given me. I was so thrilled to see it, safe in that familiar sheath with its pattern of golden leopards, that I wanted to fill the sky with cries of happiness.

I contented myself with grabbing it with both hands and hugging it fiercely to my chest. "Oh, Telys,

I can't thank you enough for this," I said quietly. "How did you get it?"

"After Lord Theseus recognized you, he ordered one of the guards to fetch all your belongings from the inn where you and—where you were staying. He said it wouldn't do for a common innkeeper to own anything that was the property of a princess. I was there when the man returned, so I saw where he put your things."

"Do you think you could go back there again without anyone seeing you?" I asked. "I could use one of my tunics. It'll be hard to teach you swordsmanship if I'm forced to wear a dress all the time."

"I can do it. I'll bring a sturdy box too, so you can keep everything here."

Telys's confidence stirred me with a fresh hope. "I want you to look for one thing more," I told him. "I had a belt-pouch holding a little gold and silver. If we're lucky, it's untouched."

Telys smiled. "I remember that pouch. I came across it while searching for your sword. It was so wrapped up in your clothes I doubt anyone else noticed it."

"The gods grant that's true." I took a deep breath and slowly drew my sword. The day was cold but bright. Sunlight sifted through the oak branches and dappled the blade. I looked at Telys. "Let's begin."

Days went by, swift or slow, depending on whether I spent them helping Telys learn the right way to wield a sword or having Lady Aithra scold me for making a mess out of every piece of handwork she gave me to do.

Theseus's scorned half brother turned out to be an impressive fighter once he got lessons from someone who wanted to see him improve, not fail. He would have been even better if his sword hadn't been a disgrace. Like all his gear, it was a bad fit, intended to make him look absurd. By the time the moon had passed completely through two changes, it no longer mattered how inferior his blade was. He'd mastered enough skills to turn the worst sword ever forged into a formidable weapon.

One morning, when the warmth of early spring was in the air, I called a halt to our practice and declared, "You're ready."

Telys lowered his sword and wiped sweat from his brow. "Are you sure, Lady Helen?"

"I wouldn't say it if I wasn't," I replied. I sheathed my sword and wrapped it up before replacing it in the wooden box he'd provided. It lay safe beneath the oak and held all the useful things he'd brought to our makeshift training ground. This included my belt-pouch, though it turned out to be much too light for my liking. The most skillful haggler couldn't trade so little for three sea passages away from Athens, or even one. It had been a long time since I'd first filled it. Most of the gold, silver, and gemmed ornaments were gone, bartered for things Milo and I had needed in our travels.

Milo . . . I prayed daily that his spirit was at peace.

"It's time you found us a ship," I said. I picked up the dress I'd left neatly folded at the oak tree's roots and slipped it on over my tunic. "And time to make your fellow guardsmen pay for our passage to Mykenae."

"*And* pay for calling me clumsy all these years." Telys wore a wolfish grin.

"Careful," I said. "My plan depends on your reputation for being inept with weapons. Don't be *too* eager to lose it until we're on our way. In the meanwhile . . ." I knelt beside the box under the oak and took out my sword once more. "Here, Telys," I said, giving it to him. "Use this to win our sea passage."

His grin was gone. "Lady Helen, your own sword?" He accepted it with reverence. He knew what it meant to me.

"I trust it and I trust you. You're a capable warrior, but you've got to be an unbeatable one."

The following morning, Telys brought me to visit Lady Aithra. The spring weather was fair and balmy, so she'd chosen to do embroidery in one of the palace courtyards. Her women tittered over how curtly she dismissed Telys the moment we arrived and how quickly she had a slave bring another guard to mind me. They must have been starved for amusement, because that was how she always treated him. The queen couldn't stand the sight of her rival's son.

I wish she hated me enough to set me free, too, I thought. *I want to watch Telys make my plan unfold.* Besides my sword, I'd given him the last few gems and gold and silver bits left in my belt-pouch, the seeds of our escape.

I was struggling over my needlework when I heard the tread of heavy feet and the sound of stormy voices. The queen's chosen courtyard lay at the heart of the palace, a lively, broad, much-crossed space. I looked up, along with Lady Aithra and her women, saw a half dozen grim-faced guards marching through, and overheard their heated words:

"—cursed luck!"

"And he was *drunk*! He can't fight when he's sober, so how did he manage to win a match against our best swordfighter when he was *drunk*?"

"What *I* want to know is where that oaf got his paws on those gems and silver and gold trinkets to stake against us."

"Who cares? I lost everything on that wager. That's what matters to me."

"—swore by the Styx he'll fight a rematch against any man we pick. We'll win our own back then. Him winning this time had to be some cruel joke of the gods. It won't happen again."

"I say we all should've rushed him after the duel and *taken* back what we lost right away."

"—say that *now,* when he's nowhere near to hear it."

"Are you calling me a coward? I ought to——!"

They marched into the palace and out of earshot. When they were gone, one of Lady Aithra's women remarked, "Well, I wonder what that was all about?"

The queen shrugged. "Gambling again. Didn't you hear them mention a wager? Men." She went back to her handwork. She never noticed that I was almost quivering with glee. The guardsmen's angry words were sweeter to my ears than any of Orpheus's songs.

According to the pattern I'd chosen to follow, I was supposed to go to Lady Aithra again the next morning, but I didn't. I wanted the freedom to celebrate Telys's victory, and the only place I could do that was in our special place between the walls, old and new.

As soon as we got there, I began to dance around the oak, crowing, "You did it, Telys! You won! I knew you would."

"Thanks to you, Lady Helen." He looked a little embarrassed by my praise. "You were right about everything. The men thought I was a bungler with a blade. They saw the glint of silver in my hand, smelled that one mouthful of wine on my breath, and expected to win an easy wager." He plucked my battered pouch from his belt and dropped it into my hands. "So much for *that*," he said with a smile.

I marveled at how loudly the pouch jingled. "This is excellent, Telys, but what about the rematch? I overheard some of the men talking about it."

"I told them I owed my win to Artemis because she'd promised me victory in a dream. To honor her, I vowed not to fight again until the moon's full. That gives me at least five days to find us a ship. It won't be hard. Now that spring's here, the harbor's teeming."

I felt a stomach-twisting qualm. "You—lied about Artemis? Telys, what if she takes offense?"

"The gods don't notice everything we do. How many prayers go unanswered? But if Artemis is offended by what I've done, I'll take full blame." He sounded strong and sure of himself, a warrior who didn't need a sword to prove his worth as a man. Then he added, "I suppose I'll soon find out if I've made Artemis my enemy. If someone from the palace spies me seeking three passages to Tiryns today—"

" 'Tiryns'?" I interrupted.

"That's the port nearest to Mykenae. Then we've got to travel overland. If I find a ship headed there, I'll take it as a sign that Artemis isn't angry with me after all."

His lighthearted words made me realize just how close I was to regaining my freedom. "I'm going to see my sister, Clytemnestra, again, Telys!" I exclaimed.

" 'Clytemnestra'?" A note of uncertainty had crept into his voice.

"Didn't I speak of her to you before? She's married to Lord Thyestes' eldest living son, Prince Tantalus. When we reach Mykenae, she'll surely help you and your mother begin a new—"

His pockmarked face lost color. "Thyestes no longer rules Mykenae. He was driven from his throne by his nephews, the princes Agamemnon and Menelaus. We heard that Prince Tantalus died trying to help his father. If I'd known that he was your kin—"

"What! When?" I grabbed his arm hard, as if I could squeeze answers out of him more quickly.

"The news reached Athens not too long before you arrived, in late autumn." He released my grip gently. "Agamemnon, son of Atreus, is the new lord of Mykenae."

"I don't care if they've put a one-legged donkey on the throne!" I cried. "What happened to Clytemnestra? Tell me what's become of my sister!"

"Lady Helen, hush, don't fear. She's alive and well. I *thought* I recognized her name when you spoke it just now. I first heard it from the herald who brought the news of Thyestes' overthrow. Lord Agamemnon made her his bride. She's queen of Mykenae."

"Queen?" A wobbly laugh shook me. "Just what she always wanted. Poor Tantalus. This Agamemnon had better treat my sister well. If not, he'll answer to Sparta."

"I pray it won't come to that, Lady Helen."

"So do I." The shock I'd felt at Telys's news was gone. Cold anger took its place. "She *knew.* Lady Aithra knew what had happened in Mykenae, but she never said a word to me about my sister."

"Lady Helen—" Telys began, a cautioning note in his voice.

"Don't worry, I'm not about to draw my sword against the queen." I smiled to ease his mind. "I'm satisfied just imagining Lady Aithra's face the moment she learns we're gone. Let's see her explain *that* when her precious son comes home! Tell your mother to be ready to leave Athens at a moment's notice, Telys, and find us the ship we need. Hermes help me, before another sun rises, I'll have a way to get out of the palace when it's time to board her. *Nothing's* going to stop us from reaching Mykenae."

14

THE LAUGHTER
OF GODS AND MEN

I'd declared I'd think of a way to escape the royal citadel of Athens before another sunrise. Two days later, I was no closer to finding a practical solution. The problem occupied my mind above all while I was in Lady Aithra's company, and I was with her daily to give Telys as much free time as possible to find us that ship.

The long-dead king who'd ordered the construction of this building had taken care to make it a point of defense first, a royal home second. Besides the main gateway, there was only one other, and it was watched jealously. The walls were tall and thick, their ramparts inaccessible except by four stairways, each guarded. I thought about climbing the oak tree that grew near Lord Kekrops's haunted ruins to see if one of its branches was strong and long enough to let me get to the stronghold's outer walls.

"And then what?" Telys asked when I shared the idea on the third morning. He was escorting me to the queen's quarters, as usual.

"Then I'd drop down over the wall and—"

"—break your neck. Lady Helen, have you *seen* how high those walls are? Two stories tall in most places, higher in others."

"If I could get a rope—" I wasn't about to give up.

"There's a parapet that's supposed to keep you from falling over the edge, but it doesn't even come up to my knees. In some places along the wall, it's nonexistent."

"So that's why he put you up there so many times, and in the dark, too," I said bitterly.

Telys gave me a wry smile. "My poor, disappointed brother; I never *did* manage to trip and tumble to my death. But you see, Lady Helen, I know the walls. You can't climb down a rope if there's no place for you to anchor it."

"Stupid walls," I grumbled.

I spent the entire day doing embroidery with Lady Aithra, sitting under a green myrtle tree in one of the smaller palace courtyards. The queen wore the most comical expression of alarm and despair whenever she reviewed my work, so I began making one huge blunder after another on purpose, toying with her and amusing myself.

When the light began to fade, she looked positively relieved. "That will be enough for today. Will you dine with me, or would you prefer to eat in your own quarters?" It was an invitation without warmth.

I didn't want to spend any more time in her company than she did in mine. "I'm very tired," I replied. "I'd like to eat alone."

She didn't try to coax me into joining her, merely summoned the guard who stood in for Telys when I visited the queen. "See the lady Helen to her room," she said, and turned her back on me.

That evening, I was seated on my mattress, finishing the last of my dinner, when I heard a gasp from the night guard posted outside my room. "Lady Aithra!" he exclaimed, and tore the door curtain aside so violently that he nearly pulled it off its hanging rings. I looked up from my plate to see the well-dressed regal woman enter my room. She'd pulled her mantle up over her head, putting her face into darkness, but a few gray curls escaped into the light and trailed down one shoulder. I wondered what she wanted from me now. She had a thin blanket draped over her arms. Even if the night were cold, why wouldn't she simply order a slave to bring that to me?

"Lady Aithra, is anything the matter?" I asked, setting aside my dish and rising to my feet. She shook her veiled head, then turned and pulled the curtain all the way back across the doorway. That done, she edged past me and went into the farthest corner of my tiny room before settling herself into a very un-queenly squat against the wall, the blanket still covering her hands. She sighed happily, then nodded for me to join her. For a moment I hesitated, convinced that her son's long neglect had broken her mind at last. Who knew what she had concealed under that blanket? Medea had taught me to keep my distance from madwomen. Then I realized my error.

I knelt beside her and peered into the shadows cast by her mantle. "You're not the queen," I whispered. "Who are you?"

"A grateful mother," she replied softly. She let the blanket slide to the floor, revealing reddened, rough hands. No one who saw such work-hardened hands could ever mistake her for a queen.

When she pushed back her mantle, I drew in my breath sharply in shock. "You're the woman who sold me the offerings I needed for Hades' shrine," I said, struggling to keep my voice to a murmur.

"True." She reached inside her gown and pulled up a thin leather thong hung with the same amber bead I'd traded to her. "Telys is my son."

We spoke as softly as we could to keep our conversation from the guard outside. Telys's mother thanked me for all I'd done for her boy.

"I still can't believe I ever took you for a lad," she said. "Look at you! I don't think I've ever seen a more beautiful young woman, body and spirit."

I made haste to change the subject. "And I can't believe you simply walked in here unquestioned, as the queen."

She smiled. "It's easy enough. I know the ways of the palace. When I'm clad like this"—she held up a fold of her fine gown—"the guards see only the dress, not the woman."

"Where did you get such clothing?" I asked.

"It was a gift from my boy's father." She looked wistful as she stroked the supple wool covering her knees. I'd imagined that she'd gone to the old king's bed because she'd been a slave and had no choice about it, but her eyes told a different story. "These garments are old, but I preserve them well. This disguise is the only way I can see my son as often as I'd like." She held up her hands and studied them ruefully. "As long as I keep *these* hidden from sight, no one questions me. I've also learned it's not wise to linger too long under *her* roof."

"I'm sorry, I can't help you," I said. "I don't know where Telys is right now."

"But I do." Her smile was much like his. "Tonight I've come to see *you*, Lady Helen. I'm here to let you know my son's found us the right ship, a merchant vessel that sails for Tiryns tomorrow."

Tiryns, I thought. *So Telys has his sign that Artemis forgives him. Good.* "This is a gift from the gods," I said with more enthusiasm than I felt. "I wish you both a peaceful voyage."

Her brows met in a puzzled frown. "You speak as if you're staying here."

"It's not what I want. To leave Athens, first I need a way out of the royal citadel. It's all I think about, but the only thing that fills my mind is the sound of the gods laughing at me." I bowed my head, dejected.

"We're not leaving Athens without you." Telys's mother spoke in a voice that forbade argument.

"Nonsense. I'll be fine." I smiled as boldly as I could manage. "You could carry a message to my sister from me, asking for help. I don't want to drag Mykenae into war, but if worse comes to worst—"

"If worse comes to worst, you'll be pregnant with Theseus's child by summer," she said bluntly. "Lady Helen, sometimes what's simplest works best. At dawn tomorrow you're going to walk out of the palace, through the great citadel gates, and down the city hill to the sea. No one will stop you."

"They won't?" My brows rose sharply.

"Why should they?" She spoke with calm assurance.

"Haven't you done the same thing a dozen times before, when the queen takes you with her to the temples to pray for her son?"

The sun was a sliver of gold on the eastern horizon when we approached the great citadel gate. There were five of us—Telys, his mother, myself, and two elderly slave women. They were the same age as Telys's mother and were her dearest friends. Each carried a large basket on one shoulder, apparently brimming with offerings for the gods.

The air was still cool from the night before, but we women would have kept our mantles up over our heads even if the day had blazed like Hephaistos's hottest forge. The pair of guards on duty peered at our group in the faint light and saw what they expected to see.

"Lady Aithra." The two men on duty saluted Telys's mother solemnly. One of them added, "My lady, please join my prayers to yours when you ask the gods for Lord Theseus's safe return." She inclined her head graciously in response and he smiled, basking in "royal" favor.

The second sentinel looked annoyed at being left out. He stepped forward, keen to grab his share of the "queen's" attention. "My lady, perhaps it would please you better to have a *different* guardsman accompany you to the shrines?" He looked meaningly at Telys. It was clear he hoped to win "Lady Aithra's" approval by shunting aside the man she most despised.

Telys's mother shook her head emphatically but said nothing. If she spoke and the guards realized how different her voice was from the queen's, we'd be doomed.

"Are you sure, Lady Aithra?" he persisted. "Say the word, and I'll—"

"Are we going to waste the morning here, listening to this jabber?" I demanded loudly, drawing all eyes to me. "Where I come from, guards *take* orders and keep silent."

I stalked toward the gate as though exasperated with the pushy fellow. Telys overtook me in two strides. He clamped one hand to my shoulder, turned his head crisply toward the "queen," and coolly said, "Lady Aithra?" His mother responded by standing taller, turning her back on the abashed sentinel, and sweeping past Telys and me, out of the citadel, the perfect image of regal pride. The two slave women hurried after.

"That was close," I whispered to Telys as we all walked down the path to the heart of the city. "For a while, I was afraid I'd have to use this." I patted the familiar weight on my left hip. I had my sword at my waist again, hidden beneath my cloak.

"You sound more regretful than relieved," Telys

joked. "If that man had challenged us, you'd have given him a fight to remember."

"I did *not* want to fight my way out," I said vehemently. But in truth, this wasn't how I'd pictured my escape from the citadel. In my more fanciful moments, I'd imagined the clash of swords, the shouts of soldiers, the rumble of running feet, maybe even the reek of smoke and the crackle of fire.

We reached the temple of Athena as the city was waking up. Soon the streets would be crowded. Many eyes followed the five of us as we entered. I could just hear what those people would be telling their families that night: "You'll never guess who I saw this morning: Lady Aithra herself and the king's young bride-to-be, visiting the shrines. Yes, *again*. Mark my words, with so many prayers constantly in their ears, the gods won't fail to bring Lord Theseus home soon."

"Lady Aithra" had her slaves give the priest wine and olive oil for Athena while she and I stood together before the image of the goddess. Before we left, she removed a necklace and placed it at Athena's feet. I saw the priest beam with approval.

Looking less queenly than before, "Lady Aithra" proceeded downhill to Aphrodite's shrine, where she and I each gave the goddess one of the more splendid pieces of our garb. The priest was too busy admiring our offerings to notice how much more we resembled ordinary folk than royalty.

In Apollo's temple we left behind wine, cakes, and one of the slave women. I admired the inconspicuous way she faded into the shadows. Telys also took the opportunity to find an out-of-the-way spot and hide his sword inside the basket she abandoned. When we headed for Zeus's temple, we looked like a well-to-do family attended by a single slave woman, but when we left the god's house, only three of us remained. The same sort of Athenians who would have stared at "Lady Aithra" and her escort didn't give us a second glance as we passed them now.

By the time we reached the ship, we were just a mother, a son, and a *very* modestly veiled daughter. The sailors had gotten the ship into the water already and were too preoccupied with their own tasks to bother about us. Once aboard, we were sent to a place in the stern of the ship between the last bank of oars and the helmsman.

The captain gave an order and the men bent their backs over the oars, rowing the ship into deeper water to wait until it was time to set the sail and let the wind do most of the work. I pulled back the folds of cloth concealing my face and felt the familiar touch of sea spray on my cheeks. It filled me with elation and memories.

Lord Poseidon, forgive us, I thought. *We didn't have time to go to your shrine and ask for a safe voyage. I ask that favor now, and I promise you that when we reach Mykenae, I'll make you a worthy offering.*

I rested my hands on the ship's rail and turned my eyes toward the prow. I remembered all the voyages I'd known since leaving Sparta, chief among them the quest for the Fleece. *Where are they now?* I wondered. *Are my brothers well? Has the* Argo *brought them safely back to Iolkos? Oh, Castor, Polydeuces, I do miss you!* My thoughts painted their faces against the bright sky, and other faces, too. Hylas and Herakles, Jason and Argus, mad Medea and sweet-voiced Orpheus. Above all, Milo. When I wiped the sea's breath from my face, it was mixed with tears.

The voyage from Athens to Tiryns was pleasant enough, though I missed the freedom I'd enjoyed when I'd traveled disguised as a boy. My new identity was Telys's younger sister. Telys, his mother, and I agreed that I'd keep my given name for simplicity's sake.

As the daughter of a humble but respectable family, I couldn't speak to strangers. Thankfully, my "mother" and "brother" didn't have to live by such rules, so by the time we neared Tiryns they'd made friends with the two merchants aboard our vessel.

"They're heading to Mykenae, too," Telys told me one day as we watched a flock of gulls dive for fish in our ship's wake. "They said we can travel there with them."

"That's a stroke of luck," I said. "I guess Artemis *really* wants you to know she's forgiven you for that lie."

Telys looked sheepish. "I *did* dream about her. Last night. I was scared at first, afraid she was going to curse me for what I'd done. But all she did was look at me and laugh."

"Maybe sometimes it's *good* to have the gods laugh at us," I said.

The ship landed at Tiryns the next morning and we set out for Mykenae with the merchants and their trade goods. After the ease of our voyage, the overland trek to Mykenae was a trial. The only diversion we had turned out to be unwelcome: One of the merchants developed an annoying attraction for me. When I ignored him, as a modest maiden of good family should do, he persisted. The road to Mykenae became a strand of days filled with gifts, sighs, languishing looks, and the occasional love song. There was nothing I could do to stop it.

"I almost feel sorry for that man," Telys's mother said one evening as we made camp. "I think he loves you very much. He's breaking his heart over you, child."

"Is that supposed to make me love him? Suppose I *did* marry him, just because he wouldn't stop pestering me until I gave in. Imagine that another man arrives, years later, and he's breaking his heart over me as well. What am I supposed to do then? Run away with the new pest?" I shook my head. "Is love just a matter of badgering someone until you get your own way, like a spoiled child? If that's so, Aphrodite ought to carry a hammer as a warning." Telys's mother didn't say another word on behalf of my exasperating suitor after that.

One blessed morning, our group emerged from a grove of trees high on a hill and saw a most welcome sight: the city of Mykenae. "We'll be there well before nightfall," Telys said, shading his eyes and gauging the distance. "It looks like easy going from here, downhill and then fairly level land until we reach the city heights."

I sighed happily and said a prayer of thanks to Hermes for having guided us well. I wanted to hike up my skirt and race across the plain to the citadel gate. Already I saw myself embracing my sister, Clytemnestra, and my heart ached to make that vision real.

When we reached the outskirts of the city, spread out below the slopes of the royal stronghold, my impatience got the better of me. I didn't run, but unconsciously I began to add speed to my stride, until I was rushing ahead of the rest of the group. Telys and his mother were too busy staring at everything around them to notice. Before I knew it, I'd left everyone behind.

As I climbed the hill toward the Lion Gate, my mind raced faster than my feet. A practical voice inside my head spoke up, saying, *Slow down, Helen! Do you think the guardsmen at the gate are just going to stand to one side and let you through unchallenged? They don't know who you are. If you proclaim that you're the queen's sister, they'll probably burst out laughing. No princess arrives on foot, covered with the dust of the road.*

I didn't want to listen to common sense. All I wanted was to see my sister again. I wasn't going to let anyone or anything stop me.

As I ran, my eyes skimmed the faces of the people I passed. Had there been so many soldiers in the streets when Lord Thyestes ruled? Was the new king, Lord Agamemnon, so insecure that he needed to put more troops around him, like human armor? When I reached the towering stone gateway, would these men try to keep me from seeing Clytemnestra? I scowled at each warrior I passed, yet as I did, I noticed that not all of them were Mykenaeans. Their garb, their hair, the shape of their shields and the decorations painted on them, all stirred my memory. Here and there I saw a face I thought I recognized.

"Helen! Helen!"

I heard a voice ring out through the Lion Gate, a voice I thought I'd never hear again until Lord Hades' ferryman, Charon, carried my own spirit across the river Styx into the land of the dead. Sandaled feet

came pounding down the path from the royal stronghold and a shouting, flying blur struck me so hard that
it was more like an attack than an embrace. And
through it all, my ears filled with the joyous, familiar
sound of my name being called out again and again:
"Helen! Helen! Helen!"

I pushed him back to arm's length and stared into
his eyes, afraid that one word would break the spell
and send his ghost wailing back into the Underworld.
But I couldn't stay silent forever.

"Milo?" I whispered, shaking. He grinned and
nodded happily in spite of the bandage binding his
head. "Oh, *Milo!*"

I hugged Milo tight and tighter, unable to let him
go, until a new hand closed gently on my shoulder and
I heard a beloved voice murmur tenderly, "May all the
gods be praised, this is a miracle."

I released Milo and turned to look into my father's face. He closed his arms around me, and though
I was still far from Sparta, I was home.

15

IN THE HOUSE
OF AGAMEMNON

My father, my sister, and I sat together in the queen's apartments. How strange, to look at my sister and realize that now she *was* a queen. We spoke in low voices, our eyes on the slave women who drifted in and out of our sight on silent feet. I got the feeling that their main purpose was not to bring us food, pour our wine, sweep the floor, or fuss over the queen's belongings. They were the ears of Agamemnon, but we didn't have to make it easy for them to hear.

"He's clever, your new husband," Father said to Clytemnestra very, very softly. "He offers to let us have time alone to ourselves, but makes certain that he'll know everything we say or do."

"That's his mistake," I replied, also in a nearly inaudible voice.

"And who's a better authority on mistakes than you, Helen?" Clytemnestra said tartly. "When that boy of yours came stumbling up to the Lion Gate, babbling about how you'd been taken captive in Athens, the gods must have been protecting him like a priceless jewel. If one of Father's men hadn't been there and recognized him, my husband's soldiers would have struck him down."

"Milo is not my *boy*," I responded sharply, striving to keep from shouting in Clytemnestra's face. "He's my friend."

"I'm sure he is." How *could* I have forgotten my sister's mastery of the insufferable smile?

"Girls, girls, please." Father reached out and took our hands. "Is this how we thank the gods for having brought us together again?"

"I'm sorry, Father," Clytemnestra mumbled. "I didn't mean to say that. I rejoice to see Helen again." She clasped my other hand. "I'm just—just a little nervous lately. It makes me prickly."

"I understand." I lowered my eyes and gave her hand an affectionate squeeze. "I heard what happened to your husband, Prince Tanta—"

"Shh!" She tensed sharply, her hands clenching. "Lord Agamemnon is my husband now."

"I marched north with my men as soon as word reached Sparta about how things had . . . *changed* in Mykenae," Father murmured. "We received too many conflicting reports about what was happening here. I couldn't stand by, waiting to hear about my child's fate. I had to come, to see that she was well and happy. If not . . ." He didn't bother elaborating. We all knew that if anything had happened to Clytemnestra, Mykenae and Sparta would be at war.

"Are you happy, Clytemnestra?" I asked. I didn't know whether or not she'd been happy with Prince Tantalus, but I wasn't concerned with the past. I cared about the life my sister had to live *now*.

She lowered her eyes. "Lord Agamemnon has been very kind to me, very gentle and loving. The alliance between Sparta and Mykenae can go on."

"But are you *happy*?" I pressed.

Father spoke before my sister could reply. "Everything is settled here, Helen. I've recognized Lord Agamemnon's right to the throne of Mykenae. My men and I would have returned home by now if he hadn't insisted on marking our new kinship with one grand banquet after another. I wanted to get back to Sparta, but it seems that the gods had their reasons for keeping us here."

"You mean for Milo's sake?" I asked. Then I laughed. "He walks with luck. I thought he'd been killed."

"He told us all about what happened that night," Father said. "He was knocked senseless and took a bloody head wound, but there was no deep harm done. The widow you'd lodged with bandaged him up and spirited him off to her brother's house in case the king's guards came back."

"Father, I want to reward that woman," I said.

"That was my intention, too. I meant to do it as soon as I'd rescued you from Athens." He patted my head, as if I were still a little child. "Now I see that you need no one's help."

I smiled. "No, Father, sometimes I do. There were many times in my travels that I was grateful to have it." And with that, I began to tell my father and sister about my adventures.

Five days later, Milo vanished. At first I thought nothing of it. As happy as we were to be together again, we often found that after our first reunion, many things forced us to spend our days apart.

Meals were a problem. The closer we came to leaving Mykenae, the more my sister clung to me. She insisted I share her rooms, which also meant sharing our daylight meals. She would have tolerated Milo's company, but by order of Lord Agamemnon himself, the queen's quarters were forbidden to any man outside her family. When darkness fell, Milo still had to eat in the palace kitchen, while I attended the nightly feasts Lord Agamemnon gave in the great hall to celebrate my arrival. Though Milo was my dearest friend, he was still a freed slave. There could be no room for him at Lord Agamemnon's table.

Other matters also conspired to separate us. Father put Milo to work running errands as we all prepared for the journey home. Though I swore I'd be able to cover the distance on foot, the same as our men, or riding beside Father in his war chariot, or even on horseback, if a horse could be acquired for me, Father insisted that I'd travel in the style suitable for a princess.

As for me, I had certain tasks to see to before we left Mykenae, above all repaying Telys and his mother for their kindness. With the help of Prince Menelaus, they joined the household of the freeborn potter who supplied the best families in Mykenae. When I thanked the king's brother for using his influence to help reward my friends, he became flustered.

"I did nothing," he said, not meeting my eyes. "That woman has a talent for painting, and her son—" He hesitated a moment, then earnestly asked me, "When you traveled with those people, was he— was he *respectful*? He didn't try to—that is—I heard that you pretended to be his sister. Did he treat you like a sister? Always, I mean?"

I was mystified by so many odd questions. "Of course. Why do you ask?"

"Oh! Oh, no reason. It's just that you're so beautiful, I don't know how he could have— Never mind. Telys is a virtuous man. It will be my honor to make him my friend, if he'll let me. And I promise you, Lady Helen, that I'll gladly continue to look after him and his mother . . . for your sake."

"Um . . . thank you," I replied, still puzzled.

Prince Menelaus also helped me when my thoughts turned to Milo's future. I remembered what my friend had told me about wanting to become a merchant, like the Corinthian who would have carried us from Athens. I determined to make Milo's ambition come true.

I shared my intentions with Prince Menelaus, since he'd been so gracious helping me reward Telys and his mother. He sent for the two merchants who'd accompanied us from Tiryns. I admit I was glad when only the younger of the pair appeared, and *not* my unsuccessful suitor. It spared us both some awkward moments.

The younger merchant beamed when he saw me. "So it *is* true," he exclaimed, taking in my royal garb, a gift from Lord Agamemnon. Once again my gown was bright with gloriously colored patterns, my tiered skirts jingling with precious ornaments. "You *are* a princess. When you traveled with us, we thought you were no more than an ordinary girl, though I must say, there was never anything ordinary about your loveliness."

"Enough of that." Prince Menelaus gave him a

stormy look. "The lady Helen of Sparta wants to question you. She wants answers, not insolence."

"It's all right," I said quickly, wondering why such a mild-mannered man as Prince Menelaus had turned suddenly stern over a trifling bit of flattery. "There's a kind of kinship between travelers. I don't think he's being insolent at all."

"I wouldn't dare," the merchant reassured us. He was carrying a polished olive-wood box, which he set at my feet. Opening the lid, he took out a long-handled mirror, very much like the one my mother owned, and offered it to me. "Noble Lady Helen, why should you be the only one unable to enjoy the gift of beauty you give to all the world?"

I took the mirror from his hands and looked into the circle of polished bronze. How long had it been since I'd last seen my own face? I recalled sharp features, harsh lines, the same awkward angles that had taken over my childish body and turned it into a gawky, gangling thing. But now . . .

I knew my body had changed again. I'd learned to master my long limbs, to move with the grace that successful swordsmanship demanded. I'd also experienced changes that made passing as a boy more than a simple matter of throwing on a tunic. Now, gazing into the mirror, I saw that my body wasn't the only place where new curves and softness had made me a stranger to myself.

"Does my poor gift please you, Lady Helen?" the merchant asked.

Before I could answer, Prince Menelaus declared, "If Lady Helen likes it, it will be *my* gift to her. You will receive its weight in silver before you leave the palace, I promise you."

The merchant looked stricken. "Mighty prince, I didn't come here intending to make a profit. I only wanted to make the lady Helen smile."

"You don't need to concern yourself with Lady Helen's smiles," Prince Menelaus snapped. "You heard what I said. If she likes the mirror, she'll accept it from *me.*"

"I'll take nothing from anyone." I put the mirror back in the box and looked at the merchant. "This isn't about gifts, it's about the future of a dear friend of mine." I told the merchant about Milo as briefly as I could, including his bravery in defending me that night in Athens. I ended by asking, "If you agree to help him, will you promise me not to think of him as a former slave?"

The younger merchant laughed. "Only if he promises not to think of me as the son of a former slave. But tell me, does this Milo have a bandaged head?"

I nodded. "He was wounded trying to save me."

"Ah, well then, I'm afraid he's been too fast for you, Lady Helen. He came to us two days ago and said he'd heard we were the ones who'd brought you safely to Mykenae. He wanted to thank us. He thinks very highly of you. *Very* highly indeed." He winked at me, in spite of Prince Menelaus's scowl. "He's also quite the clever lad. By the time he left us, he'd convinced my partner to take him on as a student of our trade. They left yesterday for Corinth. If he's half as good at swaying customers as he was at persuading us—"

I didn't hear the rest. I picked up my skirts and ran from the room, my bare feet pelting through the palace halls until I found my father. He was seated in an inner courtyard where violets bloomed and the sweet scent of a green myrtle tree perfumed the air.

"Milo's gone!" I cried, throwing my arms around my father's neck. "He's gone, and he never even told me good-bye!"

"You're wrong, dear one," Father said. "He did tell you good-bye. He just couldn't say it to you himself. He came to me two days ago to let me know he'd been given a wonderful chance, the chance to make a new life for himself, and he was going to take it." He stroked my hair. "I understand why you're upset, but this is for the best. I wish I knew why the gods play tricks on us. That boy has an honorable spirit and a brave heart. If he'd been born into a noble family, even if it weren't a royal one, I wouldn't mind having you marry—"

"Marry!" I stared at him. "Father, I love Milo dearly, but as a friend, nothing more."

"Is that so? And does he know it?" I nodded firmly. My father sat back and stroked his beard. "Then perhaps his departure really is for the best . . . for him."

I nestled against my father's chest and he put one arm around me. I was aching with misery. "Is that why he left?" I asked. "Because I didn't care for him the way he cared for me?"

"I think that was a part of it," my father replied. "Don't brood about it, child. Only Aphrodite can change what we feel in our hearts."

"I hope he'll be happy," I murmured. "I pray Aphrodite will help him find someone who loves him as much as he loves her."

"That's a good prayer." Father gave me a hug and stood up. "Now let's find her shrine, and make sure she hears it."

I smiled sadly. "Don't the gods hear our prayers wherever we are?"

"Yes, but I think it's best to speak with them in their own houses and bring them a little gift when you *really* want them to pay attention to what you've got to say."

I followed him to the goddess's temple, where we both made a sacrifice of wine and honey cakes. I prayed for Milo's safety, for success in his new life, and for someone to share his heart. When I finished, one of the priests tried to sell me a pair of doves as an additional sacrifice, but I couldn't bear the thought of shedding their innocent blood. Instead I took them from his hands and tossed them into the sky. I imagined them flying to the heights of Olympus, bearing my prayers in a whir of wings to the foot of Aphrodite's throne. I hoped with all my heart that the goddess would stretch out her white hands and welcome them home.

EPILOGUE

A year passed before I saw Milo again. He arrived in the company of the young merchant I'd last seen in Mykenae. They were brought into my father's presence because of the richness of the goods they had to offer, things too beautiful and costly to be acquired without the king's own say-so. Mother and I were there when the trading party was escorted into the great hall. We came as soon as we heard that Father was receiving men who'd traveled far before they reached Sparta.

We were always avid for the news that merchants carried along with their wares. After all, a band of tradesmen brought us word that my brothers were alive and well when the *Argo* finally returned to Iolkos and the crew went their separate ways. The merchants also carried dark and bloody tales of the Argonauts' escape from Colchis, all involving Medea. Had she really contrived her own brother's murder to distract the king from pursuing Jason and the Fleece from Ares' shrine? I wouldn't have put it past her, and I was glad Castor and Polydeuces were safe after a voyage in *that* company. I only wished the quest for the Fleece hadn't given them such a taste for heroism. Once they left the *Argo*, they'd promptly set out on fresh adventures. The gods alone knew when they'd come home, but their exploits were often on the tongues of traders.

There was another good reason for my attendance in the great hall. Ever since my return home, Father had insisted that I be present whenever he gave anyone a royal audience. He said it was best I started learning how to govern Sparta sooner rather than later, even if he wasn't about to hop aboard Charon's ferry tomorrow.

I nearly didn't recognize Milo. I saw a tall, strong-limbed young man with long, gleaming curls and a neatly trimmed beard. His bright blue and green tunic was banded with rich red and gold, a far cry from the cast-off garments he'd been forced to dress in before. He was hard at work, spreading out all manner of glittering wares at Father's feet, when he looked up at me, and all at once I knew him again. I couldn't help uttering a cry of delight. If he hadn't been holding an especially fine vase in his hands just then, I think I would have rushed into his arms.

"Well, well," Father remarked fondly. "I think our daughter has seen something she likes."

Milo's presence transformed the trading party from merchants to guests. As Mother said, it was the least we could do for the people who'd helped me in one way or another ever since I struck out on my own. That night, over dinner, the younger merchant told us the fate of his absent partner, my persistent suitor.

"He died on the way back from Corinth. He thought he knew how to tell good mushrooms from bad. He was wrong. That was when *this* one proved himself." He clapped Milo on the back. "It was just the two of them on that first journey, because my partner wanted to test the lad. When there are tasks to do and only one extra set of hands to do them, you learn soon enough whether you've taken on a worker or a drone. So there Milo was, left all alone with a load of valuable goods. He could have vanished into the hills with it all. Instead he came straight back to Mykenae, handed me my late partner's tally sticks, and apologized because he'd had to trade off part of our profits in order to give the poor man a decent burial. I've trusted him utterly ever since. He'll be ready to undertake his own trading journeys before you know it. And I think we all know the first thing he's going to do when I let him go out on his own."

"I'm afraid we don't," my mother replied pleasantly.

"Why, marry his sweetheart, of course!" The merchant grinned. "She's a nice little thing, just a fisherman's daughter he met when we sailed to Delphi, but there's something about the way she carries herself that almost makes you think she's a princess in disguise."

Father looked at me closely. I don't know what he was expecting to see.

That night, when I was already undressed for bed, someone scratched at my door. It was Ione, my former nursemaid. Even though all of us royal children were grown up, my parents had kept her on. Just the sight of her face called up comforting memories of childhood, before my sister left to become a queen and my brothers set out to win the fame of heroes.

"I've a message for you," she said. "From him. That boy you bought." Like my parents, Ione knew the full tale of my adventures, including how Milo got his freedom.

"That *boy* is going to be rich enough to buy all of Sparta someday," I replied lightly. "What's the message?"

"He wants you to meet him somewhere . . .

private. He says he's got something to tell you. News from an old friend." She bit off the words sharply, just to let me know that she didn't believe them for a moment.

I asked her to send him to the rooftop shrine my parents had dedicated to Aphrodite. She trudged off so slowly that I wondered whether she'd obey me or conveniently "forget" all about it. But by the time I'd put my clothes on again and climbed the stairs to the sanctuary, Milo was waiting for me in front of the painted image of the goddess.

"It's wonderful to see you again, Helen," he said. "I'm sorry I left Mykenae without—"

"No need for that," I said, smiling. "It's past and pardoned. I'm just glad to learn everything's going well for you. So you're marrying a fisherman's daughter. *That* fisherman's daughter?"

"Alkyone." Milo pronounced her name so fondly that I didn't need to ask if he'd found true love and happiness. I was delighted for him. "She did a very good job of pretending to be you. Too good. She told me that when your father's messenger arrived at Delphi to announce you were back in Sparta, half the priests and servants at Apollo's temple refused to believe it. The Pythia herself had to swear an oath with one hand on the holy tripod before they'd accept it. Of course, then they wanted to punish Alkyone for fooling them. Eunike stepped in again and said that Alkyone would become her personal servant in order to make up for what she'd done."

"Eunike's servant?" I laughed. "A very hard job, I'm sure." We both knew that the Pythia had asked very little of the girl.

"Almost as hard as pretending to be a princess. It's a good thing I'm going to be so wealthy. My Alkyone's got a taste for the finer things in life. But she's worth all of them to me." His gaze drifted to the statue of Aphrodite. "I should make a generous offering to the goddess for such a blessing."

I studied the clay image. She looked much smaller than I remembered, and her paint was no longer bright, but I knew that Aphrodite's true power came from something greater and more enduring than what mortal eyes could see.

"I'd be honored if you'd bring your offering here," I told him.

"The honor would be—" Milo stopped short, then slapped his forehead. "It's so good to be able to talk to you again, Helen, that I forgot the reason we're here. I have a message for you."

"News from an old friend." I mimicked Ione's disapproving tone. "Who?"

"The Pythia."

"Eunike!" I exclaimed happily. "Oh, I do miss her. Maybe I can convince Father to let me travel to

Delphi again. I could say I wanted to hear what the future holds for—"

"It wasn't Eunike who sent me, Helen," Milo said solemnly. "When she sees the future, there is no Eunike, only the holy Pythia."

I felt the hairs at the nape of my neck prickle. "She saw my future, didn't she? What did she see, Milo?"

"This." He stepped to one side. It was only then that I saw the cloth-wrapped bundle on the ground behind him. He stooped to pick it up and handed it to me. I drew back the swaddlings and found myself staring into the shining depths of a mirror. At first I thought it was the same one that the younger merchant had tried to give me, the gift that roused so much anger in Prince Menelaus. But that mirror was made of polished bronze. This one was silver. I turned it over slowly and saw the breathtaking artistry of a master craftsman.

Frozen in glimmering metal, sheep wandered untended over the forested slopes of a great mountain. Their shepherd had a more urgent task at hand. His face was hidden from me, but not the faces of the three goddesses before him. They towered above the trees, their streaming hair becoming a part of the clouds. Their faces were as flawless as their bodies, but there was a dreadful intensity in their gaze. All three stared greedily at a single dot of gold, the perfect apple shining in the palm of the shepherd's hand. What was so special about that tiny golden apple? Why could I almost feel the mirror vibrate with the intensity of the goddesses' desire and the fateful, breathless *waiting* that hovered over that unknown shepherd in the moment before he made his choice?

"How can a contest among three goddesses have anything to do with me?" I asked, looking up. "And why did Eunike—why did the Pythia send me her message like *this*?" I held out the mirror to Milo.

He took it from me calmly. "She didn't. She only summoned me into her presence, described her vision, and ordered me to take her words to you. Bringing her prophecy to you like this"—he turned the mirror over and forced it back into my hands—"was my doing. I owe you everything, Helen. I want you to be as happy as I am now. Most of all, I never want you to be afraid. No matter what the Pythia saw in your future, I never want you to forget—"

"—that it's *my* future." I held the mirror by its long, elegant handle as if it were a sword and looked steadily into its smooth silver face. There were no goddesses there, was no golden apple and no shepherd. There was only me.

My future, I thought. *May the choices that create it all be mine!*

"SHE CAN'T DO THAT TO MYTHS!"

One of my all-time favorite movies is *Jason and the Argonauts.* It showcased some fabulous pre-CGI special effects done by the master of the art, Ray Harryhausen, who also co-produced the film. The effect that impressed me the most (by which I mean it scared the daylights out of me) happened after Jason slew the Hydra and took the Golden Fleece. Infuriated, King Aetes of Colchis planted the Hydra's teeth in the earth and intoned, "Rise up, all you dead, slain of the Hydra! Rise up out of your graves to avenge us!"

After so many years, I don't know whether those were King Aetes' exact words, but whatever he said, it worked. A skeleton army of the Hydra's previous victims slowly and creepily emerged from the ground, bearing swords and shields. They formed ranks and did a grim, inexorable, step-by-step advance on Jason and his men. Then, with a bloodcurdling shriek, the dead *attacked!* Harryhausen didn't just give us the sheer horror of living, moving, armed-and-dangerous skeletons (with the added fear factor of *How can you defend yourself against an enemy who's already dead?* Some of the skeletons kept on fighting even after their heads were knocked off!). He took the trouble to make those skeletons look angry, vicious, and bloodthirsty. They went after Jason and his men with a vengeance. I didn't sleep well for *weeks* afterward.

It was wonderful.

In the myth of Jason and the Argonauts, Jason *doesn't* slay the Hydra. The Hydra belongs to one of the myths about Herakles. Jason *does* have to overcome the dragon that guards the Golden Fleece, but he never gets the chance. Medea sings the dragon to sleep so Jason can take the Fleece from the branches of the tree that the dragon is guarding.

Before this, however, Jason *does* have to deal with an army of men who spring up out of the ground, but it's nothing like the movie version. When he asks King Aetes for the Fleece, the king tells him he must first yoke two fire-breathing bulls to a plow, till a field, and plant the furrows with dragon's teeth. Sowing the teeth *does* cause a host of armed men to leap out of the earth, spoiling for a fight, but they're not skeletons and they don't get into a scary, thrilling battle with

Jason and his men. Instead, heeding Medea's advice, Jason throws a big stone into the midst of the dragon's-teeth men as soon as they emerge from the ground. This makes them turn on one another, fighting among themselves until all are dead.

Was Harryhausen's *Jason and the Argonauts* true to the myth? Not entirely. Did that matter to me and all the other people who were entertained by the movie over the years? No. And why should it? Sticking to the facts is important in many aspects of our lives, but myths aren't facts. If truth be told—and it should be—wildly differing variations on the same story do exist in Greek mythology. There are at least three separate versions of Jason's story, all of which disagree about who was and wasn't a member of the *Argo*'s crew.

Helen's own story isn't immune to this. The best-known version has her carried off to Troy by Paris. Her husband, Menelaus, seeks help from his brother, Agamemnon of Mykenae, in getting her back. A huge Greek army is raised, but contrary winds prevent it from setting sail for Troy. To appease the angry god who sent the wind, Agamemnon sacrifices his own daughter, Iphigenia. The Greeks reach Troy and fight a war that lasts ten years. In the end they are triumphant and Helen is carried back to Sparta.

But that's not the only way the story goes. Some versions have Helen running away with Paris voluntarily. Some say that Iphigenia, who died in order to buy the Greeks a favorable wind, was not the daughter of Agamemnon and Helen's sister, Clytemnestra, but was actually the child of Theseus and Helen herself, born while Helen was his captive in Athens. As for Iphigenia herself, in one version of her story, she dies on the altar, but in another, the goddess Artemis replaces her with a deer and whisks her away to serve as her priestess in the far northern land of the Taurean tribe. Some accounts of Helen's adventures report that she never even reached Troy. When Paris's ship landed in Egypt, the Pharaoh found out that the Trojan prince had abducted another king's wife. He did *not* approve and forced Paris to leave Helen behind to await the eventual arrival of her husband. Unfortunately, no one got the message to Menelaus, and the Trojan War went on with a phantom Helen, sent by the gods, as the prize.

So perhaps my story of Helen's life before Troy doesn't recount the myths exactly as we know them, but at least I'm in good company. And who's to say it couldn't have happened this way? Remember, myths aren't history, and even the "truth" of history depends on who's telling the story.

ABOUT THE AUTHOR

Nebula Award winner ESTHER FRIESNER is the author of thirty-one novels and over 150 short stories, including "Thunderbolt" in Random House's *Young Warriors* anthology, which led to her first novel about Helen, *Nobody's Princess*. She is also the editor of seven popular anthologies. Her work has been published in the United States, the United Kingdom, Japan, Germany, Russia, France, Poland, and Italy. She is also a published poet and a playwright and once wrote an advice column, "Ask Auntie Esther." Her articles on fiction writing have appeared in *Writer's Market* and other Writer's Digest books.

Besides winning two Nebula Awards in succession for Best Short Story (1995 and 1996), she was a Nebula finalist three times, as well as a Hugo finalist.

She received the Skylark Award from NESFA and the award for Most Promising New Fantasy Writer of 1986 from *Romantic Times*.

Ms. Friesner's latest publications include the novel *Temping Fate*; a short story collection, *Death and the Librarian and Other Stories*; and *Turn the Other Chick*, fifth in the popular Chicks in Chainmail series, which she created and edits. She is currently working on a young adult novel about the great beauty Nefertiti, which carries on in the spirit of her Helen of Troy books.

Educated at Vassar College, receiving a BA in both Spanish and drama, she went on to receive her MA and PhD in Spanish from Yale University, where she taught for a number of years. She is married and the mother of two, harbors cats, and lives in Connecticut.

IF YOU LIKED WHAT ESTHER FRIESNER
DID WITH ANCIENT GREECE,
JUST WAIT UNTIL YOU SEE WHAT SHE
HAS PLANNED FOR EGYPT. . . .

SPHINX'S PRINCESS

Turn the page for a sneak preview of the
thrilling adventures of Nefertiti—
available September 2009!

PROLOGUE

From the time of my first memories, my dreams were filled with lions—fierce, impossibly huge monsters with fiery manes and eyes as black and cold as a starless night. There were no lions of such colossal size in all of Pharaoh's realm, not even in the wild Red Land, the desert where the waters of the holy Nile never reached. I was only a small child, barely four years old, but old enough to know that the lions haunting my dreams could not be real. And yet I was still afraid.

The dreams were always the same: It was daytime, and I was playing with my doll in the shade of the sycamore trees in our garden, when suddenly the earth under my feet turned to sand. My doll sank out of sight as the lions clawed their way into the blazing sunlight, their mouths gaping, ready to devour me. I ran toward the house, crying for help, but no one came, and my home slipped beneath the surface of the sand before I could reach it. Then I was running, running across the Red Land, where nothing grew but stones and bones. I saw strangely shaped mountains in the distance, and though I somehow knew I would be safe if I could reach them, I never did.

No matter how fast my dream-self ran, the lions always caught me. When they did, they surrounded me in a ring, and that was when their faces underwent a frightening change: They became the faces of men. Before I could marvel at the transformation, their lips parted and I saw that though their mouths looked human, they still held the keen, bloodstained teeth of lions. Their roars shook the desert.

In every nightmare, the last thing I saw before I woke was their fanged faces. As soon as I felt the first hot touch of their breath on my cheeks, my eyes flew open and I found myself shivering and sobbing in my bed.

I can't count how many times my terrified tears brought Father running. He was a very patient man who never once scolded me for waking him. If my beloved nursemaid, Mery, was already there, trying to calm me, he would dismiss her. Then he'd pick me up in his arms and hold me until I fell asleep again.

The older I grew, the worse my nightmares

became. Sobs and tears became shrieks and howls that roused everyone in the household. One particularly harrowing night, I woke up to find myself not in my own bed, or even in Mery's comforting arms, but beside the pool of blue lotus flowers in our garden, only a stone's throw from the very spot where the lions appeared in my dreams. I sat bolt upright and screamed.

"Nefertiti, hush, it's all right, I'm here." Father's arms were around me, strong and sheltering. He was down on one knee beside me, his face filled with sadness. "I thought that if I brought you out here to sleep, the Lady Isis would take pity on you and banish your evil dreams forever." He gestured to the delicately painted stone image of a woman, whose serene face and welcoming arms were reflected in the waters of the lotus pool.

"Isis?" I was very young, and the name was new to me, even if the statue itself was already one of the eternal, unchanging parts of my childish world, like our house, our garden, the city of Akhmin beyond our walls, and the great river that flowed beside them. "Will she make the lions go away?"

"Lions?" Father echoed. "What lions?"

"The ones that come to hunt me every night," I said. Though everyone in our house knew I suffered from nightmares, that was the first time I ever spoke about the images those nightmares contained. No one under our roof—not even Mery or Father—had ever asked me to describe them. By night, their chief concern was getting me to go back to sleep. By day, they might have been afraid to remind me of my midnight terrors. *If we pretend the evil dreams don't exist, maybe she'll forget about them tonight, at last!*

My father settled himself cross-legged on the ground and took me into his lap. "Tell me about the lions, Nefertiti," he asked solemnly, as if I were a grown-up and not a child who had lived to see only four Inundations of the sacred river.

So I told him everything about the dream that haunted me, and when I explained how the lions' faces changed, he hugged me close to his chest. "My poor little bird," he said. "The same dream, time and time again, and I never knew. All of your unhappiness for so long, and I could have put an end to it so quickly if only——!" He sighed. Then his expression changed from regret to determination. "Never mind what's past. *Now* I can help you."

I never doubted it for a moment. Of course he could help me! He was Father, strong, all-loving, all-powerful, the only true god in my eyes. All the rest—Amun, Osiris, Thoth, Ra, Hathor, even Min, for whom our city was named—were only names to me. (Indeed, I had *heard* Isis's name many times before that night in the garden, but I'd never thought to attach the sound of it in my ear to anything solid, the way hearing the word *table* or *cat* or *tree* called up a specific image in my mind.)

Now Father got to his feet, still holding me in his arms, and carried me to the statue of Isis. "Hail, Isis, lady of life, light-giver of heaven, queen of the earth, lady of the words of power!" he cried. "Have mercy on your servant, Ay, for he has been a great fool. O Lady Isis, this is my sweet daughter, my only child, my Nefertiti, my greatest treasure. Banish her evil dreams and send them to haunt me instead as punishment for my stupidity. For this, I promise you many rich gifts. O Lady Isis, hear my prayer!"

I was astonished to hear such words coming from my father's mouth. How could he call himself a fool and stupid? Didn't he know his own power? I had no time to ponder such disturbing thoughts: As soon as he ended his plea, Father bowed to the image, then turned and marched off. His brisk pace jounced me roughly, all the way to the edge of the raised bank where our property looked down on the green rushes and reeds bordering the Nile. Here, Father lifted me so high that I was nearly sitting on his shoulder, then pointed upstream and asked, "Do you know what lies in that direction, my Nefertiti?"

What a question! Even if I was only four years old, I knew the answer well enough. It was part of a game that Father and I played when he wasn't busy with whatever grown-up business filled his days. "The gates of the Nile," I replied. "The birthplace of the holy river. And . . . and . . ."—I wanted Father to be proud of how clever I was—"and that's where Pharaoh lives, too!" I cried in triumph, then quickly added: "May-Amun-bless-and-protect-the-living-Horus-son-of-Ra-lord-of-the . . . lord-of-the . . . um . . . I forgot."

Father chuckled. "Good enough. But do you know what wonderful birthplace lies *there*?" He pointed down the shimmering river. I shook my head. "Yours, my darling."

"I thought I was born here," I said, my eyes darting toward our house.

"You would have been, but then as now, I served Pharaoh, and in those days it was Pharaoh's pleasure that I travel with him when he sailed down the river to view the great monuments and tombs of his ancestors. Ah, what wonders!" He lowered me so that I could put my arms around his neck. "There is one above all that steals your breath away, a pyramid of such size that it's like seeing a mountain. We call it Khufu's Horizon, because it is the place from which the soul of that Pharaoh rose to sail the heavens with the other gods. Its sides are sheathed in slabs of the finest white limestone, and the crowning stone is covered in a mix of gold and silver. When Ra's sunlight strikes it, it dazzles the eyes."

"Oh! Can *I* see it, Father?" I asked, pressing my cheek to his. "Will you take me there with you? Please?"

He looked at me wistfully. "That was almost exactly what your mother said. You are very much like her, my dear—just as beautiful, just as charming. I couldn't tell her 'No,' though I tried. I reminded her that it was almost time for her to give birth, but she argued that it wouldn't happen for at least thirty days. Then she reminded me that we'd be traveling with Pharaoh and his Great Royal Wife, Queen Tiye. 'Tiye, who is your own sister!' your mother said to me. 'You know she'll see to it that nothing happens to me or the child.'" He sighed.

I felt strange. This was the first time I'd heard Father speak about my mother for so long. I knew she had died very soon after I was born. That was why Mery—whose own husband and baby had died—came to be my nursemaid. The three of us often went to Mother's tomb to leave offerings of food and drink for her *ka*, the part of her soul that remained in this world. Apart from those solemn occasions, Father seldom spoke of her at all, and he looked so sad when leaving the offerings that I didn't want to add to his grief by asking about her.

He looked even sadder now.

"It's all right, Father," I said, hugging him. "You don't have to talk anymore. I'll go to sleep. And I won't have any more bad dreams, I promise!" I knew the promise was empty, that the monstrous, man-faced lions would come back for me the next night and the next, but all I cared about at that moment was easing his spirit. "Please don't be unhappy."

Father patted my head. Like all children, I had it shaved clean except for the single braided lock of hair trailing down the right side. The warmth of his hand was comforting. "Are *you* trying to protect *me*, dearest? Only four years old and already you're such a brave girl. Your mother named you The-beautiful-woman-has-come, but perhaps you should have been called The-beautiful-warrior."

I hung my head. "I'm not brave, Father," I said. "If I were, I wouldn't wake you up every night. I could fight my bad dreams myself. I'm sorry."

His smile, bright even in the moonlight, lifted my heart. "Don't you see, my sweet bird? Being brave doesn't mean always having to fight alone. You have me, and Mery, and as you grow older, you'll have friends who'll stand up for you, too. But on the night you were born, you were given a guardian who's stronger than all of us put together."

"Stronger than a lion?" I asked timidly.

"*Part* lion," Father replied. "Part lion and part man—the creature we call a sphinx, just like those in your dreams—except *this* one is mightier than all of them. His face is the face of Pharaoh—not our lord, but a Pharaoh who ruled the Black Land in ancient times. So you see, he is lion, man, and god. He ascended to Ra so long ago that his divine powers are more than a match for any bad dream. And he is *your* protector, my Nefertiti."

"He is?" I gave my father a skeptical look. I couldn't imagine the almighty sun-god Ra making room in his Boat of Eternity for such a monster.

"Do you doubt me?" Father smiled and chucked my chin. "Someday, my princess, I will take you sailing down the river and show you the place where you were born, the place where the pyramid tombs guard the kings and queens of our past. That's where the great sphinx crouches on the sand and rock, greeting the sunrise. You were born in one of the rest houses that stand near the temple where our own Pharaoh worshiped his divine ancestor. Before you were one day old, I brought you out into the light of your first dawn, held you up before the god's eyes, and asked him to watch over you. He heard my prayer, and now he is your special guardian. I should have asked him to help you long ago, when your nightmares first began, but I wasn't thinking. Will you forgive me?"

I pressed my forehead to his. "It's not your fault, Father," I said. "He's *my* guardian. I'll ask him myself." Then I yawned widely, making Father laugh before he carried me back to my bed.

The following night, before I went to sleep, I made Mery take me outside to the riverbank. There I stood, gazing downstream to where my unseen guardian kept watch over the splendid tombs of ancient rulers, until I found the right words in my heart to offer up to him: "O great sphinx, come into my dreams and don't let the bad sphinxes hurt me!" It wasn't much of a prayer, but the great sphinx must have made allowances for a four-year-old child.

It worked. That night, when the same dream came back to trouble me, when the lions surged out of the sand that swallowed our house, when they chased me and caught me, when their faces became the faces of men and their fanged mouths opened to devour me, I didn't scream. Instead, I stood my ground, stooped to pick up a rock, and threw it right at the biggest, fiercest one of all. The rock struck him squarely between the eyes, and he broke into pieces like a clay jug dropped on stone. I grabbed more rocks and threw them as well, smashing sphinx after sphinx until my arms ached and I was panting like a dog at midday, but I was the only being left standing.

I did a little victory dance in the middle of that ring of shattered sphinxes until a shadow fell over me. I looked up and saw a sphinx so huge that he could have made a single mouthful of all the others. His human face was grave and severe, but somehow I knew that he wasn't angry at me for what I'd done to the other sphinxes. I raised my right hand to my chest the way Mery taught me to do when we prayed to the gods, and he smiled at me. It was a smile of approval as beautiful, comforting, and good as when Father smiled at me. Then a whirlwind out of the Red Land swept over the two of us, he vanished behind a curtain of swirling sand, and I awoke.

After that night, whenever I dreamed of lions, I was the one who ruled them. I dreamed of riding them through the streets of Akhmin, or across the desert, or even from the earth to the heavens. They became as tame to me as the cats who blessed our house, and they never hunted me again.

But no matter how far I rode them—to the ends of the world or the pathways of the stars—there was always a protective shadow over me. If the road grew too rough, or I became afraid that I had lost my way, I only had to glance up and he would be there, the great sphinx who had seen me born, the shadow of strength that was always with me.